True Blue Cowboy

True Blue Cowboy

A Blood Brothers Romance

Debra Holt

TULE
PUBLISHING

Hello all,

The first book in my latest Blood Brothers series has arrived! *True Blue Cowboy* introduces us to Josie Monroe and Chance Braxton. This contemporary romance is about a young woman who faces a real challenge in proving herself in a 'man's world'…the running of a ranch after her father's unexpected death. And Josie is also harboring a secret love involving her next-door neighbor…Chance's younger brother, Devlin.

Devlin presents himself as the quintessential devil-may care young man, appearing and disappearing at odd times, much to his brother's disapproval. He is adept at leaving a trail of broken hearts…most notably Josie's. And always there in the background to pick up the pieces, to provide a strong shoulder to cry upon, a hand to hold, and words of encouragement stands the ever patient, ever determined Chance.

Chance is the epitome of what any of us would describe as most deserving of that true-blue cowboy label. His shoulders are broad and strong enough to shoulder the responsibilities of running a large ranch, being seen as an example to those who look up to him and depend upon his decisions. His word is gold and his handshake is an unbroken bond. His heart is large, and he has an enormous wealth of patience. Patience is what he needs the most because his heart has belonged for years to Josie. But Josie's been blinded by her 'worship' of Devlin.

The day comes when Chance must step forward and show Josie the man standing before her is the man she was meant to share her destiny with. It won't be an easy road to a happy-ever-after, but Chance is the one cowboy who will not give up in proving to Josie that real love will withstand the test of time and nothing will shake his faith in their future together.

This is for all of you who dream of finding your own true-blue cowboy... or maybe you already have! They truly do exist. In the meantime, I hope you enjoy sharing the rocky road to a love to last a lifetime with Josie and Chance.

Happy reading,
Debra

Prologue

CHANCE BRAXTON GLANCED up at the slate-colored sky overhead as he approached the old building. A weather change was on its way. He could feel it in his bones and in his spirits. His brain told him he should be out on the range, helping his crew roundup the last of the horses and move them to winter ground, but instead he was here. *Same story, different day.* His gaze latched on to the fact that the door to the old hay barn was partly open…just wide enough to allow someone to slip through. If his hunch was correct, he would find the person he sought inside. He eased the door open just a tad wider and slipped his tall, broad-shouldered frame through as quietly as possible.

Once inside, he paused to allow his eyes to adjust to the dim light. Ears were attuned to any sounds, and it didn't take long before he heard a soft sniffle…and then another. Familiar sounds that had a way of tugging at the heart Josie professed he didn't possess inside his chest. Chance moved deeper into the large room with its overhead loft and his gaze swung upward to where the sounds came from.

He moved to the stairs and eased up them, not wanting to startle the person he sought. On the top rung, he stopped as his gaze lit on the slight figure sitting with her back to him, now and then her slender shoulders moving in a soft shudder. Taking a deep breath, Chance kept his tones low.

"So what's my brother done now?"

In an instant, the girl's hands went to her face in a quick wiping motion. It was evident she didn't want her tears to be seen. But Chance was used to seeing them and, each time, he had to harden his resolve even more. The problem was, he didn't know how much more *resolve* he had in him. She didn't answer him right away, but when she did, it was with a question of her own.

"Do you ever wish it was a different time? You could maybe fast-forward into the future…ten or fifteen years? When your life would be settled, and you'd know where you belonged…and who you would be with for the rest of your life?"

It was about his brother. Chance blew out a deep breath and eased forward, to settle on the edge of the hay bale beside her. The loft door was open before them, and a soft breeze filled the area around them in the late afternoon. He swept his Stetson off his head and ran a hand through his thick mahogany-colored hair. It was important to give the question some consideration.

"That's a mighty interesting idea, Josie. I guess each of us does that now and then. But trying to look for a glimpse of the future is sort of like looking into a crystal ball. I never could make out too much in those things, either. Guess I prefer to stay in the here and now and leave tomorrow to itself. It's going to come in its own time. And if you're so intent on the future, you'll be more likely to miss something important in the present."

"Chance's sage words of advice… you'll probably have met your soul mate and gotten married and had kids by then."

The rancher slid his gaze over at the girl beside him. It was getting more difficult by the day to remain in the role of the "big brother" that Josie Monroe had cast him in over the last few years. But he also knew it was as much his fault as hers for allowing it to happen. He used to be able to give her his shoulder to cry on and then wipe away her tears. She had outgrown that need…and holding her nowadays lent itself to a whole different set of complications so he made a concerted effort to keep his distance.

"I can only hope that'll be my future. It sounds pretty good. I think the same could be said for you."

"I doubt that. I'll probably be an old maid rancher."

He couldn't help it. The laugh burst out of him before he could stop it. The rising of her hackles was immediate and matched with the fire in her eyes.

"It's not funny."

"Yes, it *is,* little one." His voice softened a bit, and he settled his blue-eyed gaze on her profile. "Look at me and listen."

"What? Do you have some more of Chance Braxton's words of wisdom to share? And why do you continue to call me by that silly nickname? I'm not 'little' any longer. And you're not all that older than I am… six years doesn't make you an expert on everything." Her chin came up in pointed stubbornness, and her tear-washed gray eyes settled on him. She was just a week past her eighteenth birthday but had always been a lot more mature than others her age. Except for when it came to her bruised heart. He had to keep reminding himself of that fact…plus the fact she fancied herself head over heels in love with his brother.

"I realize you aren't little any longer, Josie. It's just a habit. I've called you that since you were a little girl in pigtails, and I can't seem to break it. And I have no words of wisdom. They just come from having lived a few years longer than you and having a good deal more experience with life under my belt. Slow down…don't be in a hurry to grow up and skip over too many years. Life isn't a race. Trust me. You'll find your soul mate one day. When you least expect him…he'll be in front of you. And then all the tears and the pain you felt along the way, they'll vanish from your memory." A few long moments of silence surrounded them.

"But he won't be Dev, will he." It wasn't a question…more like a sad statement of an undeniable truth.

Chance drew in a slow breath and then eased his words out. "I doubt that very much, Josie. You deserve someone a lot better than my young brother. Just keep your mind and heart open to allow for someone else to have a chance to win that heart of yours. It's a treasure the right man will guard and cherish with his life."

"You really think there's someone better for me in my future?"

"I think once you let go of the idea that you've built around Dev as being the 'perfect' person, standing on a high pedestal, your heart will open to other possibilities."

She rounded on him in an instant. "Why do you say such things about your brother? Just because he isn't like *you*, doesn't mean he is less."

"I didn't say he's *less* anything, Josie. It just seems that more and more of late, you get defensive anytime anyone says anything about him in your presence. Maybe you need to look at why that is. It's not like he hasn't given people plenty of reason to look at him without blinders on over the years."

"I know why I defend him. *Someone* should be on his side. He can't help it if he isn't tough as nails as you are, if he doesn't care about staying on a ranch all his life. And maybe I know how it can be… always having people make assumptions about you without any real facts to back them up. People look at me, a girl trying to be a rancher…they think I'm playing dress up or some silly game. It isn't a game to me…it's my life. They just don't want to see that. That's how it feels at any rate.

"I may not be a male, but I can ride and rope and work cattle just as good, if not better, than a lot of the guys around these parts. But seems like I have to keep proving that each day the sun comes up. And, one of these days, the people around here will know I'm just as good as they are. And that's the same for your brother. Dev's going to be a success, and you'll end up envying him."

Chance was silent for a few moments…more so to gain control of his mounting frustration than anything else.

"Maybe I already do." The words were low and said in a

disgusted growl. He stood at that point. If he stayed, he might say too much. "There are already a good number of people who admire what you're trying to do with this ranch and the way you're trying to help your parents out. There will always be those old-timers who will go to their graves with their beliefs because that's the way they were raised and have lived for decades. But times are changing every day, and female ranchers can hold their own…they just have to be tougher than most. Now, I've got work to get done, and you've got your chores. Just don't get in such a hurry to grow up…*little one*."

Chance left the loft, but not before catching the look of confusion in her gray eyes. He could understand confusion…and frustration…and nerve-bending patience. He had made his decision a while back where Josie Monroe was concerned. He had prepared himself, because it meant he would have to have a thick hide and a deep well of patience. But it really was the only choice he could make, because once you found your soul mate…you'd face whatever came in order to have that person's heart. In the meantime, he'd remain where he was…by Josie's side…a silent protector.

Chapter One

Ten years later…

"MY BROTHER NEVER deserved you."

"Did you stop by today just to cheer me up?" Josie Monroe threw the words over her shoulder, intent on adjusting the cinch on the saddle of her horse. "If so, it isn't working."

"Just stating a fact. And, since today is your twenty-eighth birthday, I hoped to find you doing something a bit different. You know a person can take a day off now and then…maybe celebrate."

"Said the pot to the kettle. I've not seen *you* taking days off. It's just another workday on a ranch like this one. And you're wasting your time. Dev and I were kids back then. It was just a silly, childhood crush. One I outgrew a long time back. Whatever he does or doesn't do now, it's his business and no concern to me."

"Except your heart got broken just the same…more than once."

"Look," Josie began, as she faced the cowboy with his dark brooding eyes the color of sapphires fixed on her. "My heart is just fine. And, as I've told you more than once, I'm not a child any longer, and my life is none of your business. I outgrew the need for a 'big brother protector' a while ago. Why are you *really* here?" She turned back to the horse, threading the reins through one gloved hand as she stepped easily into the stirrup and swung herself up into the saddle, the creaking noise sounding louder than usual inside the old cavernous barn.

The man stepped forward, settling long, muscular arms along the top of the weathered planking of the stall door. His Stetson covered a good deal of his face, but the part Josie could see was not smiling. "Thought I should deliver the latest news about Devlin Braxton in person. There was a phone call this morning."

His gaze didn't miss the fact her body subconsciously steeled itself for whatever might be coming. It was something she had practice doing over the years, particularly where Dev was concerned.

"Plans changed, I guess? So, he won't be coming home anytime soon? Nothing surprising about that one."

"Dev's engaged...*again*. Wife-to-be number three is some showgirl from Vegas. Needless to say, his trust officer is coming down hard on him, but Dev never was one to pay attention to anyone or anything else but what *Dev* wants at any particular moment."

"And this concerns me how? I appreciate you dropping by with your family's good news, but I do have a ranch to run. I don't have a crew to delegate the work to."

"All you have to do is ask, Josie," he countered, fixing his steady, unreadable gaze on her. "You just never want anyone's help. You're just too stubborn or too proud to ask, and one day that just might land you in a heap of trouble."

"Nice chatting with you, Chance. Congrats on your family's news." Josie left him leaning on the fence, watching her retreating back as she rounded the corral and touched her horse's flanks, sending it into a gallop toward the distant hills.

"Stubborn as a mule," he muttered under his breath at her retreating back. The only one around to hear him was the black and white barn cat sitting just inside the open doorway, licking its paw after a morning feed on barn mice. "Why should I care?" The toe of his boot kicked a small rock out of his way since there wasn't anything bigger around at the moment. "That's the problem…I *do* care." And it was high time he did something about it, once and for all.

"WHY DIDN'T YOU invite Chance to stay for your birthday supper?" Dianne Monroe asked the question as she set the pan of chicken enchiladas on the kitchen table, their aroma filling the kitchen. "You knew I was cooking his favorite dinner tonight. And I made *your* favorite cheesecake for dessert."

"He had other things to do, mother." *Like darken someone else's door with the glad tidings of his brother's nuptials.* Josie helped herself to the enchiladas and then pushed her fork into the food on her plate. "It's just another day around here. Besides, it means more dessert for me."

"Chance is such a kind and thoughtful young man. He brought over some bags of shelled pecans this afternoon for my holiday baking."

"You realize he has an ulterior motive in doing that, don't you? He knows you'll bake extra pies and goodies for him, also. Besides, he isn't a *young man* anymore. He's over thirty now…almost thirty-four. You still see him as some sort of teenaged god or something. He's no longer the rodeo star or the class valedictorian. He's just getting older. Like the rest of us mortals." Perhaps she got a bit carried away in her reply, but Josie felt more and more unsettled around the man who just would not stay away from their ranch. One would think owning the largest ranch in the western part of Texas would keep him too busy to mind the business of others. In particular, *her* business.

"Well, I still think of him as the kind and thoughtful young man he's always been to us, from the first day he rode over to meet us. Hard to believe that's been almost twenty years now…or is it more? Good manners never grow old or go out of style," her mother replied, casting a measured look toward her daughter.

Seated at the kitchen table, in her usual jeans, old work boots, gray and red plaid flannel shirt, Josie took little pains with makeup or hairstyles. Dianne had tried to instill in her daughter some of the female qualities that interested most other young girls growing up. However, Josie had always been independent of thought and followed no other trend but her own.

"I also remember how the three of you were thick as

thieves in the summertime around the ranch. Your father called you 'the three amigos.'"

"That was a long time ago when we were just kids. We all grew up." Josie laid her fork on the plate and took a long sip of her tea, a light shadow crossing her eyes.

"Not so long ago. It's a shame Chance hasn't found someone to settle down with. He needs a good woman to help him run Braxton Ranch."

Josie was no fool. Her mother was testing the waters, and she wasn't about to dip her toe in that particular pond. "Good luck with that. He's too picky and too stubborn. Most of the girls in school certainly tried to land him. They still *are* trying from what I hear around town. He's just too serious all the time."

"Well, he's had a lot to deal with beginning at an early age. He had to mature quicker than most. Chance missed out on a lot of things most young boys got to experience for fun. He wasn't allowed time to be carefree. You know that better than anyone. I think you should take a closer look at the man he's become." Dianne smiled at her daughter. "Maybe he's found the one he wants, but she might be too hardheaded for her own good."

Josie pushed back from the dining table and stood. "Any female who wants to put up with him is either crazy or a glutton for punishment. I'm heading to the barn to check on Cookie and deliver the apple I promised him earlier for all his hard work today. Then there'll be more room for another slice of that cheesecake. Love you." She dropped a quick kiss on her mom's forehead. "Thanks for another great birthday dinner."

DIANNE WAS FINISHING up the last of the dinner pots and pans when a swift knock on the back door caught her by surprise. It was followed by a familiar tall figure stepping through the doorway, hat in hand, and a wide grin on his face. "Didn't mean to startle you. I just came by to drop off a tractor part I told Zeke I would pick up for him when I ran into town earlier. I left it at the bunkhouse and then I saw you through the window standing in front of the sink. I thought I…"

"That you might stop by on the off chance there was a plate of chicken enchiladas with your name on it?" She finished the thought for him with a laugh and shake of her head. "I put it in a container for you already, but I can also heat it up." Dianne moved to the refrigerator and reached inside.

"Don't bother heating it. I do need to get back to my place and tackle some paperwork tonight." His gaze had already traveled around the room when he entered. "Don't see your daughter around this evening. Guess she had an engagement in town maybe?"

The container was placed in Chance's hands. "Now you know that Josie has only two interests in her life, the ranch and her horse…and possibly one other."

"That goes without saying. My brother Dev has always been high on her list."

"I've tried to figure that one out a time or two. It's been that way almost since the time they laid eyes on each other in elementary school. True, he does have those movie-star good looks and that devil-may-care smile. But I can be honest with *you*…he wasn't the choice of either my husband or myself. We just kept hoping, as time passed, Josie would mature and see that looks will fail with time, so there better be some substance underneath it all. I'm sorry if that came out too harsh."

"Don't worry. It's not anything I don't already know. Dev was always treated special by our parents for whatever reason…things were made easier for him; more allowances were made for his wanderlust. I've had to get used to that early on. We all have our own roads to travel. His is just always *away* from Braxton."

"And you were always older and wiser beyond the years in your age. And you know how we feel about *you*. After Josie's father passed away, without your steady presence in the background, always offering to help wherever need-ed…well, I don't know how we would've managed. And I'm also mindful of how much patience you've had to exercise of late in dealing with my stubborn daughter. I wish we could return to the days when Josie used to follow you around like your second shadow. That would certainly be easier for *you*."

"I appreciate your kind words, but my helping is all part of being a good neighbor as far as I'm concerned. You certainly helped both my brother and me when we lost our mother. And as for Josie," his voice trailed off and he tried to keep things light. "Well, Josie is Josie. I don't think any of us would change her. Besides…my hide is tough."

"Good." She smiled, patting his arm. "Just hang in there.

I'm pulling for you. And Josie's down at the barn if you want to stop by and visit or anything."

Dianne gave him a knowing smile. He met her steady gaze with his own.

"I think it's best not to push my luck any more today. Thanks again for the enchiladas. I'll be on my way home."

"Don't wait too long," Dianne said into the silence of the kitchen after the door shut behind him. "Time is growing shorter by leaps and bounds." The smile faded within her.

Chapter Two

"AFTERNOON, LADIES." CHANCE strode into the hardware store two days later, and when he caught sight of the two women standing at the counter, a grin lit his face, and he swept his hat off his head. "I should come into town for plumbing supplies more often if this is where the prettiest girls gather."

"Chance Braxton, if you were Irish, I'd say you had kissed the Blarney stone this morning…but maybe you've just been out in the sun too much today and it's gotten to you." Mitzi Lewis stood behind the counter, shaking her head with a laugh at the cowboy.

"Oh, shush, Mitzi," Dianne Monroe said, stepping into the circle of the cowboy's arm and sharing a hug with him as she had done for most of his life. "Chance has never been a flirt," Dianne went on. "He knows beauty when he sees it…so enjoy the compliment. At our age, we take them whenever we can get them."

"Too true," Mitzi agreed. "What can we help you with today?"

Chance gathered the items on his list, and Mitzi checked them out soon enough. He turned to the other woman, who sat on a stool at the end of the counter, joining in their easy banter now and then. Chance had the two women smiling, but his gaze took in certain telltale signs while being unobtrusive in his surveillance. He was well aware of the new paleness in Dianne's features. She had been more tired-looking than usual two nights ago when he had stopped by and been gifted with the enchiladas. And there was just something that had been "off" in her usual demeanor. She seemed to not be as spry of late as she had once been. Whatever the "something" was had amped his concern level.

"Mama Dianne", as he and Dev had come to call her after they lost their own mother when they were still young boys, had always been there with words of encouragement, home cooking, and special hugs when needed. There had also been her brand of quiet stare when they needed a reminder to straighten up and fly right.

Chance had taken it upon himself to do as much as he could to always be there to lend a hand after she and Josie lost Ben Monroe to a stroke. That is, he was *there* as much as Josie would allow him to be. More often than not, she let him know that his presence was neither needed nor wanted. That had been a change over the last half dozen or so years.

When she was growing up, they had been closer. He was like the older brother she never had. At least that was how her mom and dad had treated him to a large extent. Of course, he was glad to not be cast in that role any longer. Being a brother was not the connection he wanted with Josie. And he had a sneaking suspicion that Mama Dianne had realized that fact long before he even had admitted it to

TRUE BLUE COWBOY

himself. She had hinted at that more than a couple of times in recent weeks.

"I'll have these things picked up this afternoon by one of the hands when he picks up the other items from the lumber yard," Chance replied to Mitzi's question about packing the purchased merchandise. His gaze fell on the seated woman and the two bags sitting at her feet.

"How about I take those to your truck for you, Mama Dianne...if you're done visiting?"

Her eyes brightened at his offer. "That sounds like an offer I'll gladly accept." She slid off the stool and threw a parting wave at her friend. "I'm going to let this handsome man escort me to my truck. It'll make all the young females jealous!"

Chance shook his head and returned Mitzi's goodbye as he followed the woman out of the store. Once on the sidewalk, he offered her his arm, and she slid a hand around his elbow. They walked across the two-lane main street toward the Monroe ranch truck.

"How about you stop by on Sunday afternoon and I'll make my meatloaf you like so much? Followed up by some blueberry cobbler?" They reached the truck, and Chance placed the two bags into the back bed before he turned and smiled at the woman.

"Hadn't you better check with your daughter before you issue that invite? I have a feeling she might not be too thrilled to have me at the dinner table."

Dianne cocked her head to the side and gave him a long, considering look, her hands on her hips. "Since when do I have to check with my daughter about who I invite into my own house? And you aren't just *anyone*…you're part of our family. You've done well to keep coming over and helping despite the fact Josie seems to have misplaced her manners. I taught her better."

"It's understandable," Chance replied. "She thinks I'm butting in, and it's hard enough for her, being a young female and trying to run a ranch and all. I've tried to tell her that I think she's doing a good job, but she doesn't want my compliments, either."

"Yet, you keep coming by and doing what you've always done. You take a lot from her, and I *used* to not understand why you would put yourself through it all."

His eyes focused in on hers and they shared a silent gaze for a couple of moments. "You're a shrewd woman, Mama Dianne. No one ever could put anything over on you for very long."

"You know, I've missed having you call me that. And I know you try not to do it whenever Josie is around. She's headstrong. You know that. You can't break her spirit to your own will. You know that, too. I wish I could say that she'll lose the blinders where you and your brother are concerned soon enough…but I can't. I thought it would happen long before now. Just know that both Ben and I have always thought a great deal of you, and no man would be as deserving…or as *welcome*…as a son-in-law into our family as *you* would be. I just hope you hang in there and don't give up on our girl. Promise me that?"

Something in those last words seemed to carry an undertone of a soft pleading. Chance gave a responding nod. He reached over and opened her door for her to step into the driver's seat. "I made that promise a long time ago. Don't worry about me. I'm not going anywhere. Josie's heart is her own to follow. Maybe it'll head in my direction one day. In the meantime, *you'll* just have to be my best girl." He gave her a wink and a grin as he shut the door behind her. "See you on Sunday for that meatloaf."

DIANNE DIDN'T HEAD straight back to the ranch. She had another appointment to keep in town. Braxton was a bit on the small side to actually be labeled a "town" by most standards. It had formed over a hundred years back when the railroad put in stock pens and a depot as a regular stop to load the thousands of head of cattle that made their way to markets in the other states. Stores came along to supply the ranches, and then a school, church, and before too long, it had grown to its present-day size of almost four thousand…scattered across a county that was bigger than some states were. Of course, it carried the name of the person who had the most cattle and the most money in the area…the first Royce Braxton. The elder Braxton left not only his sons and his ranch as his legacy, but his family name on the town.

It was the typical small Texas community, centered by a shaded square in the heart of it and then spread out like a wagon-wheel…making use of the tall oak and pecan trees to create an oasis on the southern plains and plateaus of the region buffering both the hill country and the southern plains of the Panhandle region. It was a good, solid small town with big-hearted, hard-working country folk who revered their state, their country, and each other.

Rounding the corner and going three blocks south, she pulled into a parking space in front of a one-story brick building. She fed the old-time parking meter her quarters and went inside. The receptionist smiled and buzzed her straight through and into the office behind her. There was important business to discuss.

"I'm going to die, Phillip." The spoken words hung heavy in the silence of the lawyer's office as she advanced and took the chair in front of the large desk.

The man leaned forward, hands clasped on top of the paperwork in front of him. One hand removed the wire-rimmed spectacles from his nose and laid them on the desktop. His shrewd gaze narrowed on the woman seated across from him.

"Of course you are, Dianne, we're *all* going to end up that way sooner or later. You've got a lot…"

"No, I do *not* have a lot of anything left. That's why I'm here. I've been seeing Doc Winters for a few years now. He and those medicines of his have done all they can for me. My old ticker is tired out and that's just as well. I've lived a good life. I miss my Ben. I've kept him waiting awhile on me now up there," her head gave a slight nod toward the ceiling and beyond. "But I'm leaving behind an awful mess for my beautiful Josie to have to deal with on this earth. That's why I'm here today. She thought she was keeping things from me, so I wouldn't worry. Ben tried that, too.

"But I had my ways of finding things out. We had to make some decisions a while back to keep the ranch afloat. I'm afraid those decisions may prove to be just the opposite. And Josie will be left with a mess. She's too stubborn to admit when she needs help. That's why you're gonna help me do what needs to be done for her own good and protection when I'm gone. There's no time to waste."

"I can see where Josie gets that stubborn streak of hers."

"Stubborn, yes…*determined,* you better believe it. I've given this all a lot of consideration and serious thought over the past few months." She reached inside the bag on her lap and withdrew a sheaf of papers. She pushed it across the desk toward the lawyer. "This is my will and final instructions. Josie knows nothing about what it contains. Can you see this gets carried out the way I want it?"

Phillip Banks reached for the glasses again and slid them on his nose. He began to read the words she had written. The attorney made no comment until he reached the end of the document. Then he withdrew the glasses and left them to dangle in his fingers as he cast a shrewd gaze in her direction along with a slow shake of the head.

"This is quite something. My first thought is that your daughter is going to go straight through the roof. I can't say that I want to be the one to deliver this news to her or be anywhere in a twenty-mile radius when she gets it."

"Can I trust you to do it or not?" She leveled her steady gaze on him.

For a few long moments, the man scanned the paper

once more. A sigh left him and then he shook his head at her again. "I've never seen or heard of anything like this before. However, if all parties involved agree to it, then that's the way it will be. Have you spoken to Chance Braxton about this? Is he going along with these wishes?"

"I believe he will. I'm going to inform him what I've done when he comes over this weekend after I make certain you'll handle all this just as I have written. If he refuses, which I doubt he will, then I have another will ready to go as a backup." She sat forward in her chair, ready to move on. "What's it to be?"

"I've taken care of your family's legal affairs since I became a lawyer almost forty years ago. I've known you and Ben since we were in grade school. I'm not about to let you down now. All I ask is, just make certain all the guns in the house are unloaded and ammunition hidden when the day comes that I have to deliver this news to Josie."

⚜

TWO DAYS LATER, Josie sat on Cookie, her black Quarter Horse gelding, breathing in the changing air. Her slate gray eyes were on the darkening, thin blue line approaching steadily from the north, over the flat plains below the ridge where she watched in silence. A cold, "blue norther" was barreling down across the plains between the Canadian border and Texas. Fall was on its way out and winter was coming. Another season was changing, and the unusual feeling of restlessness increased within her. Her thoughts were as bleak as the weather headed their way.

She had just found another section of fence line that had come down with help from the previous night's strong wind. It seemed like she was standing with her finger in a dam that was springing too many holes all at once. Maybe it was the dull, overcast sky that had her so down in spirit. Or maybe it was reality weighing in on her. More likely, it was a combination of both.

Josie tried to stay positive, if for no other reason than to keep her mother placated. However, when she was alone, she could admit she was lonely and just a bit scared. *Okay...maybe more than a bit.* In such moments, she missed her father and his large, comforting presence. The missing ache should have lessened with the passing of the years, but it had never done so. He always seemed to know what to do to make things better. But he was gone...much too soon.

The ranch that had been her only home since birth was draining their bank account dry with bad winters and drought-ridden summers. Thirty-five hundred acres didn't put them on the same scale as many other ranches in their area, or by most Texas standards. But it felt like triple that to Josie sometimes. The writing was on the wall...and on the letter the bank had sent to them last week.

A "*friendly*" warning notice. *Right.* Nothing friendly about being told you could lose everything you ever loved in a matter of weeks. Only Josie tried to not look at that wall, and she had crumpled the letter and tossed it into a drawer and locked it. No need to worry her mother with it...not until she could figure something out. Her brain had been on overload trying to do just that.

Without the ranch, what would they do? Where would they go? It was the only life she knew. While her friends graduated and moved on to college and to lives outside their small town, she had stayed behind. Then her world had been turned upside down a few days after her twenty-first birthday.

Her father was gone in a blink of an eye. He never even felt the stroke that took him, or so the doctor said. All the questions she still needed answers for were left unanswered. It was suddenly up to her to make decisions and keep the ranch moving forward. She tried to look like she knew what she was doing, but inside herself, she felt woefully inadequate. Her mother tried to help, but she wasn't as young as she once was.

Her father had always cherished her mom, as if she were delicate china, and never burdened her with the business side of the ranch. At least not that Josie ever knew about. Too often, especially over the last year, Josie had noticed how her mom's brown hair had become more silver-infused, her movements not as quick, her visits to the doctor in town more frequent. Whenever she had questioned her about the reasons for the visits and such, her mother had given her some reasonable excuse and changed the subject.

Josie liked to think the woman was stronger than any of them gave her credit for being. However, everyone had a limit to their strength. Josie realized that with each passing day. She also realized that not even her mother could stem the tide that was rising around them. For seven years, Josie had done her best to fight the battle. Her fear was that she would lose the war and she would have failed her father. The naysayers in town would be proved right…it was nonsense to think a young girl could run a ranch on her own.

The sudden shift of the wind brought her back to the present. The storm front was almost upon them. Soon, the temperature would begin to drop twenty or thirty degrees within an hour. This was the part Josie did enjoy. She turned Cookie and, with the swirling wind at their backs, she let the animal have its head, and they were off across the plain, literally on the wind itself, leaving all dark thoughts to chase behind her.

JOSIE TOPPED THE final rise before reaching home and quickly brought the reins back against her chest, her gaze taking in the two vehicles in front of the ranch house. One was Tom Herndon's older white pickup. Tom had been the ranch's foreman since Josie was twelve. The other bore the markings and lights associated with the county sheriff's department. Two men stood conversing beside it. A sudden chill went down her back that had nothing to do with the weather. Touching the horse's flanks with her boot heels, she covered the remaining ground in a matter of minutes, leaving the saddle almost before the horse came to a halt.

"What's wrong, Tom?" Her eyes and attention went immediately to the older man.

She didn't care for the quick look the two men shared.

"We tried to reach you on the cell, but you were out of range. Don't worry, Josie, but your mom has been taken to the hospital. Seems she was having some chest pains, and she called for the ambulance herself."

"No. *No*," she denied more forcefully. "I've got to get to her. Where are the keys?"

"I'll drive you there, Miss Monroe," the deputy spoke up. "We'll make better time with lights and siren."

"Call and let us know what's going on when you get there. I'll get things settled in here, and then Mary and I'll be on to the hospital," Tom said, his hand at her elbow, as he moved with her toward the vehicle.

Somewhere in the recesses of her shocked mind, Josie knew it had to be more serious than they were letting on. Why else should they need lights and siren? An ambulance had been called? Why hadn't she been home? She hadn't come in for lunch as she normally did. Why did she have to do something different today of all days? So many questions flew through her mind and no real answers. Panic pushed everything into her chest, making it difficult to breathe or even speak. The ride, normally a forty-minute drive, into the closest city of Abilene, was accomplished in just over twenty.

The SUV barely came to a halt in the driveway before she was out of the vehicle. Josie flew through the doors of the emergency room, totally lost as to where she was going in her panic. Luckily, her eyes fell on the familiar figure of their pastor, Reverend Morrison. He was an anchor she recognized and grabbed hold of as though her life depended on it. Beside him, were his wife and a couple of other people she recognized from her mother's circle of church friends. They were all trying to keep encouraging smiles on their faces, but their eyes held something different, and Josie tried not to look into any of them for too long.

"Your mother is still being examined," the pastor spoke in his quiet, calming manner. "They have the chief of cardiology in there, along with her own doctor. She's in the best medical hands possible. We need to keep positive thoughts and prayers in our hearts until they can bring us definitive news." Josie heard the words, and knew they were correct, and all well and good, but her mind kept going to places that scared her. She felt as if she were drowning and couldn't pull herself out of the deep water.

People tried to ply her with cold drinks and coffee and food. She wanted none of it. She needed answers. The hard-plastic chairs of the waiting room and the glare of the overhead fluorescent lighting closed in on her as the minutes turned into an hour. She resorted to pacing the floor, her arms wrapped around her chest. Her eyes flew to the double doors each time they opened. Always, the news coming through them was for someone else in the waiting area. Just when she thought she would scream, a familiar figure in blue scrubs and white lab coat pushed through the doors and she flew to his side, controlled panic etched in every line of her body.

"How's my mother? Can I see her? I need to see her."

Calming hands went to her shoulders as the short, balding doctor smiled at her. "She's alive." He knew that was the way to get her attention, and all the words her fevered mind could process needed to be right up front. Josie visibly drew in a long breath and the rigidness left her small shoulders.

"Thank you, Doctor Winters."

"She isn't out of the woods yet," he added, obviously needing Josie to comprehend the issues at hand. "She did have a heart attack. Luckily, she knew the signs and placed the call for help sooner rather than later. The ambulance crew did a good job of stabilizing until they could get her here.

"We have her sedated, so she'll calm down and allow her heart to rest. We'll know more in the next few hours, but for right now, she's holding her own. You can see her through the window in the ICU, and then you need to relax. I know it won't do any good to tell you to go home, but I do want these good people to take you out of here for about an hour or so and get you something to eat besides our cafeteria food." He gave her a slight smile at that point. "You'll help *us* to help Dianne by doing as I say."

Josie didn't argue but nodded her head in mute agreement. She just kept running the words through her mind over the next couple of hours. *She's alive.* It was a talisman that she held on to with all her might.

Chapter Three

"WERE YOU ABLE to see your mother?" Tom asked as he and his wife arrived in the waiting room later that evening.

"Only for a couple of minutes and they had her sedated at the time. The doctor came around a little while ago again. 'Cautiously optimistic' is the term he used."

"Miss Monroe." The nurse's voice brought all their gazes to the double doors. One of the ICU nurses stood there, motioning for Josie to join her. Josie wasted no time in crossing the room, the others following. "Your mother is awake. Normally, the doctor would have you wait until the morning to talk to her, but she's being very insistent that she speak with you right now. Is there a Chance Braxton out here with you?"

Josie was taken aback for a moment when she heard the second question. "No. He's not here. Someone said he's out of town. Why do you ask?"

"Your mother keeps asking to see him, also. If your friends will wait here, I'll take you back to her room now."

Following on the heels of the uniformed woman, she walked the long hall with her heart hammering in her ears.

The woman stopped and nodded for her to step inside the glass-walled room. Josie's heart jumped to her throat. And she swallowed hard. Her eyes quickly took in the monitors at the head of her mother's hospital bed, and the others situated in the corner. She didn't have any idea what all their numbers and squiggly lines meant, other than the fact that her mother was still alive and with her. Her focus fell on the pale face on the pillow. The blue eyes were a little less blue, but they still had her spirit in their depths, as she managed a slight smile up at her. Josie folded her palm around the one hand that didn't have needles and lines into it.

"The nurse said I can't stay long. She said you need to rest."

"I'll rest when I'm ready. I wanted to make sure you were okay and not worrying yourself sick. I'm in good hands here. It won't do anyone any good if you don't take care of yourself. You've got to be strong now, Josie. Stronger than you've been before."

"I know, mom. I don't know why you couldn't tell me that you had a problem with your heart. There are specialists and…"

"Enough of that, Josie. You had more than enough on your shoulders without worrying about what might or might not happen to me. It's my life, and I handle it the way I see fit. Specialists can't do me any good."

"We'll find ones who can. We just need you to hurry up and get out of here."

"I want you to listen to what I need to say." The woman's tone was different, and Josie felt a strange uneasiness pass over her and a chill settled around her.

"I'm listening."

"I know how much you love the ranch. How much you have fought to make a go of it since we lost your father. But you can't let the ranch be your only reason for living. If you do, it'll end up being the death of you. You've given your father and me every ounce of yourself, practically since you could sit on a horse all by yourself. You didn't go out and enjoy what other girls were doing, go to parties and dress up, have lots of boyfriends…"

"That stuff never mattered to me. I did what I wanted to do. Why are you talking about it now?"

"Because it *does* matter. *Life* matters, Josie. You must live it and enjoy it along the way. Stop hiding on that ranch. Open yourself up to new things, and open your heart, too. That's the only thing that really matters in this life…that you love someone and are loved in return. I want you to find the love you were meant to have. To have the family you deserve and children to enjoy."

"Mom don't worry about me. I'm happy right where I am." Josie noted the worried look that crossed her mother's eyes. She hastened to chase it away. "I promise that I'll find that someone special one day, and then you'll have a few grandchildren that I know you'll spoil rotten." She hoped her smile was more genuine than it felt.

"I'll hold you to your word to do just that for me. You being happy and safe is all that I ask," her mother said, squeezing her hand. Then she looked around her daughter's shoulder. "Is that you, Chance? Come over here."

"Yes, ma'am." The tones were low and steady.

As the man progressed into the room, Josie felt the chill of the room lessen and an unexpected calm settled in its place. She didn't stop to reason the why of it. Her walls did their automatic rise at the sight of him being there at that moment. Chance moved to stand on the other side of her mother's hospital bed. His eyes were steady on the woman in the bed. There was a tug in her chest as Josie noted the warm smile he gave her mother.

"I would have been here sooner, but I was down in Austin when I got the news. It took me a while to get a plane here with the front moving through."

Dianne smiled at him. "You're a good man, Chance. Your mother, dear Emmaline, raised you right. You've been a good neighbor and more like a son we never had. When you give your word, you keep it. I know you were coming over to have dinner with us this Sunday but looks like we might need to postpone that right now. However, I do want to have a conversation with you about something that can't wait until I get out of here. There's another favor to ask of you."

Josie had no idea where her mother was headed with any of this. She certainly had no idea why Chance Braxton had to be here, taking up her time with her mother.

"I hope you know how much your words mean to me, Mama Dianne. Name the favor and I'll do my best."

That was the other thing which grated on Josie's nerves more and more over the years. Since they lost their own mother at an early age, and as long as she could remember,

Chance and his brother, Dev, had been encouraged to call
her mother by that nickname. It used to be amusing. Now, it
just seemed to be an irritant for some reason. However, that
irritation was soon replaced by shock, which left her speechless, when she heard her mother's next words.

"Take care of my little girl, Chance. You know better
than most, she is hard-headed and too stubborn for her own
good at times. She'll fight you tooth and nail, but you've
always had a way with managing her. You've known when to
let her have her head and when to pull in the reins. If
anything happens to me, I'll rest knowing you'll be there for
her."

"You don't even need to ask that." The words were just
above a whisper in the room. "I do give you my word,
though." He didn't meet Josie's gaze but continued to keep
his focus on the woman lying in the bed.

"Josie, I need you to give Chance and me a couple of
minutes alone. There's some business we need to discuss."
Her mother's eyes were on hers. She wasn't asking, she was
stating a fact. Josie wanted to immediately react and say no.
To order the man from the room. Chance's eyes finally rose
to look at her and that one look from those serious blue eyes
made her bite back the rest of her thoughts. This was neither
the time nor place, and her mother didn't need to be upset.
Josie would bide her time.

"I'll be just outside the door." Josie bent and placed a
quick kiss on the cool forehead, feeling her mom give her
hand a responding squeeze. The door whispered shut behind
her.

DIANNE TURNED HER head to look up at the man standing beside her. "She's fuming right about now. She'll likely take it out on you."

A slight smile creased his face. "I'm sure she'll try. But I've gotten several layers of tough hide over the years. No need to worry."

"It's had to be over the years." The woman expressed a weary sigh. "It wasn't easy for you watching my daughter pine for your little brother and always giving her a shoulder to cry on. You've loved my Josie for a long time now. When do you aim to do something about it?"

Chance's smile left his face, as his eyes grew to a darker sapphire in their solemn regard of the woman and the consideration of her unexpected question. "When the time is right, I'll know."

"That's not an answer."

"As I told you the other day, I'll be here for her as long as she needs me. Hopefully, that might be an eternity or two."

"Then I'll trust in that. Any man who loves Josie has to be very patient."

The half grin seemed almost forced. Chance was already walking a fine line where Josie was concerned. He had loved Josie for too many years to count. But he had also had to come to the realization that there would be little hope of him having her heart if she couldn't get past her fixation on his brother. There was no future in being second-best. He had stood by and watched his ne'er-do-well brother break her heart time after time and stepped in to help her family with the ranch more times than he could count, but he wasn't certain he had any more "patience" left. However, the woman needed reassurance in her fragile state. He couldn't deny her that. "I have the patience of Job."

"I trust you've given thought to what we discussed briefly on the phone yesterday? The terms that are in my will?"

"Yes, I've thought of little else."

"What's your answer?"

"I gave you my word that I'll be here for Josie. I'll give you my word that I'll see that she always has her home here…no matter what happens at the end of the time period. But I can't say that I know how this will all play out. There are trustees and bank managers to keep in mind. Everyone has a say. But I will do my best to find the best course of action to protect Josie and your home."

"I trust your word. I know you'll always do the right thing. I also trust in my faith that my daughter will listen to her heart and make the right decision when the time comes. I can rest easy now that this is all settled. Josie's future is safe in your hands."

THE SKIES WERE cloudless and as blue as a sea of bright bluebonnets in spring. Winter halted its advance with a reverent pause. A light breeze brushed over the sea of pale winter grasses and around the crowd of dark-clad mourners gathered in the small cemetery in the grove of leafless pecan trees. Their vehicles mostly ranch pickups and SUVs, filled the parking area around the native stone church, which sat a few hundred yards distant on a small knoll. The site was on the outskirts of Braxton and about ten miles from the Monroe ranch.

Dianne Eileen Monroe, aged sixty, was laid to rest next to her husband, Benjamin, in the family plot, which held three previous generations of the Monroe clan. Reverend Morrison extolled the many virtues of the woman who touched so many of her neighbors' lives. While modern medicine had worked its wonders on keeping her on the earth another four days after her sudden heart attack, it wasn't in the Master's plan to leave her with them.

Josie saw it all as if she were standing apart from the crowd, watching it all play out before her. She was impervious to everything...numb. The moments that had ensued after the call from the hospital causing her to race back to the ICU; being told her mother's heart had arrested and nothing they could do to bring her back; to standing among the granite tombstones in the present moment...she had functioned on autopilot. She moved and spoke and did what was expected of her. All the while, there was a stark emptiness where her heart had been. Josie didn't know if it would ever go away. Part of her hoped it wouldn't. It somehow made it possible for her to go through the motions expected of her, keeping the sharp barbs of pain at bay.

She stood dressed in the one black dress she owned. It was the same dress she had worn at her graduation and then for her father's funeral. She did add the blue shawl her mother often wore around her own shoulders while reading at night. Josie told herself it was to keep the slight chill of the wind away. Her heart knew it was an attempt to keep her mother close beside her. To pretend it was her mother's arms gathering her inside, away from the pain. Josie's fingers drew the material closer around her shoulders as the time neared to walk away. *Alone*...that was how she would leave. That was how she truly was now. The starkness of the word had become a double-edged sword in her heart.

Chance, dressed in a tailored, western-cut dark suit, black hat in one hand, stood across the casket from her, having done his duty as pallbearer. A couple of times, she had looked up and found his gaze upon her, and she quickly brought her eyes downward. He had never been far from her side over the last couple of days...not being obtrusive, just *there*...if she needed to reach out. But she hadn't. The look in those blue depths was too painful for her to see.

She didn't need, nor want, people's pity. It seemed that was all she saw as she stood quietly, receiving the well-meaning expressions of sorrow and condolences over the last few days. All she really wanted was to bolt from the place and ride as far and fast as her horse could take her. To outrace every ounce of pain and never look back. Her eyes locked on the distant hills as if seeking refuge.

A few minutes later, it was over. "Amazing Grace" had been sung. The last prayer had died away. People began to file away in twos and threes. They would return to their busy lives soon enough. Josie continued to stay seated in the folding chair for a couple of minutes, her hands clenched in her lap. Finally, the Reverend and his wife offered to walk her to the reception hall at the church, where food and more condolences and pitying glances awaited. She thanked them and said she would be along shortly. At last, with their departure, she was alone.

Standing, she walked toward the casket of burnished wood and steel. There was no need to draw things out. Her mother wasn't really in that box. She was walking in a golden meadow of her favorite sunflowers, hand in hand with her Ben once more. At least that was the vision Josie held in her heart. She kissed the single white rose she held and laid it on top of the rest. Taking a deep breath, she turned and walked away. As hard as it was, she didn't look back.

Looking back would have been her undoing. Besides, her mother had said often enough, looking back can cause you to miss what is right in front of you. At the entrance to the cemetery, she saw Chance, standing quietly, his hands running the brim of his hat through his fingertips. Her steps slowed and then stopped as she came even with him.

Neither of them spoke for several moments. Josie kept her eyes on the toe of one of her black pumps she was wearing instead of her usual cowboy boots. She kept them there until a soft jangle of keys seeped into her thoughts, and Chance's palm caught her attention. He extended it towards her. A key ring lay on it. She looked up at him.

"You can take my truck back to your ranch. I'll catch a ride with Tom and pick it up later. If anyone misses you inside, I'll make an excuse for you. I figure it's a good afternoon for a ride."

Josie was closer to tears at that moment than at any other time over recent days. Chance's unexpected act, and the fact that he *knew* what she needed more than anything at the moment, was almost her undoing.

"Don't speak. Just go." He motioned with his head toward his truck.

She caught the keys in her hand and did just that.

Chapter Four

SOMEWHERE ACROSS THE far distant plain and hills, Chance could imagine Josie and Cookie riding in solemn quiet. In times of inner struggle or painful moments, he knew that Josie's solace was much the same as his...to be on the back of his best and silent companion, surrounded by both the majesty and stark vastness of nature. It was a balm to both the spirit and body. But he doubted Josie ever thought about what they both had in common.

And now times had changed on them once more. In the past, he could be a help and a shield for the spirited young Josie. But the years had changed them all. And, while he tried to remain steadfast in his silent stance not far from her side, he knew that other forces were moving to place invisible barriers and choices between them. Maybe it was all for the best. He had said he was patient...he could wait for Josie to recognize him for the man he wanted to be to her.

But then, maybe, he would just be the one always in the shadow of his brother. More and more, he had found that thought weighing heavily in the corners of his mind. What if Dev did come back now? What would Josie's reaction be? Was she truly over him? Or would she hand him her heart again to be broken? Would I need to step in and pick up the pieces once more of my brother's undoing?

But it wasn't just between Josie and Dev and himself any longer. Dianne had asked him to make promises that he had no idea if he could keep…or even if he should try. The will would soon be made known to Josie, and that would ensure an explosion. And lest they forget, there were the trustees to be satisfied. Business was business. But Chance knew it wouldn't seem like that to Josie's heart. No matter what was coming over the distant hills toward them with a relentless speed, there would be changes and decisions to be made. And he had no idea what to do. So he would just sit and wait…waiting for Josie.

JOSIE RETURNED TO the ranch from her run just as the sun began to set in the western sky. She had spent her tears with Cookie as her silent solace. To her surprise, Chance's truck was still parked where she had left it. Someone had left the porch light on for her. For just a little while, she forgot. For a moment, she imagined her mother would be inside with a home-cooked meal on the table and a bright smile on her face. Nothing would have changed.

Then reality came crashing in as she slowed her mount's steps across the ranch yard. There would be no one inside waiting for her. There was no one left but her. Her mind numbed. She took her time in the barn, rubbing down and putting away Cookie, until she could put it off no longer.

It wasn't until she mounted the last step to the porch that she noticed the quiet figure sitting in the rocking chair to the side of the porch. Chance sat, sans suit coat and tie, seemingly relaxing in the quiet of the oncoming dusk.

"I thought you'd be gone long before now. Did you and Tom just get back?" Josie spoke first, an uncertainty settling over her.

"We've been back a while. I thought I'd just sit a spell and enjoy the peace. I've always liked the view from this porch. I figured you'd be along soon enough."

He didn't fool her a bit. She had never seen Chance sit still for very long.

"You didn't have to wait for me. I'm okay. I left your keys in your truck for you earlier, so you wouldn't have to wait."

He pushed himself out of the chair and paused to stretch his legs a bit, before picking up his hat from the side table, his jacket folded over an arm. Then he moved to stand closer to her, his shoulder leaning against the pillar of the porch. "I figured you'd say that." His eyes brushed over her face, and Josie felt the air around them grow heavier. There was something new in those eyes, but she didn't want to dissect it, because she knew it had to be some new kind of pity.

"I know you'll get your bristles up if I mention that Tom and Mary have offered to come stay here at the main house with you for awhile...*if* you want them. Just in case you don't want to be alone right now."

Josie was about to set him straight, but something stopped her. They were all trying to help her. They had cared for her mother, too. And her mother would be the first to remind her about being rude. She simply shook her head instead. There was a knot in her throat, and she was afraid she was about to make a fool of herself. It was okay because, once again, Chance seemed to know what she needed.

He stepped forward and simply gathered her inside his strong arms. She didn't have any desire to fight him. Her head came just to the top of his shoulder, yet it seemed the space was a perfect fit. It always had been over the years. There were no words. He simply held her. Her arms found their remembered path around his waist as they had done many times before. For a few minutes, they stood like that on the front porch, as the shadows grew, and night fell around them. His warmth eased the pain, and his arms held the world at bay for just a little while. For a moment, the world righted itself.

He continued to hold her as she found her voice, her words muffled by his shirt front. "Everything is falling apart. I don't know why. I don't know why you put up with me, either. I'm mean to you, and you don't deserve it. You've always been the one person in my life who never changes and the one I know I can trust to stay the same."

Chance didn't respond at first. She was aware there was a change within him though. She felt his muscles tighten beneath her cheek and in the arms around her. Had she embarrassed him in some way? When she raised her head to look up at him, his eyes didn't meet hers. He didn't stop her when she loosened her hold and stepped back.

Chance's gaze settled warmth over her, and he chose his

words with care. "And as I recall, I always seemed to have some advice for you. From experience, I can tell you that it seems like your world has cratered around you right now. I can't fix this. No one can. But I can tell you that tomorrow will come, and you'll do what you have to do because you're one of the strongest people I've ever met. As for you being mean to me...I might have pushed a bit harder sometimes than I should have...stuck my nose in things that were better left alone. But it's going to take a lot more than any rudeness on your part to run me off. Just remember that, whatever comes your way in the coming days...keep in mind that I always keep my promises. My word to someone is my bond."

His words were cryptic, but he didn't give her time to question anything. Placing his hat on his head, he gave her a quick peck on her forehead and then stepped around her, heading down the steps. "Get some sleep, Josie. I'm always just a phone call away if you need me." She stood in the spot he left her. Once his truck pulled down the drive, she was truly alone.

As Josie entered the quiet house, there was a light in the kitchen, and she found there were several containers of food on the table, and a note stating the fridge and the freezer were also full. Their neighbors had been busy. She had no idea how she could possibly eat all the food by herself, especially when she had little appetite. Switching off the lights, she went upstairs.

Instead of going to her room, she went to her mother's. She stood in the doorway for several long moments, her eyes taking in the emptiness. Her things were still as she left them…as if she would return any moment. Josie knew that one day she would have to deal with the items, but not soon, and certainly not at that moment.

As she was about to turn, her gaze caught the scrapbooks her mother kept on the bottom of her nightstand. It was a hobby the woman had picked up after the loss of her husband. She had said it reduced her stress and brought her peace. Josie picked them up and carried them to her room. Removing her boots, she settled in the center of the bed. She opened the first one.

There were photos of her parents on their wedding day. Her mother had been a beautiful bride, all smiles and candlelight lace. Her dad looked so nervous. Gazing into each other's eyes…her heart constricted at how much love their eyes held for each other. They seemed so excited to begin the unknown adventure ahead of them. She turned the pages, and then there was a ton of photos of a little pink-blanketed baby girl named Josie. Her life was on the pages for her to see. For the first time, she really examined the photos.

Halfway through the first album, photos of Dev and Chance appeared. There was even one of their parents… the Braxtons. She barely remembered their mother. Their father was a different story. A tall man, he rarely smiled, and always seemed to have better things to do than be around his family. He ran his ranch with a tight fist, and people always seemed to breathe easier when he would go on his business trips for a week here or there. She couldn't remember ever seeing the man extend any warmth to either of his sons. What had it been like for Chance…and for Dev…growing up in such an atmosphere?

As Josie turned more pages, she saw very little of Dev in the photos. It was Chance who stood beside her in her party dress for her first real dance. Then, he was beside her again at her prom. The first time she branded a cow…he was in the background watching her. Her first cattle auction…he had taken her. She learned to drive in his old ranch truck…and he had stuck it out when she had put a couple more dents into it along the way. Through the years, it continued.

In more than a few photos, Chance was somewhere in the background, and his gaze was in her vicinity…like a watchful big brother. She hadn't needed a big brother…but he had been labeled that more than once. She was more than aware he was often thought of as the son her parents never had. That thought jarred inside her. Often times, it had felt he was a measuring stick in her mind…she had to measure up to Chance. And, just as clear as that thought came, another took its place…she never would. So she had to be tougher and stand on her own. She silently fought against him and his interference. She rebuffed him for helping. She tried to push him away, but he was just as stubborn. He kept her tied in knots, and her life was already difficult enough.

She learned early that, to have respect in the ranching world, you needed to be tough…doubly so if you were a female. Chance had seemed, at times, to step in where she didn't need him to be…and that angered her. She had to do things on her own. And the fact was, that now, she was truly on her own. People would be waiting and watching, expecting her to fail. As much as she might wish there was a strong hand to hold once in a while, or a shoulder to lean on when she felt inadequate to the task, she had to get through it. If she failed, she would have to fail on her own.

The final photo in the book was one taken last spring. It was of her and Chance, astride their horses, and Chance had said something, and she had laughed out loud. He threw her a grin in return just as the camera snapped. Something caught in her chest as she looked at the pair in the photo. They looked *happy*…with each other. It had been a really good day. *Chance.* Why did he frustrate her so much of late? Why couldn't they be like they once were? Things used to be so much easier…so much was changing, far too fast. Everything was slipping through her grasp.

She shut the book and shoved it away. Memories hurt too much. Pulling back the covers, she slid into bed and buried her head in her pillow. Josie prayed sleep would come quickly and shut out the memories and any dreams would stay at bay.

Chapter Five

TWO DAYS PASSED. On the third day, Josie repeated the other two. She rose before the sun and dressed in her usual work clothes...flannel shirt and jeans. The warmth of the previous day was gone. The temperature was in the upper forties, which made her parka and heavier gloves necessities. As she came out on the porch, she saw Tom's truck parked beside the barn. She joined him a few minutes later and found he had their horses saddled and ready.

"I figured you'd want to tackle the east pasture fence to-day," he said, swinging into his saddle as she did the same. "Roy Morgan volunteered some of his time today, and I sent him ahead with our couple of hands and the truck and materials."

She nodded her head. "We can start on it. Then we need to see how much more hay we need to add to the hay barn. If we can't get a better price than McGuffey's, I'll need you to head over to Sweetwater and see what you can get there." While they raised as much hay as they possibly could for their cattle, they fell short this season due to the drought conditions. With the early arrival of the first cold front, they would need to supplement even more than they had originally ordered earlier in the season. It would be another expense to add to the long list she calculated almost continually in her head…that and the looming business with the bank note. But, at the moment, she had to tackle what she could in the day before her.

Topping the second hill, they brought their horses up short. Josie blinked a couple of times to make certain she wasn't seeing things. Several men, not just her two ranch hands, and a work truck loaded with wire and toolboxes stood beside a section of their fence in need of repair. By their actions, the crew was intent on making fast work of it.

Before Josie could speak, her eyes caught the movement of the familiar big paint horse headed their way. Its rider, bundled in a navy work jacket, his black hat pulled down on his head, leather chaps protecting long legs, eased toward them. Chance Braxton sat a horse as naturally as if he was literally a part of it. She had caught herself a time or two almost mesmerized as she watched him cutting a herd of cattle or racing ahead of a remuda of horses.

However, she wasn't mesmerized at the moment. The irritation rose inside her. Did he take it for granted that she couldn't manage the re-fencing without his help? The wall came up. She wasn't smiling at his approach. She hadn't seen nor heard from him in almost three days, and then he appeared on her land, doing repairs he had no business making without her permission.

"Are your men lost? They happen to be on *my* land, not yours."

Chance ignored her remarks for the moment. He dipped

his head in a greeting to the man who sat between them, obviously wishing to be someplace else, instead of in the line of fire.

"Morning, Tom. Could you show one of my men which section you plan to restring next?"

"Sure thing." He didn't need a second invitation to leave the pair alone.

Chance waited until the man cleared earshot before he turned to look at Josie, moving his horse to stand close beside hers, their legs almost touching in their respective stirrups.

"Looks like we're back to normal." His sarcasm-edged remark wasn't lost on her. "As I said in an earlier conversation, you can push me away all you want, but I'm not going anywhere. You and Tom can't hope to get all the fence repaired before the next front hits. Adding a few of my crew can get it done in half the time. That frees up your men to do other things that need their attention. Don't worry…Tom gives the orders, and my men will follow."

"Why, Chance? All the times you send your crew along to help us out over here? Is it because you think, like everyone else, that I can't handle things on my own, or is it because you think you still have some misguided notion of atoning?"

"First of all, I don't think you can't handle it. You know better. You're more capable than most men I could name. As for atoning? For what?" By his expression, it was evident he was in the dark in regard to where her remark came from.

"For your father."

"What in the world does *my* father have to do with repairing your fence line?"

"My father asked for help from your father when the bulls your father had just purchased ran through our north pasture fence. Your father refused. That's why my father had to stay out in hundred-degree heat half the day, trying to fix it himself. That's where the men found him after he had suffered the stroke that killed him. I just think, sometimes, all this helpfulness on your part is some sort of way to make up for not helping back then. And, if that is the case, I can tell you that you can stop right now. That time is over and done with."

Sheer disbelief showed in Chance's gaze. He took his time responding. He appeared to be making an attempt to choose the best words, while holding back his own frustration. "I know you're still in the throes of grief over your mother, and I'm trying to keep that in mind. I've also tried to call you numerous times, and you refuse to answer me. Now I'm trying to do the *neighborly* thing and help with the downed fences, and all you can do is throw some ridiculous accusation from what my father did years ago in my face? I swear Josie, my patience is almost at the end of its tether." He took a deep breath then before he continued, and it was evident he used a great deal of self-control at the moment.

"Our fathers were lifelong neighbors, Josie. The day your father asked for help, mine said he would gladly give it, but the cowhands had to finish up with the repair of the well-head first. Water for animals in a heat wave comes before a fence repair. Your father was impatient, a trait you inherited from him. What happened was no one's *fault,* Josie. What is this really about?"

Part of her brain registered his words and their validity. He was right about the wellhead and everything else. What he said about her being impatient only made matters worse, along with the fact that he was *right,* and she was tired of admitting that truth. Downed fences were part and parcel of maintaining a ranch. If she couldn't take care of something as basic as that, what did that say about her ability to keep the ranch? She was failing…failing everyone and everything. That realization made her response sharper than it should have been. "We don't need your help. When we do need something, *I* will ask for it."

The look in his eyes should have warned her to back off. She waited too late to move.

"You need something all right. I can't decide if your father should have tanned your hide more when you were growing up or you just need a strong man to rein you in now."

Her mouth opened and then clamped shut. His words surprised her to the point of shock. So she didn't move. "I don't need either."

"That's where you're wrong." His hand snaked around her neck, bringing her toward him and holding her steady as his head immediately followed, his lips landing on hers as fast and white hot as a branding iron on a calf at roundup, and just as searing. Josie felt it through every fiber in her body, to the very tips of her toes in the stirrups. Just as her mind registered that fact, his lips left hers, his hand returning to the saddle horn.

Not a word was spoken. Chance gathered his reins into his gloved hands and turned the horse around, heading it away from the work crew, and away from Josie, at a fast clip. But not as fast as Josie's world had just turned upside down.

Chapter Six

"IT'S BEEN A while since I was last out here. I'd forgotten how far you can see once you get beyond the mesas and ridges." Phillip Banks was the senior partner of Banks and Banks, Attorneys at Law. He was close to retiring and letting Banks Junior take over the practice, but he had handled the legal affairs for Ben and Dianne Monroe since before Josie was born. He was always a kind man and not one to put on airs. He often shunned the suits of the courtroom for a pair of jeans, boots, and a white shirt with a bolo tie. Such was his attire at the moment, along with the heavy parka he had just shed after coming in from the cold afternoon. "That wind cuts right through you, too."

"Nothing to stop it between here and the Arctic Circle." Josie nodded in reply. "That's what my dad always said."

"Your dad was usually right."

"I have some fresh hot coffee in the kitchen. Have a seat in the living room and I'll bring you a cup."

"Nonsense. The kitchen table is the place to drink coffee on a day like today. And it's the best place to conduct business, too."

He followed her into the bright, homey room with its

myriad of cabinets and aroma of coffee and freshly baked muffins. Josie placed the muffins a little closer to his spot at the table.

"Are those banana nut?"

"Of course. I remember my mother always sending a basket of them to your office at Christmas. Mine aren't quite up to her level, but I think they're edible."

The lawyer chose one and took a bite, and he closed his eyes in obvious enjoyment, as he chewed slowly, savoring the experience. The sound of a truck pulling up outside, the slam of a door, and then purposeful strides of boots across the porch alerted them to the arrival of a third party. The front door opened and then shut, and before Josie could clear the chair, Chance strode into the room, removing his hat and placing it on the hook by the cabinet.

"Sorry, I'm late. I got held up by a phone call I had to take from a potential horse buyer. Have I missed anything?" He drew out a chair across from Josie and slid into it, an affable smile on his face as he addressed the pair.

Josie was speechless for a moment, trying to wrap her head around a reason he should even be there to begin with, much the less the easy familiarity he used when entering her house without a knock or an invitation.

"You're just in time. We haven't started," Phillip answered. "Josie got me sidetracked with one of these delicious muffins. Have one." He pushed the plate toward Chance, who didn't hesitate in taking one. "You'd probably like some coffee to go with that, too."

Josie realized the older man was looking in her direction.

She was expected to be the hostess for this new addition. She hadn't seen Chance since their explosive kiss three days before and she didn't care if she ever saw him again. He had taken their whole relationship and turned it upside down. Now, he was seated in her kitchen as if he had every right to be there. She kept as pleasant a smile on her face as possible as she rose, poured another cup of coffee, and returned to put it in front of the man. She didn't meet his eyes as she did so.

"I had no idea that Chance was invited to be here for this," Josie spoke, resuming her seat, her gaze on the attorney.

"Of course he has to be here. Your mother named him executor of the estate. Didn't you know?"

⁂

DIDN'T YOU KNOW? The words kept repeating in her brain even as she listened to the beginning of his reading of the will. How could she know? Her mother had never said a word to her about the terms of her will. Of course, Josie had to admit she had never wanted to discuss it with her. In her mind, the death of her mother was years and years away. That hadn't been the case.

Her mother had known for the last two years that her heart was not functioning as it should. She kept the news to herself and maintained her regular appointments and took the prescribed medications. All without Josie being the wiser. That was how the woman had wanted it. The doctors and

Phillip Banks all confirmed that point. She hadn't wanted her daughter to worry about her on top of running the ranch. Whenever Josie would ask about a doctor's visit, there was always a pat answer available...allergies, lingering colds, coughing fits, fatigue. The list went on.

In addition to that news, the fact she had appointed Chance Braxton as the executor of her estate was a shock. Josie had always assumed Mr. Banks would be the person in charge of carrying out her mother's wishes. Not their next-door neighbor. *Not Chance.*

Although, she should have guessed there might be such a possibility. Her mother and father always had a soft spot for the man. She had grown up hearing her father sing his praises almost daily. There wasn't a finer rancher to be found...and any man would be proud to call him son. And that highlighted the inevitable truth...she would never be the son her father had wanted. Of course, he had adored her, and never let on that she was ever a disappointment, but she wasn't stupid. And then Chance had come along, and her father...and her mother...had welcomed him into their little world, and he had not hesitated. He was perfect in their eyes.

Their opinion might be quite different if they knew about the kiss he had forced upon her. *Sure.* They would have ordered wedding invitations immediately, once their celebrating died down.

Only now, they weren't here. She was. And she faced the biggest decision of her life. The ranch was in bad shape financially. She had managed to barely make ends meet the last year, but the bank had always been willing to work with her. That is, until now, when an unfeeling conglomerate had replaced the hometown bankers who knew her and her family and cared about helping people in the community. She needed to talk to the attorney about all that, but not with Chance, the *outsider,* present. That hope of doing so was fast fading.

"I know this has come as a shock to you, Josie, on top of everything else that has transpired over the last couple of weeks in your life." Phillip's words brought her back around to the present situation. "I've laid out the basics for you. You inherited the ranch and all the problems with it. There's something else we need to discuss and that's the financial situation of the ranch. It's never easy reducing something you care about to cold, hard numbers on a balance sheet, but it's reality. The ranch has been in financial decline for a number of years."

She forestalled the man from continuing. "I don't think we need to bore Mr. Braxton with these details. He can read a report on his own. I think he can leave, and we can discuss these matters between you and I."

Chance met her gaze with his own steady blue one, arms folded across his broad chest. "I'm not bored. This is business, and I'm well aware of what Phillip is about to discuss. Your father and I already discussed some of these issues before he died. Your mother and I also had a talk about them a few months back. So I suggest we let Phillip state what he needs to say, and then you and I can discuss it."

Josie sat in stunned silence. How dare he sit there so cool and composed and stating what they should do? And the fact that her parents had discussed their private business with him only added fuel to the simmering fire. Anger mixed with a bitter pain of betrayal that her parents would do such a thing and not let her know about it. "Fine. Guess everyone knows everything about my business anyway, apparently." She sat back in her chair, trying to hang on to whatever shred of dignity she could find and wait to face whatever was coming.

Phillip shot a swift glance over at Chance, and then he turned his attention to the notes in front of him, clearing his throat. "The ranch went into the red about five years ago. The bank issued two loans, one of which went into default prior to your father's death. They would not consider extending the note as it was, but your parents were able to establish alternate financing. The second note became due and, as you know, the drought and drop in cattle prices and all, put a lot of good ranchers out of business the last couple of years. Anyway, this ranch has been kept afloat by these two notes administered through Mr. Peerman at the bank. The bank sent you a letter a couple of weeks ago, I believe, based on the copy they sent to me recently."

"I am well aware that the bank wants this ranch. I plan to go in and speak with this Mr. Peerman on Monday and try to get them to give me an extension. I've been working over some figures, that I think they need to look at, that I've forecasted for the spring calves." Josie spoke up and tried to sound like a businesswoman with a solid plan. But she had to admit, it sounded hopeless even to her own ears. Banking conglomerates didn't care about small ranchers like herself. Panic flitted through her stomach, but she wouldn't dare allow it to show to the two men seated at the table with her.

"Well, Mr. Peerman really has very little to say about the loans. It isn't…" Phillip responded, but was cut short when Chance broke in.

"The bank didn't issue the loans…that is to say, the bank isn't the lienholder on the ranch, Josie. The bank wouldn't underwrite the loans to your dad. I did that. The bank simply is acting on behalf of the lender of the funds…which would be Braxton Ranches Incorporated."

Josie sat stunned at the news. All along, she had blamed strangers sitting at a long, polished boardroom table in a distant city making their decisions. But all along, the enemy had been coming and going on her own land each day. Chance Braxton had always wanted their land, and here was proof of it! Her parents had played right into his hands. She stood.

"Get out. Get out of my house right now." She shot the words directly at the silent cowboy, her hands clenched in fists at her side.

"Josie, I think…" Phillip's words didn't get far.

"I am not angry at *you*, Mr. Banks, so please take no offense at this, but I really need to be left alone right now." Her words went to the attorney, but her eyes still blazed steel-colored fire directed at Chance.

The two men stood. The attorney gathered his papers and his jacket, while Chance solemnly eyed Josie, sliding the hat onto his head, but not bothering to put on his coat.

"Stop by my office this week, Josie, if you have any questions. I'm sure there's more that you and Chance will need to discuss together. If you need anything, please call me."

She accepted the hug from the older man and watched him head to his Lincoln in the driveway. She did not look at Chance as he stepped around her, but the moment he cleared the doorway, she shut the door firmly behind him. Only then did anger mix with pain and with a sense of betrayal which brought tears down her cheeks.

She felt betrayed, but by whom? By her parents who never once told her about the loans really being from Chance, or betrayal by the attorney for holding the secret from her? Or by Chance...who she had once trusted with her most secret confidences and dreams and who showed he only wanted to increase his own land at her family's expense? So much for *trust.*

Wiping the moisture from her cheeks with a swift swipe of her fingers, she moved to stand in front of the fireplace...seeking warmth to comfort somehow. The front door opened, and Josie turned swiftly to see Chance walk back into the living room. She thought he had left right behind Phillip. *Evidently not.* She crossed her arms over her chest and stood glaring at him.

"You don't own this ranch yet. A closed door means keep out unless you're invited inside."

"We needed to talk in private...and the sooner, the better." He laid his jacket on the back of the couch and placed his Stetson on top of it. Her words had no apparent effect on him. Chance walked to stand not far from her, warming his hands in front of the fireplace.

"*I* don't think so," she bit the words out.

Chance swung his dark gaze to focus on her, and she clasped her arms tighter, as if she needed to bolster a shield against him. "Okay, Josie. You've had a lot thrown at you in a short time. However, there isn't the luxury of time to sort things out and think things through. If you don't want to talk, at least you can listen."

She turned away to face the fire. She would have preferred to run upstairs to her room and slam the door and not come out again until he had disappeared down a dark hole, but since that wasn't going to happen, she needed to let him talk and get it over with.

He took her silence as agreement.

"Your mother asked me to be the executor that night at the hospital. I gave her my word to ease her mind. Phillip and I discussed it, and it was easier to agree with her at the time. In the true legal sense, it wouldn't be right for me to hold that position and be involved financially, as I am in the disposition of this ranch. I've asked Phillip to act in my behalf. I want everything to be as open as possible between us."

Josie looked over at him. "Open and honest? Are you *serious*? You knew all along that, sooner or later, this day would come, and you would have everything you wanted. You had more than enough time and opportunity to mention these details to me, yet you never did. Not until Phillip Banks made you own up to it today. You're just like the others, who think I'm some weak female who hasn't got any business trying to hold on to this ranch."

Chance's voice held a strange tone to it as he looked

down at her. "This isn't quite the day I envisioned, Josie. I didn't want to ever stand here with you thinking I'm the devil wanting to take away all you love and have worked so hard to hold on to. I made those loans because I respected your parents and what they were trying to do. I also didn't want to have to watch what the worry and stress was doing to you. There's nothing you could have done any differently, Josie. You've done your best to keep this place running. Time and Mother Nature dealt you blows that would defeat anyone."

"Not *you*," she ground out. "It must be nice to know that soon you'll be able to get your hands on this land."

The sapphire gaze came alive with smoldering fire as he rounded on her. "That's a low thing to say. It may come as a surprise to you, but I neither want nor need this property. But *you* do. Or have you decided that it's too tough after all and want to cut your losses and head to the big city?"

There was fire sparking from *her* eyes then, and her hands went to her sides, palms balling into fists as she faced him head on. "This is *my* home. I'll fight to my last breath to keep it, no matter what."

His gaze softened in its regard of her, as did the hard set of his jaw line. "That's more like it. There's the spirit and the fight I was counting on. You're in a bad spot right now, and I think you realize you're out of options if you want to keep this place. And, while I wish I could say that was all the bad news, I can't. I need to explain that it isn't exactly me who has the say-so over the calling of the loans. So, if you'll let me finish, we can then discuss options that will, hopefully, keep this ranch in your name."

"There's more bad news? What more could there be?" Her eyes narrowed as she watched him. What was he up to? Did he really have a way to help her keep her home? Why would he? No matter, if it was a viable plan, she'd listen. He was right about one thing...she had no other options at the moment.

"The loans are due. You can't get money from anyplace else to pay them off before they default. I may sit in the head chair at the table, but I have trustees to answer to, also. They expect the loans to be repaid, or equal value compensated for them. So I can't just void them. You need an infusion of money, but that takes Mother Nature cooperating, with a wet spring and a good herd of calves. You don't have the time for all that to happen."

"Tell me something I don't already know. Just get to your plan."

"Don't interrupt and I will do just that."

She bit back her retort. It was a hope to keep her home, and she would listen, for whatever it was worth.

"I'll give you an extension on your notes and place my own funds in your ranch account to cover expenses for a year. You'll satisfy the trustees. I'm placing a bet, if you will...on your abilities to put this place into the black. At the end of that year, if you have brought the ranch back into the black, then I sign off on the loans and guarantee the board will be agreeable. All you have to do is say yes."

Josie blinked a time or two. Had she missed something? She wasn't certain she had heard him right. She was rendered speechless, until wariness caused her to look directly into the steady gaze for what might be lurking there.

"I can't believe what I just heard. Why would you do that? Are you serious? What's in it for you? What strings are attached? You'll give me the money to make the bank note payments and keep the ranch going. Then, after a year, you'll forgive them, and all will be just fine. And I am supposed to believe all of that?"

"You can believe it. I would do it because I believe this place is worth it, and I think you can turn it around with a little help and time. I want you to have the chance to prove it. There are other reasons, but this is business. And, yes, I am *very* serious."

He watched her with a look in his eyes that she couldn't fathom. Chance Braxton was a good businessman…everyone knew that. His ranch was a premier operation, and his word carried weight in a lot of areas in their part of the state and beyond.

"You say you don't want the land. I keep wondering what's in it for you? What do I have to say yes to?"

He looked at the fire again and silence lengthened. Josie noted how the firelight flickered over his face…a face that she felt she was seeing perhaps for the first time, with its strong cheekbones, square jawline, and high forehead. A solid face, and too handsome for a female's peace of mind, in a rugged cowboy way. Strange, she hadn't really noticed that about him before. Her eyes gravitated to the mouth that had kissed her so unexpectedly and her gaze quickly darted away from it. She didn't need any thoughts of a personal nature clouding this discussion. He turned his eyes upon her at that moment, and she was drawn into the dark blue depths, as warmth crept through her, and her breathing became a little more difficult to maintain. His warm tone drew her in.

"You love this ranch. You'd never survive away from it…it's your heart. I've been buried in my own ranch, building it up and maintaining it. For what? I have no one to leave it to when I'm gone. Dev certainly doesn't care for it…he'd sell it in a heartbeat to a developer, who would cut it to shreds. You and I have more in common than you think. Time is passing us by. But there's a way we can help each other out. I'll help you keep your home, Josie, by giving you the time you need to prove it can be done. In return, you'll help me make a home…a legacy."

She slowly shook her head, trying to comprehend. "You lost me on the last part. How can I help you leave a legacy?"

"By marrying me. We'll be each other's family."

Silence was deafening. The chiming of the grandfather clock in the hallway cut through the thickness. Josie closed her eyes for a moment thinking her brain would clear itself and all would be sane when she opened them again. When she did, Chance stood watching and waiting. He wasn't an apparition, and he actually did just say those words to her. He had proposed? Never having a proposal before, she didn't have much to compare it to, but she was fairly certain it wasn't the way most of those things went. Marriage? To *him?*

"We could stand here and waste a lot of time, with you pointing out what an idiot you think I am, and how ridiculous this idea is, and a lot more, but the bottom line is really simple and won't change. If you can come up with a better option, I'm listening. Marry me and you'll get what you want and so will I."

"What about love?" She wished she could take back those words the moment she had spoken them. The look on his face became unreadable. "I mean, what if you…or I…what if we find we fall in love with someone else? How could you live your life with someone you don't love?"

"I'm willing to take my chances. Stranger things have happened…friends have been known to fall in love. Maybe I'll grow on you."

Was he trying to be funny? "You can't be serious. This can't be happening."

"This is very serious. You need to make a decision. Make no mistake, Josie…if you choose to not agree to these terms, then the loans will be called in by the trustees. I can't help with that once it starts. However, you also need to know something about me," his voice grew softer, as did his gaze, reaching a place deep inside her that responded without hesitation. "I mean what I say and, when I give my word, I keep it. This marriage won't be just a business arrangement. It's a commitment I'll be prepared to make to you for the rest of my life. I made a promise to your mother, and I make the same promise to you…I'll always be here for you. I'll do everything in my power to give you a good life…one you'll never have reason to regret. Once upon a time, you used to think I wasn't such a bad guy. I think we can find that again. It's something to build on."

"You said you'd give me a year to put the ranch in the

black. If I did that, then the loans would be cleared. What happens at the end of the year if we're married? If I want a divorce?"

His eyes and his demeanor both became unyielding in that moment. "Fair is fair. You put the ranch into the black, and if at the end of the year, you find you want out of our marriage…I won't keep you. You're taking a gamble on keeping your ranch…and I'll take a gamble, too."

"You and my mother talked about all of this? She knew? That's why she made you executor?"

"This was part of what we talked about, yes. It gave her peace in the end…knowing you would be taken care of and not have to lose this place you love so much. It wasn't that she didn't have faith in your ranching abilities, Josie…it was just that the hole was too deep for you to climb out of by yourself. As for the marriage part and my agreement to give you your freedom at the end of a year if you want it…that's my addition."

"My mother always wanted you for a son. She thought the sun rose and set with you…my dad did, too. There are a lot of memories in my life and my family's lives that have you in them. As much as I've tried to ignore those of late, it's still a history we share. But what sort of basis is that for a marriage?"

A knot formed in her throat. If Josie didn't know better, she'd think she was about to cry. Would it be because she was angry or because of something else she suddenly felt…a feeling that was foreign to her and made her both excited and afraid at the same time? "I need to think about…everything."

He took a deep breath and his shoulders relaxed a bit. "That's reasonable. I'll stop by tomorrow for your decision." Chance picked up his coat and shrugged into it, then settled his hat on his head. He moved to the front door and then paused, giving her a last look.

"We've always been friends, Josie. That's more of a foundation than many people have to build upon. Trust in what we can do together. I'll be cheering for you the loudest when you prove to everyone what you can do with this ranch. I believe in you. You need to decide if you can believe in *me*." For a moment, he seemed to want to add something else, but then evidently thought better of it. He stepped through the doorway and closed it behind him. This time, Chance did leave her alone.

Chapter Seven

I T WAS MIDMORNING and Josie had just finished feeding the horses in the barn and was crossing the porch when Chance's big black truck pulled in to the stable yard. The tall man exited, his eyes shaded by the brim of his hat, so she couldn't see his expression, but she could tell by the set of his jawline that he was determined about something. Maybe he had second thoughts about their strange conversation the day before? Was that wishful thinking on her part? Or an attempt to protect her feelings in case he came to tell her that his proposal was off the table after he gave it more thought? He could declare that now the loans were due?

His stride was purposeful and aimed directly for her. He looked too good, in jeans that fit snugly to long legs and hips, and the sheepskin-lined jacket covering the broad shoulders of his six-foot-three frame. And all that caused a stirring in her mid-section that she couldn't ignore. He was like rich bourbon that slowly snuck up on your senses and had you lulled under its spell before you knew what hit you.

Where had that all come from? He was Chance. She had watched him walk across a yard many times over the years and never noted such things before. What was happening to her and why wouldn't it stop? *If only there hadn't been that kiss.* She had to really concentrate in order to keep the memory of his kiss out of her brain and from their business at hand. It was all about her ranch and saving it. *Period.*

Josie had laid awake most of the previous night, her mind working over the words he had spoken and the future he proposed. She had tried to find a different solution, but each one met a dead end, with the same outcome…her losing the one thing she loved the most…her home. Chance had been right on that score.

"I would have been here sooner, but we had a stallion go down. The vet is there now, so I left him and my foreman to handle it," he explained, stepping onto the porch.

Josie turned and moved inside the house, leaving him to follow, which he did, closing the door behind him. She was aware of him moving behind her down the hallway and into the kitchen. Nervousness began a slow crawl in her stomach.

Chance removed his jacket and hung it and his hat on the pegs beside the door. He waited for her to open the conversation.

"There's coffee made if you want some." She turned to look at him, crossing her arms and leaning her hips against the cabinet.

"I've had my quota this morning, thanks. We might as well get to the elephant that's in the room. No use making small talk. I trust you've given thought to what I said last night."

"That goes without saying. I can't wrap my mind around it. You say you don't want the land, but that's the only plus side there is for you. You say you want a legacy…a family to leave everything to, but I know there is no shortage of females in this county more than willing to step up and help you out on that one. You don't need to choose someone that you don't care about and who certainly doesn't…." She cut her own words.

"Who doesn't care about me." He finished the sentence for her. A muscle twitched in his jaw, and he moved to the cabinet, taking a mug from the shelf and obviously deciding to pour himself a cup of coffee after all. The silence lengthened as he added a couple of spoons of sugar.

"I didn't say that."

"No, you didn't. I said it for you." His gaze settled on her over the rim of the mug as he took a sip. "Don't presume to think you know my motivations or my feelings. In all the years we've known each other, I doubt you've given much thought to how I feel about things at all. You've always been too busy worrying about others…most notably my absent brother. Well, this is just between you and me now. I stand by what I proposed. I meant every word of it."

His words totally rattled her for a moment. Of course she cared about him and his feelings. They didn't talk as much as they used to, but they weren't kids any longer…*okay so she wasn't a kid*. Chance had always been older. He couldn't say she didn't care. She always sought out his opinion and tried to follow his advice. *Wow*. The fact hit her like a light coming on in a dark room. He was right. Looking back, almost every conversation they had usually concerned her infatuation with Dev, or what was needed for the ranch. Or

Chance had been picking her up and putting her back together after Dev had done something to break her silly heart. Had she ever had a conversation with Chance that involved him and not his brother? She didn't like the answer to that question. She sought to change the direction of the conversation.

"*Proposed*…that was some proposal, I must say. No one could ever accuse you of turning a girl's head with hearts and flowers." Her attempt at levity fell flatter than a pancake.

Chance set the mug on the cabinet and took a step closer, his eyes intent on her. "I didn't think those things would help my case any, but I can certainly remedy that if it'll move you in my favor and not get me knocked flat on my butt by you."

Josie pushed away from the counter and moved to put some space between them. For some reason, his presence was making the space smaller, and the air in the room was heavier to breathe. "That won't be necessary. I was joking. It would just be a mockery anyway. What we have to handle is business and strictly that. While I've tried to think of any other way out of the mess I'm in, I can't come up with anything in the timeframe I'm faced with. But I can't help think that, sooner or later, one of us will come to regret making this deal."

"That seems to be what's giving you the most issue with this. I know myself and can speak to that without the least bit of concern. I realize that you have a different viewpoint. I'm willing to agree that, should the day come you find yourself in love with someone and want to end our marriage,

I won't stand in your way…after the year is done and you've done your best to meet me halfway…to give things an honest try."

Had she heard correctly? It gave her pause and a hint of suspicion filtered through her mind. "You'll simply let me out of the marriage?"

"As long as you have made every effort to work with me on this situation, to try to make a reasonable effort between us, then I wouldn't want to hold you if your heart was elsewhere."

"If I say no? If I try to save this ranch on my own?"

"Then the trust will move to secure the collateral of the loans and to take control of the ranch and all its assets. You would take away nothing but your personal belongings."

The words were cold and chilled Josie to the bone. How could he talk so dispassionately about things that were her very life? Because it wasn't *his* life. At the end of his day, he could walk away. At the end of her day, she would walk away with nothing…no home, no land, only memories. And the sense that she had failed her father and mother.

"How would you dispose of the 'assets' as you call them?"

"I think the Richter brothers have always had their eye on this place. In fact, I have a message from Paul Richter to call him. Seems he wants to know if you're planning to sell. He might…"

"My father would turn over in his grave if he thought a Richter would ever set foot on our land!" She spoke up with vehemence at the very idea. "You can't be serious. They don't even run their own place and cattle in a decent way."

"Calm down, Josie. I didn't say it was a done deal. You asked about the options. That's an example of where I would have to go next to recoup the loans. Braxton Ranching is a business, too, and those loan amounts would have to be covered somehow. I am aware of what this ranch means to you and to your family. I wouldn't have suggested what I did last night if I didn't know just what this place means to you."

His tone was softer, almost soothing now. "We're on the same side, Josie. If we can find a common middle ground again, I think we have a chance."

Josie returned her gaze to the crackling fire behind the iron grate. She was standing on the edge of a deep canyon, and she couldn't see the bottom. Dare she trust him? She had trusted him for so long...and then something had changed between them. And he had kept secrets from her...about her own ranch and the loans and all. There was no one to seek advice from. All she had was her brain and heart, and they weren't in agreement by a country mile.

"What still worries you?"

"The marriage part...is that really necessary? I mean...what is it that you expect would be any different if we..."

"It's marriage or no deal." He made the statement as succinct as possible. His gaze was steady and locked on hers. "You aren't a child any longer. I intend to make a commitment to you...to us. I expect the same from you. Will I force you into any situation you aren't okay with? Will I force myself on you?" Chance took a step closer, just a hint of a gleam in those sapphire eyes, as they floated over her already heating cheeks.

"I won't force anything. We'll find common ground. I've learned a lot of patience over the last few years, for some odd reason." And then there was a slight grin. It lasted for a moment, and then he was all business again. "So what's it to be?"

It was no use postponing it any longer. He held her with a steady gaze, no sign of any nerves on his part.

Her heart was beating faster in her chest than it ever had before. There was only one decision to make. Josie had to hold on to the last remnants of life as she knew it. All she had, all she could count on, was the land beneath her feet. It was all that remained of her family. What would come tomorrow or the day after that, she had to let it go. One day at a time was the only way she would be able to get through this waking nightmare she had been dropped into since the death of her last parent and the subsequent reading of the will.

Josie fixed her gaze on the man standing across from her. The man who she wondered if she ever *really* knew. The man who held the key to the future…for better or worse. Fighting the sudden feeling in the pit of her stomach that she might hurl the meager breakfast she had earlier, she quickly nodded her head and drew in a calming breath, her chin rising to take what would come.

"Yes. I have no other recourse but to agree. I'll marry you. But I'll run this ranch as I always have…without your interference. You have your ranch and I have mine."

Was there a perceptible twitch at the corner of his mouth? Had she said something amusing? Her gaze narrowed on him, hands fisting on her hips.

"And neither the twain shall meet?"

"I don't recall making a joke," she responded. "There's nothing remotely amusing about any of this."

There wasn't any hint of amusement on his face any longer. "You're right. This isn't amusing. But neither is it the end of the world. It's a detour, but we're in this together. So we negotiate. I agree that you'll continue to run this ranch as you have each day. I'll take care of the bookkeeping and paying the bills. When my ranch hands can be spared from my place, they'll be available to help over here. I know this is your home, and you've had a lot of change in your life lately, so, for now, I have no problem moving in here with you. We can decide where we'll make our permanent home later."

"Move in *here*?" She suddenly felt the ground shift beneath her feet again. She hadn't given much thought to the actual day-to-day arrangements. "Why can't you stay on your ranch?"

"News flash, little one. Married people usually share the same house."

Panic rolled around inside her at the prospect of sharing anything with him, much less things shared by a couple. Heat began to rise along the back of her neck, and she hoped it wasn't a full-blown blush for him to see. The knowing look in his eyes told her he had seen and knew what was in her mind.

"It's no secret that children are a necessity to pass any

legacy on to. However, first things first. We've got to get used to marriage before bringing in anyone else to the mix. So relax, Josie. As I've already stated, I'm not going to expect you to say 'I do' and fall into my bed."

Josie blocked the image that came to her mind as soon as he said those words. She needed to keep her wits about her and not let Chance Braxton get her off track and thinking about things that would only complicate everything. *One day at a time...until an exit could be found.*

"What happens next?"

"Are you accepting my proposal as it stands?"

"I am."

Chance moved slowly towards her. He stopped within a foot of her.

Her five-foot-five-inch frame was dwarfed by his. At such close range, she was able to note the little crinkle lines radiating from the corner of his eyes, eyes that weren't a dark sapphire at the moment, but a lively sky blue, as if something had given him immense pleasure. His lashes were longer than any man's had a right to be, and the slight crook of his nose, from where he was tossed by a bronc into the dirt at age thirteen and had been broken, only lent a masculine virility to a face that loomed ever closer to hers. When her gaze fell of its own volition to his mouth, she almost forgot to breathe.

"I'd kiss you right now because I'm fairly certain that would follow a normal proposal and a moment like this. But I'm afraid if I did try, you might knock my head off. So I'll just get back to my place and get things rolling, beginning with letting Phillip know what our plans are for the time being. I'll be back to pick you up about seven."

Those words jarred her back to the moment. "Pick me up? Why?"

"To celebrate, of course. It's not every day I get engaged. How about you?" The familiar, easy grin was back, warming his eyes. "We'll make it dinner…your choice. We can go to the cattlemen's club or to the country club or…except I can see by the look in your eyes you don't care for either of those. I would venture that you might prefer…Nan's Back Porch."

"I'm not a fancy place kind of female. I have work to do early in the morning. I don't need…"

"You're a female after my own heart. I saw that hint of a smile when I mentioned your favorite restaurant. The Back Porch it will be, and I'll have you home early enough. You're a smart lady…see how you're already catching on? Now get busy…you've got a ranch to run and so do I." Before she realized what he was doing, he had lowered his head and placed a quick kiss on her cheek before she could react. Stepping back, he gave her a tease of a wink and then reached for his jacket and hat. She was left looking at the closed door. *What had she just done?*

Chapter Eight

W*HAT HAD HE just done?* He had become an engaged man. Not exactly how he envisioned it to be when the day came, but, then again, Josie Monroe was an unusual girl. *Make that woman.* His course had been set years ago, when he rode over with his father to see their neighbor, Ben Monroe, and he had caught sight of a girl, red mane of hair flying behind her, as she and her horse raced across the field and drew up beside them. He should have known then that he was in for a wild ride knowing her, her silver-laced eyes challenging him even then.

And then his brother had come along, and those eyes had changed. He had to watch as yet another female fell for the Dev Braxton charm. He tried to ignore it. But, for some reason, his shoulder gravitated toward Josie more and more, and he fell into a new normal…making himself the protector of her heart. He had never envied anyone. But he knew the green-eyed monster on a personal basis each time he saw the look in Josie's eyes and then the tears shed over some careless way his brother had broken her heart.

As the years passed, that envy turned to anger on more than a few occasions. He wasn't unhappy when his brother finally left the ranch and took off for more exciting places. That left Josie alone, but Chance did his best to step in whenever needed.

Maybe he had been foolish to do so. But he had no regrets. Maybe he was still being foolish to think that Josie could ever see him as more than a business partner and a poor substitute for his brother. Maybe. But it was a chance he had prepared himself for a long time to take. Josie was worth it. They were headed down a new road...*together.* He had to trust it was the right one.

SIX HOURS LATER, Chance was headed along that road. He could set the cruise control and the truck would find its way to the Monroe ranch without any help from him. At least, that's the way it felt. He thought back over the years he had traveled the road between the two ranches. Or cut across acres of land on horseback, all to arrive in the same place...wherever Josie was.

This trip was different. Tonight, he was on his way to pick up Josie Monroe...*his fiancée.* He still found it difficult to believe. While he may have thought about it...even daydreamed about it once or twice over the years...*okay, maybe more than a few times*...he never expected it to ever be a reality. Josie Monroe was a wild combination of spitfire and tenaciousness, soft heart and natural beauty. Josie had grown from a gangly, coltish girl into a beautiful and desirable woman, and the most amazing part of all was the fact that she had no idea. There wasn't one ounce of conceit or pretense. What you saw was what you got with Josie.

Josie's secret weapon, a secret even from her, was the fact she had no idea how absolutely sexy she could be without even trying. While the jeans she most often wore might just be serviceable in her estimation, they often increased the blood pressure levels of many of the males she crossed paths with on the ranch and on the streets of Braxton. He knew that fact because he had seen it in many of those men's eyes, and he had felt it often enough first hand.

She had a glorious mane of deep red hair with lighter natural streaks of blonde highlights which she insisted on braiding or tying back out of her way more often than not. The few times he had seen it down and around her shoulders, he had to keep his hands occupied elsewhere to keep from reaching out to touch it. Those silver-gray eyes of hers were always expressive, often reminding him of a feline's eyes…and usually good at putting him in his place with one look.

Long lashes were natural concealers so that one never knew what thoughts were really behind those eyes and, yet, they drew you into them, and a man could drown there if he wasn't careful. Her beauty was natural and needed no false enhancements. And when you made her laugh, you felt as if your whole life had just been made worthwhile. His goal was to make her laugh more. She had carried the weight of the world on her shoulders for a long time. It had made her less likely to laugh and more apt to frown, to grow a protective shield around feelings that, at the slightest perceived threat, would bring out her defense mechanisms.

Chance knew none of what was ahead would be easy. From the moment Phillip Banks had dropped the bombshell of the will and the truth had come out about the nature of the loans that had saved the Monroe ranch in recent years, he had known things would not be easygoing...not with Josie and her pride and stubborn determination to handle everything on her own slim shoulders. She was strong and independent and would fight him like one of his mustangs when trying to halter them.

He couldn't blame her. His hope had to be that, one day, she would realize that he didn't want to break her or take the spirit away. That was all part of what made him care so much to begin with. *Care.* That was a watered-down word for what he did feel and had felt for quite some time where she was concerned. Lord knows he had tried to ignore it and keep her compartmentalized in a place that was far from his heart. Especially since she had never been able to see beyond his younger brother to anyone else.

He had been a shoulder for her to cry on so often he'd lost count. He wanted to tear his brother limb from limb more than a few times and shake sense into him. Dev had always had things come too easy for him. He had placed little value on a young girl's heart. Otherwise, he couldn't leave so often and stay gone so long.

But then, a day came when he realized that he didn't really want Dev to look at Josie in a different way...as another female to become a conquest...another heart to step on and leave in tatters when he was done. Dev was all about lovin' and leavin' them with a smile. Josie deserved better. So he stayed in the role of confidant and advice giver…to protect her and be there, hopefully, when the day came she woke up and put her infatuation with his brother behind her. If that made him weak or crazy, so be it. Josie's heart was worth the wait. And he was about to take a real leap of faith with his own.

THE HALL CLOCK had just chimed for the seventh time when Chance stood at her front door. For a moment, Josie forgot to speak at the sight of the man in the snug, charcoal dress jeans and crisp white shirt with its long sleeves and pearl snaps. A gray, western-cut suede jacket, sans tie, gave it a polished, yet easy, finish. The dark Ostrich gray boots and cream Stetson made him the epitome of the well dressed, well-heeled, wealthy rancher about to set out for an evening in town, and she had to remind herself with a pinch, he was still Chance…the man she had always known. Except that wasn't really the case now. He was also her fiancé. That sent her stomach rolling again.

Josie suddenly felt woefully inadequate in the soft, plum-colored angora sweater with its long sleeves and V-neck. She had matched it with a slim black corduroy skirt that fell just below the knee. A pair of black, high-heeled, knee-high boots covered her legs. She wore the small pearl studs in her ears that her mother received from her father on their thirtieth anniversary. The way Chance's eyes slid slowly over her ensemble made her more self-conscious. She had tried to appear more sophisticated and had swept her long hair onto the top of her head, but she knew even that fell short in the attempt at the sophistication department.

It was too late to wish she had paid more attention to girly things that her mother tried to expose her to along the way. It seemed they had both chosen to step it up a bit for their first "date" or whatever it might be called. People most often dressed in western casual...jeans and boots being the mainstays of wardrobe for the crowd that favored Nan's Back Porch. Special occasions brought out the polished boots and ladies in dresses.

"Punctual and very beautiful." He took the black jacket from her and held it while she slipped it on. Then he gave her his arm, and she didn't hesitate in accepting it. For some reason, her knees felt a bit wobbly. She didn't want to crash down the porch steps. Seated beside him in the luxury SUV, she certainly felt special. The way he had spoken the word "beautiful" kept rolling around in her mind as the vehicle ate up the miles.

Coupled with the dark blue velvet look in his eyes when he had spoken it, it had certainly given her pause. Besides her parents, who were more or less obligated to think and say such a thing, no one else had ever said that to her. Her insides had gone all quivery...*was that even a term*? If he kept that sort of talk up during the evening, she wouldn't know what to do. However, Chance kept the conversation on a safe subject during the drive...the daily business of their respective ranches. She was grateful for that. Anything else and she would have felt out of her comfort zone. It wasn't lost on her that he was doing his best to make her feel comfortable.

Josie was definitely glad Chance had not opted to take her to the upscale private cattlemen's club or the ostentatious country club to sit among the city's snootiest. Nan's Back Porch was situated out in the middle of nowhere, almost twenty miles from the city, down a winding country road. It looked like a weathered old ranch house with long wrap around porches dotted with rocking chairs and tables. Hanging baskets of ferns and bright petunias would hang along its length in the warm months.

Now, with the approach of late fall, lanterns hung in those spots, and most diners were seated inside the cavernous main room, at wooden tables and booths, with Texas antiques and photos on the walls. The place was always crowded, no matter the time of day, because the food was true, down-home, fresh country cooking. That reputation not only brought the locals in droves but also lured celebrities and politicians, including a U.S. President. These semi-regulars were evidenced by the signed photographs on the walls... most taken with "Aunt" Nan Lewis, whose family owned the land, and who oversaw the cooking of the family recipes for most of her seventy-five years.

It was Nan who bustled across the room and met them as they stepped through the door. She beamed her delight as Chance swept off his hat and bent to give her a peck on her upturned cheek.

"Now that's what I call a nice hello. You're always such a

sight for these old sore eyes, Chance Braxton." Her gaze lit on Josie next. Her smile widened into a full beaming grin. She stepped forward and slid an arm around Josie's shoulders and gave her a hearty hug. "Well, look here! What a wonderful surprise to see you in here again, little miss Josie. You certainly have grown up quickly." The woman sent a pointed look in Chance's direction. "Took you long enough to notice, young man."

"Oh, I noticed a while back, Aunt Nan," he returned with a wink.

"My, my...let me get Suzy to show you to our best table...and most romantic." She returned his wink with a saucy one of her own. Josie tried her best to continue to smile and hope her face wasn't blazing red, as it felt so hot.

They followed their waitress to a booth in the corner of the room next to the floor-to-ceiling windows that looked out over the sloping yard to the flowing creek that crossed the property. The sun had just dropped below the horizon and, in the dusk of the evening, a couple of deer munched on the sweet grasses still hanging on along the bank. Josie slid into the booth, and her gaze fell on a single, long-stemmed pink rose lying in front of her on the table.

A quick check of other tables told her that no other tables had flowers. She picked it up and breathed in its scent. Then she looked up and found Chance's eyes on her. The look in them definitely was new, also. It sent an immediate trilling across her nerves, and her pulse began a tap dance to an unknown beat.

"I seem to remember that you like pink roses." He noted

the inquiry in her eyes. "From prom night. The roses in the corsage…" His voice trailed off as he remembered, as did she, the catastrophe that night had been. It was so long ago; she was surprised he remembered at all.

"Thank you. Yes, I do like them. I keep thinking that one of these springs I'll plant some rose bushes around the house, but something always comes up and the time gets away."

"Maybe this spring we'll see what we can do about that." The waitress appeared at that moment with two champagne flutes, filled with the golden bubbly. She served their drinks and then left them.

"Okay, I'm thinking the special booth, the rose, and now champagne arriving as we have just sat down…this was all planned."

"I might have told Aunt Nan when I called earlier to make the reservation that this was a special occasion. Which it is."

"If you thought I would expect anything… it really wasn't necessary to go to any extra…"

"You never expect more, do you?" The question was an odd one and caught her off guard.

"Why do you ask that? I've never been one to want more than what I already have. It's been a good life so far."

"Maybe it's just that *I* expect more for you." His reply was cryptic. "At any rate," he changed the tone as he lifted his champagne glass toward her, "here's to an even better life ahead…for the both of us." She stayed silent as she took a sip of the bubbly liquid.

The meal was excellent, as usual. Chance had their signature T-bone steak, and she had ordered the pork ribs. Fresh vegetables, from the garden on the grounds of the restaurant, were cooked to perfection. As the meal progressed, Josie actually found herself surprised by the way they had settled in to a conversation. Chance seemed to lead them into subjects that wouldn't spark any debate between them. He made an obvious attempt to keep things easy, although Chance seemed to be at ease wherever he was. She envied him that ability.

Josie's gaze fell on the pink rose, and her mind flashed back on the prom night again. She had been on cloud nine for days. It had taken a month for her to get up the courage to ask Dev to take her to her prom. To her absolute astonishment, he had said yes. She agonized for days over finding the right dress and having her hair and nails done in town and being just *perfect* for him. Then she had been stood up.

Dev had gone to a bachelor party for one of his older college buddies and had been too plastered to drive. Chance had shown up on her doorstep, corsage in hand, and had taken her to the prom. He had done his best to cheer her up. The other girls all thought it was super cool that she had such an "older" and "sexy" date. She only knew the date she wanted hadn't felt it was important enough to show up for her. She begged off early in the evening with a headache, and he took her home. It hadn't been the evening of her dreams…her silly adolescent dreams. Dev had taken off on one of his long trips after that night. He hadn't even said goodbye. That had been left to Chance to handle also.

"Something made a cloud darken those silver eyes of yours just now. What's wrong?"

Chance always could read her even when she tried her best to elude his instinctive gazes. He never allowed her to get away with much over the years. He kept her grounded whenever she ventured too far out in her crush on his brother. She had fancied herself madly in love with Dev. Chance had figured that out almost before she had.

He never warned her off his brother. But he never tried to cover for his brother's weaknesses either. He had allowed her to have her foolish dreams and was there when she needed someone to tell her to get over it and get back to her studies or to work. He waited patiently for her response even now.

"Just thinking about things from long ago. Just memories."

"These things can keep us grounded. It can also hold us back. The key is to recognize the difference."

"More '*Chance words of wisdom*.'"

"Are you mocking me?"

"No. I'm just stating a fact. My father always said you were young in years but old in wisdom. He usually said that right after you had to rescue me from one thing or another. It got really old, really fast, always hearing how great you were. My dad would have loved to have had you for a son. That was a fact I had to come to terms with early on. I will admit it made me angry more than a time or two. I guess that's a big reason why I wanted to be mean to you and push you away…keep you off our land. Then I wouldn't have to compete with you, too."

"Well, he's getting me as a son-in-law soon. I think he might approve, wherever he and Mama Dianne are right now. And you were his greatest joy...you had to have realized that. I know he might not have said so in flowery words, because that wasn't his way, as we both know. But the sun rose and set with you. No one was prouder of the way you stepped forward and worked beside him, trying to absorb all that you could."

"Yes, I suppose I just felt so inadequate at times in comparison to others...to *you*. They thought you were special from the beginning."

"Too bad their daughter doesn't." He spoke the words with a lift of his mouth into a half-grin. "That was meant to get a smile out of you, in case you missed it. I admit I might be a bit rusty in the joke department, but you could take pity on me now and then and give a little smile."

She looked at him then. *Really* looked at him. Chance...*special*? Hanging the moon? *Wow*. The moon suddenly didn't seem so far out of reach. What happened? Maybe it was the champagne? Whatever it was, it was scary, and left her breathless and feeling strange sensations deep within her core.

"Is that why you tried so hard to push me away in the last months with your dad? Before he died? You saw me as a threat?" His question was direct, and his gaze did not waver from her. He deserved a direct answer.

"Yes. I suppose it was. You were always around, helping out, and if you were always there, then how could he see what I was trying to do? Sounds silly and childish now, and I realize I probably was that at times. I tried so hard to be so adult and in control of things that I ended up looking mean and inadequate. He saw that."

"Your dad knew how hard you tried, and he saw you succeed more than you know. He wanted to be able to protect you from the callous things other ranchers would say about a young female not being able to hold her own in a 'man's world,' which angered him. He took on a few of them a time or two at our cattlemen's meetings. He was a good man, a good father. You were lucky."

Instinct told her that he might have often compared her father and his in his mind. And knowing what she knew of the elder Braxton, she realized that maybe Chance spent so much time with her parents and helping them for another reason...because he found something he lacked in his life. And that made her feel even more selfish. She kept her gaze averted to the darkness outside the window. No matter how much one might wish for it, you could never make time go in reverse...get a second chance to go back and rewind the past. She finished her second glass of champagne to fortify herself for the trip back to the ranch.

"I promised to have you home before too late, so we better be on the road." Chance brought her back to the present and gave her something real to concentrate on, and she was grateful. There was a definite chill in the night air as they exited the building...which took a while as they were stopped at quite a few of the tables along their way.

Josie shouldn't have been surprised as Chance returned

handshakes and quick quips with the other diners…many of whom were neighbors or business acquaintances she recognized…some she didn't. She also noted the looks given to her companion by more than a few of the younger females in the room. Those gave her pause, too…in an odd sort of way. She might have taken him for granted over the years, but Chance was certainly of interest to the women around them. Of course she wasn't jealous.

Josie bundled her coat around her tighter as she snuggled against the leather seat a few minutes later. Chance noted the movement and turned the heater up a notch. There was a half-moon visible through the moon roof of the vehicle, and Josie found herself feeling an odd sense of peace as she looked upon the scenery outside her window. In her hands, she held the single rose…a souvenir of a most unusual evening. Chance turned on the radio, and soft, country instrumentals filled the empty spaces. There wasn't any need to make conversation between them.

It seemed no time at all they drew up in front of the house. Chance switched off the ignition but made no move to get out. Instead, he released his seat belt and ran a hand over his head…a movement Josie had seen many times and had come to realize usually preceded his having something to say that wasn't something she might be in agreement with. Josie sat up straighter in her seat…waiting.

"I spoke to Phillip today, and he's aware of our decision. I then paid a visit to the bank and squared away some things there so that there will be operating capital in the ranch account beginning tomorrow. My final stop was at the church with Reverend Morrison. He and Edna are taking vacation to visit their grandkids, but he scheduled us the minute he returns. He's agreed to marry us at the ranch in three weeks' time. Unless you want a full church wedding…then we can certainly plan on that. I know some women put a lot of store in big weddings with all the trimmings. If you want that, then we'll make it happen. It's your decision."

"Three weeks? So soon?" She had no idea it would all happen so fast. *Deep breath.*

"There's no need for a prolonged engagement. Is there?"

"I suppose not," she replied, thinking how surreal the whole conversation was once again. "There's no need for a big wedding. It's not like this is a real proposal and marriage." She realized what she had said after it was too late. Chance didn't respond right away. He simply opened his door and got out of the vehicle. She watched him walk around, and then he was at her door, holding it open for her. His expression was unfathomable in the darkness. She slid out and walked toward the house. A hand on her arm stopped her as she reached the porch. She turned to the tall man.

"Look Josie, I realize that this isn't following the norm of most engagements. I apologize that I didn't take more time and try to make it more *special* for you. For instance, right now, I'm sure there's a more romantic way to do this, but I doubt you want to hear such things from me. My mother only had a simple gold band, so I have no special family heirloom to pass on to you. I picked this out this afternoon.

The fire in it reminded me of your eyes...more often than not when I've done something to rile you...or kiss you."

Josie's gaze dropped quickly to the hand he raised between them and the velvet jeweler's box open to display a solitaire in an oval halo that was definitely the most beautiful ring she had ever seen. It had to be at least a couple of carats in a classic platinum setting. Its brilliance winked at her in the light of the porch. She was stunned speechless and could only watch as Chance withdrew it from its box and, taking her hand in his, slowly slid it on the appropriate finger.

"I made the best guess I could on the sizing. If it still needs adjustment, I can take it to the jeweler tomorrow."

Slowly, Josie was regaining her equilibrium. "It fits perfectly. It's a beautiful ring, but a plain band would..."

"I know," he interrupted her, a hint of exasperation in his tone. "A plain band would have been enough," he finished for her. "Just say, 'thank you, Chance.'"

"Thank you, Chance," she responded and found she really did mean the words. "It truly is a most beautiful ring. I've never owned anything like it."

She was rewarded with a slow smile that caused her breathing to catch in her chest...something that seemed to be happening a lot more of late.

"I'm glad you think so." Silence stretched as tight as a rubber band. Chance closed the lid of the box and handed it to her. Then he reached over and opened the front door but then stepped back.

"Thank you for the wonderful dinner. And my rose," she spoke in the awkward moment, her hand clutching the stem while her other hand still tried to get used to the ring.

Two long fingers reached out and claimed her chin, bringing her surprised gaze to his. The smile amped up and made her insides feel close to melting. "Relax, Josie. It won't always be this awkward between us. We're still the same two people we always were. Now go inside and get some sleep." He didn't kiss her cheek this time. His lips dropped to hers in a kiss that was a promise in itself.

Josie closed her eyes and she actually saw stars for a moment. Champagne-induced? She didn't think so. It was all pure Chance. The kiss ended almost as soon as it had begun and, when she opened her eyes, she thought she saw an answering look of surprise in Chance's gaze. It was a couple of moments before he stepped back, dropping his hand to his side. "Have sweet dreams, my love. I know I will."

THE DREAMS THAT came during the night were definitely not sweet. They were bordering on steamy, to an extent that Josie woke in a tangle of sheets and feeling heated, even though the temperature outside had to be in the low forties. Her cheeks blazed again as she remembered certain parts of the dreams that had Chance kissing her until she saw stars again, and her responses were definitely shocking. She needed to get a grip. Things were already confusing enough, and she needed to keep her head on straight. There was a ranch to be saved, and that was all that mattered. Pushing out of bed, she set her thoughts on doing just that.

Josie had just poured a mug of coffee when her ears detected the sound of a familiar truck's engine approaching the house. She took another swallow of the black liquid and found it bitter to her taste. Perhaps that was because she forgot to pour the usual sugar into it. Already Chance was ruining her concentration. She counted to ten and, then, grabbing her jacket, she marched down the hallway to the front door. She reached the front door just as it swung open.

"Well, I didn't expect a welcoming committee. Thanks for the hot coffee, too." His sudden appearance and words caught her off guard. Chance took the mug from her and took a sip. A slight crease in his forehead became evident as he looked into the cup. "Next time, a little sugar in this would be good. I have a sweet tooth. But I appreciate the thought." He handed the mug back to her and she took it. The movements galvanized her speech capabilities.

"That was *my* coffee. I was on my way to the barn. I wasn't expecting you."

Chance stepped by her into the hallway. The brisk air followed him, along with a faint scent of some manly cologne that caught Josie's senses and did strange things in the pit of her stomach. She wrote it off to the fact she hadn't eaten.

He took off his Stetson and placed it on the hat rack beside the entrance into the living room. He shot her a look as he did so. "Did you sleep well last night? You look a little tired this morning."

"I slept just fine." Did she look tired? *Probably*. But it was *his* fault...only she wasn't about to tell him that. She set the mug on the hall table.

"How many rooms does the upstairs have? I don't think I've ever been up there." He was on the third step before Josie came alive.

"What are you doing?"

Chance turned unexpectedly, and she almost bumped into him. His steadying hands on her shoulders made her catch the breath in her chest. Her skin was all tingly where his hands rested, something she was very much aware of. It was a reaction which made her even more upset with herself and with him.

"I'll start moving some of my things in this week, so thought I should see what room there is and that sort of thing."

"There's a sewing room downstairs that has a closet and room enough to use as a bedroom."

"What about your room?"

The color drained from her face. She struggled to keep her chin up as she felt woefully inadequate to meet his very male gaze with her own. "I just thought...that is...you might be more comfortable downstairs."

"Nice try, Josie. But I'm sure we'll make your room work just fine." Then he paused. "How many boyfriends have you had, Josie? I might have missed counting one or two over the years."

Now he was getting too personal for her liking. But she wasn't about to back down. "I dated in high school...when I had time."

"Yes, I know. Not counting the two dances I took you

to…in lieu of my brother…how many boys have you dated…have you kissed?"

"This is not a conversation that I think is any of your business."

"It is…because you seem a bit unsure of yourself when I mention the intimate side of what marriage entails. I know your mother had to have explained the birds and bees to you."

"This is ridiculous! And yes, I know about the birds and bees. I live on a cattle ranch for heaven's sake…animals are great teachers of what happens between opposite sexes, too. Just because I'm not one of those promiscuous town females you probably are used to, doesn't mean I haven't had my share of kisses with boys."

"Just kisses?"

She had to slam her mouth shut at his audacity. Counting to ten took too much time, and she cut it short. "I don't believe in kissing and telling. I know enough, thank you. And just because I'm none too keen on standing around talking about such things as where you'll be sleeping and all, doesn't give you the right to assume I'm a…whatever." She went to turn but his hand on her elbow stopped her.

Chance took a step and that brought him within inches of her. She had to crane her neck a bit to see his expression. His eyes glittered through their dark lashes and his gaze was definitely on her lips. "I think the term you were looking for might be virgin. And that is perfectly fine with me. But maybe we should wait on the tour after all. Although, I'm just now beginning to realize the full benefits of what our marriage can entail."

His words dropped her heart to her knees. "What benefits?"

His hand came up, and two fingers cupped her chin, allowing his thumb to run a light, lazy pattern across her full bottom lip. "Seeing your pretty face each morning and beginning the day as it should be started." His thumb was replaced by his lips in a quick, warm kiss. It didn't last long, and her participation was not required.

"Don't worry, Josie. I'll be putting a few things in the old foreman's room off the stables. It'll be more convenient to stay here some evenings with the branding coming up. I won't move into the house with you until we are all nice and legal. We don't need to give the town gossips any more to talk about than they already will have when word of our engagement gets around. Now, we have livestock to feed. Last one to the barn is a rotten egg."

He won the race. For some odd reason, her brain was still stuck on the bedroom issue.

JOSIE KNEW IT was a mistake…mucking out the stalls with Chance across the aisle in the other part of the barn, which was a total distraction. Only a little less than the memory of his swift kiss earlier on the staircase. It was the third time in one week Chance Braxton had kissed her. *Why?* He had never come close to her before, not in all the years she had known him.

Half the time, she never thought he even saw her as a female. In the beginning, she followed him around like a puppy at his heels. Asking too many questions and only getting limited responses. As she grew up, she followed him around like a lovesick calf. Only it was his brother she pined over, not Chance. Chance listened to her childish ramblings about his brother with extreme patience. He gave her his usual monosyllabic replies or allowed her to drench his shirt sleeve in her tears when Dev tread on her young girl's heartstrings. His patience seemed infinite with her. Not so much now.

Now, Chance was up to something else. She was certain of it, but she didn't know what. He said he could care less about her ranch land, but was that the truth? The Braxton Ranch was huge. He employed dozens of hands and had three foremen, as the ranch was sectioned in three pieces far flung in opposite directions. Why would he take his time to watch over her meager 3500 acres if it wasn't that he had other plans for it? Did he think he could throw in some kisses and hot looks once in a while and she would fall under his spell, making it easier to get what he wanted? Well, he could think again!

"Easy now with the pitchfork. You might miss and hit your foot."

She stopped and looked up to find him, leaning against the door of the stall, watching her progress. "I've been mucking stalls since I was eight, and I don't need your commentary on how to do it."

"Just didn't want you to hurt yourself. I'm concerned for

your safety. You do a good job) when your mind isn't on other things."

"Evidently not good enough," she spoke up, going back to spreading the fresh hay. "My parents wouldn't have had to go looking for a loan or take one from you if I had been able to do a better job of things…to help them out."

"Josie, no matter how many discussions you play in your mind about the circumstances, the results will always be the same. The basics don't change. They wanted you to be happy and not buried under a ton of worry all the time. Ranching is a hard life. It's doubly hard for a lone female."

"It's the life I chose. The one I want. The only one I want," Josie said, rounding to look at him, determination sparking in her silver eyes. "So get used to the fact I am not going to let this ranch go anywhere."

"I don't want you to have to go anywhere else, Josie." His tone, coupled with the solemn look, made her almost believe him. *Almost.*

"So you say."

"I'm going to do my best to help ensure you hang on to this land you love so much. I also intend on keeping my word to your mother and be here just in case you need someone."

"I don't need nor want you to look out for me. I don't need your guidance in running this ranch or my life."

"You *used* to need my shoulder. Especially when it came to my brother, as I recall."

"You would bring that up. I was a foolish schoolgirl with a crush. I made the mistake of thinking I could confide in you. You take great pleasure in embarrassing me with it now." She brushed by him and returned the pitchfork to its place on the wall.

"I don't take delight in knowing my careless brother broke your heart."

Josie turned to look at him as she reached the open doorway of the barn. "Well, you can't say you didn't warn me. I chose not to listen."

"You still choose not to listen to me."

"You're learning, Braxton." She pivoted on her heel and left him to follow or not.

REGARDLESS WHETHER OR not she wanted him around, Chance didn't seem to care. They settled into a pattern of sorts. Rising before the sun, Josie would dress and go downstairs. The coffee would already be brewing because Chance insisted on bringing over a newer model of coffeemaker from his place, one that had a timer that could be set and have the coffee already made by the time she came downstairs.

Josie begrudgingly had to admit that it was a nice change. However, what she didn't like was the fact that Chance made it a point to share breakfast with her. Until his arrival, and after her mother's death, she got in the habit of grabbing a pre-packaged biscuit and sausage, nuking it for a few seconds and going on her way. With the advent of Chance, she found herself being made to sit at the breakfast table and actually eat a full meal again. Even that fell into a routine. She would cook the sausage or bacon, and then the eggs scrambled for her and over easy for him. He supervised the toast making and setting the table. They both cleared the dishes before they headed out for their day.

Over breakfast, Chance would read the newspaper, while the farm and ranch report played on the small television on the counter. They would discuss the day's agenda together, or rather, she would tell him what she intended to do, and he would make his suggestions…and he always had suggestions. Which, more often than not, put them at crosshairs with each other on some issues.

She was happy with the reprieve she got by his not being in for lunch most days. She supposed he had lunch at his place and then caught up with his own ranch's needs until late afternoon. Usually, just before sunset, she would hear his truck pull into the drive. Subconsciously, her hearing had become attuned for it. More often than not, she had the evening meal just about ready for the table. All the food previously stocked by her neighbors had certainly come in handy.

The second week ended on a fairly benign note. She should have known it wasn't to last. Her cell phone rang while she was retrieving the mail from the box next to the road. Josie's mind was already going over the contents of the refrigerator for what might be on the dinner menu. "Hello?"

"I hope I caught you before you prepared dinner." The sound of Chance's voice on the phone both surprised her and, oddly, brought a pleasant sensation to mind. It was becoming more and more difficult to find reasons to stay mad at him or keep the walls as high between them. It was uncharted territory to be sure.

"I haven't made it back to the house yet."

"Good. I wanted to let you know that I won't be back until late. Don't worry about dinner for me. I'll be eating out."

A strange feeling twisted tighter in her chest at the unexpected news. She should have been thrilled or, at the very least, not care at all about his being gone. "Thanks for letting me know."

"Is something wrong?" His tone changed from casual to slightly worried.

"Nothing is wrong," she hastened to reply. "I'm just thinking of other things right now."

"Okay. I may be late so don't wait up."

"I wasn't planning to." She ended the call and grimaced at the phone. She knew it sounded shrewish, but sometimes the man had the most maddening way of making her feel, well... *feel*. Period. She didn't want or need to feel any particular way about him. Josie put the truck in gear and headed toward the ranch house.

The evening loomed. She watched the nightly news and caught the weather report. Not wanting to cook a full-blown meal for just herself, she had made a grilled cheese sandwich and opened a can of soup. The food didn't taste all that appetizing, and she left half of it uneaten. Josie decided to read some in the new book she had purchased a couple of months back and never opened. Even though it was by one of her favorite authors, she found her attention being caught by the tinkling chimes sounding on the porch as the wind picked up, and the deep chiming of the grandfather clock in the hallway, which punctuated the silence of the house. Eventually, the length of her day caught up with her and her eyes drifted shut.

The next thing she knew, the clock's striking woke her. She saw her book had ended up on the floor at some point, beside her chair. Picking it up, she stood and found her muscles needed a good stretch. Her gaze lit on the face of the clock, and she saw it was a little after two in the morning. She had slept for almost five hours in the chair. No wonder she had a crick in her neck. Turning off the lamps, she crossed into the hall and padded up the stairs in her stocking feet.

She entered her bedroom and crossed to the lamp beside the window. Her gaze drifted outside and then caught on something. It was the fact that Chance's truck was not in its usual spot. In fact, it wasn't anywhere to be seen. There was no light visible from the window of the apartment in the barn where he slept when at the ranch. She looked at the clock beside her bed and the time was verified again. He had said late, but this was ridiculous. What could anyone be doing out at such an hour, especially in Braxton? Maybe he had an accident? That thought sent her stomach to her toes. She shook herself. Don't borrow trouble. That's what her mother always used to say. Josie had inherited her father's tendency to always go to the worst-case scenario first.

Perhaps he was on a date? That sudden thought made her stomach want to heave the sandwich. Was the term "date" even applicable? They were engaged. Of course, it wasn't the typical engagement where both parties had professed undying love and promised to spend their lives together. Were there rules for their type of arrangement? *I am in way over my head.*

Josie told herself that Chance was a grown man. A very sexy, good-looking male, who was still unmarried and why wouldn't he want some female companionship? It wasn't like his fiancée was willing. *Right?* She turned from the window and jerked back the covers of her bed. If he wanted to stay out all night with some floozy, then that was his problem, not hers. Maybe he wouldn't come back at all. That would be lovely.

She should have known her mind could not shut down so easily. In fact, those five hours in the chair were to be the only hours of sleep she enjoyed the rest of the night. The sun rose much too soon. The throbbing in her temples was not the way to start the day. After a quick breakfast of toast, slightly burnt, and a cup of coffee, along with a couple of headache painkillers, Josie went to the barn.

She kept her eyes away from the spot where Chance's truck would normally be parked. Saddling Cookie, she decided an early morning ride would do both of them some good. She waved to Tom, who was pulling into the ranch yard as she headed out. He had his own agenda planned for the day, and she would leave him to it.

She and Cookie trailed along the ridgeline for a while and then followed the semi-dry creek for a way. The colors of the rising sun on the ranch land never ceased to remind her how lucky she was to have this as her way of life.

It was great being out in the crisp morning; however, Josie felt something was missing. She couldn't put her finger on it, but she didn't care for the unsettled way her thoughts jumbled around her. When she tried to identify why, one person kept coming to mind...*Chance.* Even without him being there, he still intruded. She didn't care if she ever saw him again. *Liar.* When had that little voice in her head become a traitor? They hadn't even made it past the first month of their arrangement. How was she to cope with the years still to come? *Years.* Josie slammed the door shut on those thoughts. She couldn't face all the issues that brought with it. Not yet.

As nice as it was to be semi-free, Josie knew she couldn't spend the entire day just riding her horse. She needed to work on the paperwork stacking up on her desk and touch base with Tom on the new grain they wanted to try. Josie turned Cookie toward home. As they topped the rise, the familiar black truck was parked once more in its usual spot. A flash of irritation sprang up within her. It didn't lessen much as she approached the corral.

Chance's familiar tall figure, in jeans and dark blue, long-sleeved shirt with his usual denim vest stepped from the barn's doorway as she approached. She didn't meet his gaze. Pulling the horse up, she stepped down from the saddle. He walked over to where she and Cookie were, his hand reaching to rub along the horse's neck.

"You two have a good ride this morning?"

"Yes." Josie's response was flat and short. She kept her

eyes on the horse, drawing the reins through her fingers and heading in the direction of the barn.

"Sorry about dinner last night." He evidently was following them.

"No problem."

"Is everything okay?"

"Just fine."

"Are you mad at me for some reason?" He leaned his arms on the rail of the stall, his eyes on her bent head as she reached and uncinched the saddle.

"No…should I be?"

"I have no idea. But you're upset about something. So what's up?"

"Nothing is up. Whether you're here or not is no concern of mine. I just find it interesting that, for someone so concerned about what the gossips of town will say, you staying out all night isn't likely to go unnoticed in this small community. But it's no concern of mine." Josie wished she hadn't said that almost as soon as she spoke the words. Swinging the saddle off the horse's back, she kept her attention on rubbing the animal down next. Except a large hand closed over hers and halted her progress.

"Look at me."

Josie had no choice but to comply. His hand was not moving from hers. She looked up at him in silence.

"I don't know what you thought up in your pretty head last night, but it probably has no comparison to the truth of the matter."

"What I think about you and any of your lady friends

doesn't matter."

His eyes narrowed a bit as a dawning light came on for him. "I see. *My lady friend.* I have to admit that she did get a bit upset when I tried to leave her this morning. We had such a long night of it last night. It wore me out."

Josie's eyes flashed quicksilver to his. She was so angry that she failed to see the mocking glint in his own. "Please, spare me the play-by-play. I don't care what you do with your time, as long as you do it away from here."

Chance's next move totally caught her off guard. He laughed. He threw his head back and laughed. *How dare he!*

"You are priceless, Josie," he said, finally catching his breath, even while he still held her hand in check with his. "Could it be that you're jealous?"

"I am not!"

"Why else would it matter to you and have you so riled up over the fact I spent the first part of the evening at the cattlemen's meeting in Abilene and the rest of it in a foaling barn at the ranch? You thought I was with another woman. That is too rich."

Besides the fact he was laughing at her, Josie felt like an idiot for having said anything at all. She was too upset to even analyze the fact that there was a feeling of relief inside her at his words.

"Whatever. It doesn't matter. I have work to do. I'd appreciate being left alone to do it."

There was no sign of humor on his face when he spoke next. "I think it *does* matter. Just so you understand something…when I put that ring on your hand, I made a commitment to *you*. I keep my commitments, Josie. You're the only female...*human* female, that is...that matters to me."

Chance stood for a long moment or two, considering her. However, he didn't say anything else. He simply tapped a long finger on the end of her nose and winked. He walked away, whistling.

Chapter Nine

"I T'S SO GOOD to see you, Josie. I've been meaning to get out to the ranch and see you, but with Charlie down with the flu, and us being one short in the store, I haven't had the time." Mrs. Ross's words met her as Josie approached the counter of the feed store with her items.

She smiled at the woman. When she was growing up, she had her first real *paying* job behind the same counter she stood in front of at that moment. For a whole summer, she worked the counter in the feed store, earning enough to pay for the bridle and saddle she wanted so badly. Josie had been all of thirteen. Her parents told her that, if she wanted something other than the plain, hand-me-down saddle she had, she would need to find a way to earn it. She had done just that.

"I haven't had much time, either. Seems like things just haven't slowed down this winter yet."

"We're all just glad you have such wonderful help with Chance and his crew. They must be quite a godsend to you," the woman remarked, ringing up the items on the counter.

"Oh, yes, they certainly are that." Josie tried very hard to keep her smile and voice even.

"I think Charlie caught his cold when he rode along with Doc Matthews out to Chance's place the other night, after the cattlemen's meeting. He didn't get home until after dawn. At least, Chance didn't lose his prize mare and her foal."

Josie nodded in agreement, as she watched the woman pack the items for her. She felt even more foolish. Chance had been right where he said he was, and the woman had just corroborated that information. Josie felt even lower than she already felt over the episode in the barn.

Mrs. Ross looked around to see where the other shoppers were and seemed satisfied they were out of earshot. She leaned forward a bit over the counter. "Your mother and father both were dear people and much respected in the community, as are you. I would hate for all this gossip that's going around to tarnish that."

Josie was caught totally off guard by the woman's words. "What gossip would that be?"

"You know. You and Chance Braxton." The woman's voice was lowered even more. "The two of you living under the same roof. What would your mother say about that? I know she isn't here, but surely you must know what people are saying."

Josie was speechless. Then, when the words came to her, she had enough presence of mind to bite them back. How dare the people, who had known her and her family for years, actually engage in such rotten gossip! Whatever she did on her ranch was her business. So many things sprang to her mind, yet she said none of them. A thin smile was fixed on her face.

"Thank you, Mrs. Ross. I know how valuable your opinion is. Have a good afternoon."

With her purchase in hand, she headed out to her truck. All the way back to the ranch, she fumed about the ridiculous gossip, and then she tried to think of a way to apologize to Chance for doubting his story. Why did things have to be so complicated? There was something to be said for wanting to be young and carefree again and not an adult. However, she tried to remember if she had ever truly been carefree, and she realized she couldn't recall the time. Josie felt older but no wiser. If she hadn't left the ring Chance gave her in its velvet box on her dresser, then she could have shown Mrs. Ross there was no need for the gossips to wear themselves out on her account.

Turning into the ranch yard, she noted an unfamiliar sports car parked next to Chance's truck. The sleek, silver car was expensive looking. Josie glanced down at her serviceable blue jeans and boots, her usual blue parka over a navy turtleneck sweater. Whoever the guest was, her appearance would simply have to do. She had taken three steps toward the house when a voice came from the barn doorway behind her.

"Hi, doll. Long time no see."

Josie whirled around, and her eyes flew wide. Without thought, she headed straight toward the pair of outstretched male arms. She felt herself lifted off the ground and swung around in a bear hug. "Dev! What are you doing here?"

"I missed you, angel. I had to come see my best girl.

You're still my girl, right?" He grinned at her, and that megawatt intensity was still evident. He finally allowed her feet to touch the ground but did not let her out of his arms. At that moment, Josie became aware of Chance and Tom, standing across the corral watching them.

Chance's face was half masked by the brim of his Stetson, but the part she could see was set in a stone mask, a frown on his mouth as he tightened the cinch of his horse's saddle. Josie was aware their conversation had to be heard by the two men, or at least parts of it, yet they made no indication they had heard anything. Neither did they make any move to be in a hurry to leave the corral.

"Oh my," Dev's voice fell to a theatrical whisper. "Big brother is watching. Just like old times."

For some inexplicable reason, Josie felt embarrassed and stepped back as much as she could while he still held her. She latched onto the first thing that came to mind.

"Your wife might have something to say about your having a best girl, don't you think?"

"My wife...to be." Dev's face lost its smile as he hastened to clarify. "Yes, well, let's just say it wasn't meant to be for her and me."

"I see." Josie did see, with quick clarity. The trustees had evidently done their work, just as Chance had mentioned they had threatened. "Surely, if you really loved her, you could find a way to make it work, to get her back."

"Dear little Josie," he said, the smile returning. "You really arc a Pollyanna at times. You're too sweet to be real. That's why I adore you. There's not a predatory bone in your body."

She hadn't noticed before how easily the charm could come and go with him. A red flag surfaced for the first time. Or maybe she just noticed it for the first time. She looked for the sincerity level in the signature Braxton blue eyes. And realized it didn't quite seem so genuine. She stepped back further and, this time, his arms didn't hold on to her.

"Was it your trustees? Surely, if you love her, you'll want to be with her no matter what."

"The trustees are a group of old grouches who act as if the money is really theirs. I deserve the money, Josie. It's my *right*. Wives come and go. Anyway, enough of that subject. Let's talk about you and me."

Josie knew the smile on her face was forced. Had Dev always been so callous and cold sounding? Where was the boy she knew? The one she thought walked on water? Would he ever appear again? A strange sadness filtered into her thoughts. Changes were happening throughout her life and to all the people around her. Or, another sobering thought took hold...was she finally catching up with changes in herself while the others were just being their usual selves?

"Are you moving back to the ranch?" she ventured, trying to find her footing.

"Oh, good heavens! No way! Punching cattle all day long is Chance's thing, not mine. There are so many wonderful places to be other than here. I could show you the world, Josie. You'd love the beaches in California. Vegas is unbelievable. It's a city that truly never sleeps."

"So I hear. However, I guess I'm just a stay-at-home kind

of girl."

"You and Chance are too much alike. What you two see in all this barren land and emptiness," he said, as his eyes moved over the space around him, before falling back on her, "is just beyond me."

"It's in our blood."

"Well, I must have had a blood transfusion when I was born, because, thankfully, it isn't in mine." Dev seemed quite adamant about that statement.

"How long are you going to be here this time?"

"As long as it takes me to talk Chance into agreeing to help modify the terms of the trust. It seems he was given the power to do that, only no one bothered to tell me, until a very nice young lady in the trust department shared that item with me."

"*Nice,* as in you sweet-talked her into telling you." Josie's words may have sounded like a joke, but she wasn't joking at all. Dev didn't seem to notice.

"You're wising up some, little one. That might have its advantages. Come play with me."

"I can't," she responded, taking another step away from him as he sought to catch her up in his arms again. "Please don't call me 'little one' either."

He gave a bit of a frown. "Why can't I call you that? You never minded whenever Chance called you that, as I recall."

Josie didn't care for the way he seemed to be studying her a bit too closely. "That was when I was in school. Which was more than a few years ago. I've grown up and out of that name," Josie replied. "I have to check on the stock tanks."

"Well, I think I need to go along and keep you company. We can catch up on everything."

Was he serious? What about Chance? A quick look and she could see that there was a neutral expression on his face, and he didn't seem the least bit concerned. It was her decision. That's how she wanted it right? She would do what she pleased on her land.

"You still know how to ride a horse?" That remark came from Chance, who was looking at his brother.

"I think I can manage. It's like riding a bike, isn't it?"

"Take one of these horses, then. Tom and I have an errand in town. That will save Josie time from having to get a mount ready for you." He didn't wait for a reply nor say anything to Josie. A fact that irritated her for whatever reason. But she kept a smile on her face, and she and Dev were soon on their way.

DEV HAD BEEN a good sport and talkative companion up until they finished the first inspection. Or, rather, he had sat and talked while she inspected. Halfway to the second tank, he had grown a bit quieter, moving to fidget in the saddle.

"Saddle getting a bit uncomfortable?" Josie ventured as they rode side by side across the flat prairie. In the distance, a tall windmill marked the site of the next tank. The afternoon was partly sunny, but the steady breeze made the chill linger through the day. Josie noted her companion's shiny leather boots, not western, but made for strolling down big city sidewalks and not across grasslands.

Dev's jeans were definitely the high-priced variety and the brown suede and leather jacket he wore was better suited to a leisurely shopping trip in New York. The scarf around his neck wasn't woolen but material which looked a lot like silk. He could be a model for GQ, not Horseman's Digest. Yet, he had offered to come along on the ride with her. She could give him credit for that. Of course, he might have done it just to irritate his brother? That thought rattled around in her mind.

"There should be ranch hands out here doing this sort of work. You shouldn't have to be out in this ridiculous cold doing menial labor like this. I'm going to have to talk to Chance about that, also. I heard about his being executor of your mom's estate and all, and he's sticking his nose into your place a lot more lately I hear. That doesn't give him any right to be a slave driver."

"Where did you hear all that?" *And what about the engagement part?* He hadn't mentioned that, but, then again, neither had she.

"I stopped in at the Tanner Mercantile before coming out here. You can hear all the latest news in that place in the first five minutes. Some things never change about small towns."

"Well, Chance doesn't supervise me," she replied quickly. "He isn't a slave driver either. Chance does his thing, and I do mine. So far, we've managed to coexist without killing each other."

"I'm surprised. If I had to be around my big brother for

very long, I think I'd go crazy. He has no idea how to have fun, always so serious, with his nose to the grindstone, especially when we were growing up."

"Maybe he had to be that way. Your father put a lot of responsibility on him." Josie didn't say her next thoughts out loud. *Maybe because he couldn't depend on you.* It sobered her even more how quickly those words popped into her brain. It wasn't all that long ago she would have fought anyone who raised a disparaging thought about Dev in her presence. The blinders really had come off…since when?

Josie road on for a few long moments in silence. Her brain was on its own course at the moment. Comparisons of the two brothers stepped to the forefront. At one time, Dev's movie-star looks had been a real plus where she was concerned. They outshone any other male in Braxton. All along, Chance had been the steadfast, working cowboy…dirt on his boots, sweat-stained hat crown, a real tan baked by hours upon hours of being outside working from dawn to after dusk.

The brilliant blue eyes of the Braxton clan was the one common trait the brothers seemed to have. Dev's seemed to stay in a perpetual sky blue mode, sparked by some joke or witty sarcasm. Chance's were different. They could have moments of the sky blue color but more often than not, they darkened to a brilliant sapphire color that a person might drown in the depths like the inviting cool depths of a lake in summer. Why had she not noticed such differences in the two brothers until that moment? Dev's response brought her back to the present moment.

"True. Chance never could do any wrong in our father's eyes. He certainly never had a trust placed over *his* money," Dev muttered. "Hey, forget what I said. I forgot how much you idolize my big brother."

Josie drew her horse up short. "Excuse me? I idolize him? Where do you get that idea?"

Dev halted his animal at the same time. He cocked his head and threw her a knowing look. "Ever since we were kids, you were his shadow. You hung on his every word. I have to admit, I was jealous of you two. Always talking so no one else could hear you and sharing those private secrets. You watched him with those huge doe eyes that never saw him do any wrong."

Josie didn't know how to respond. Was that how it had seemed to others? Of course she followed him, and they spoke in whispers. She often sought Chance out to talk about his brother or cry on his shoulder when her feeble attempts to gain Dev's attention fell short and off he went with one of his ever-present, ever-perfect girlfriends.

"It wasn't like that at all. Most of the time, we talked about you." Why had she said that? Oh well, what did it matter anyway? Those times were gone and things had changed.

Dev certainly perked up at that bit of news. "Me? You talked about me? Don't stop now. You've got to tell me about that."

Josie decided the best way to handle things was to use the truth. "Don't pretend you didn't know I had the world's biggest crush on you when we were kids. However, you didn't know I existed. Chance took pity on me."

"Well, I might have heard tell a time or two that you had a little bit of crush. I was an idiot not to have paid more attention, given how you've grown up." The words came along with a look that slid over her and made the warmth grow in her cheeks. "Besides, I doubt pity had anything to do with why Chance let you hang around him. He always had a soft spot where you were concerned. He took you to your first dance, as I recall."

Josie flashed back on that memory. Funny, it wasn't as painful as it used to be when she remembered that time. "He took me to the first dance because I waited for you to ask me and turned down every other boy who did. He said he couldn't see me sit home while everyone else went, so he volunteered. My friends thought it was cool that an 'older' man took me to the dance," she finished on a laugh. "Older man, indeed. I was fifteen and he was twenty-one. I thought of him as an older brother I never had." Flashes of the way he had recently kissed her made that statement into a falsehood. Best to keep those memories under control and to herself.

"Is that why, three years later, big brother Chance took you to the Fall Festival? And then to prom?"

"He didn't take me to the festival," she corrected. "I went with Dale Grayson, who proceeded to show up drunk at the party at Melanie Stewart's house before we ever left for the dance. I was walking home when Chance happened to see me. I was a silly mess, all tears and upset over missing the biggest dance of the fall. He went home, put on a suit, and took me. Funny...I had forgotten about that time," Josie said, almost to herself.

Chance had been a big part in her life for a long time; those memories were coming back in living color with quite a frequency of late. Seemed he had always been there to pick her up and dust her off and push her back into life again. Yet he had never expected anything in return. Had she even thanked him any of those times?

"I'm not proud of it, but I also remember a certain prom he stepped in and took you because I was under the weather." Dev had the decency to look apologetic and contrite.

"We all know you weren't sick. YOU Devlin Braxton...stood me up. And he did that for the both of us."

"Guess things tend to look different when you think back over them. Hindsight being 20/20 and all. Makes regrets even more fresh. Sometimes it's harder to see that people can often hide behind masks, and those masks can become permanent if we aren't careful. And we choose paths that might not always be the best ones for us. Then you find you can't retrace your steps...as much as you might wish you could." He seemed to say those words more to himself than her. Dev's personality changed like a click of a button to its usual demeanor. "It's getting colder. How much longer will this take?" Dev's question brought her back to the present and away from the walk down memory lane.

Josie had meant to check on three different stock tanks while they were out, but she ended up skipping the last one, making note to check it first thing the next morning.

"I'll make a quick check of this tank," she replied, sliding out of the saddle, "and then we'll get back to the ranch." Dev was a tenderfoot after all.

❧

ONCE BACK AT the barn, Dev moved a lot slower off his mount and didn't protest when Josie began unsaddling his horse for him. He leaned against the stall door and kept her company. "Of course," he said, with a flash of his bright smile in her direction, "you realize you're going to owe me a dinner after this."

"Dinner?"

"That's the plan. You and I will drive into Abilene tonight and find the best restaurant they have. Then I'll use my considerable charms to change your mind about seeing some of those amazing places with me that I spoke of earlier."

Josie should have been over the moon with the fact Dev Braxton had finally done what she dreamed of for so long…ask her out on a real, grown-up date. How many times had she daydreamed about such an event? Now, here it was, and she was shocked by the fact she didn't experience the thrill she thought would come along with it. Dev noted her hesitation.

"Don't tell me that you have another date?" He smiled for a moment, then the smile disappeared as a sudden thought came to him. "You aren't seeing someone are you? Tell me his name if you are, so I know who I have to fight for your hand."

"That would be *me*…in case it's slipped anyone's mind

in the last couple of hours."

Both pairs of startled eyes swung to encounter Chase's watchful ones as he stood leaning against the barn door, observing the pair. The words weren't uttered as part of a jest or with the slightest bit of humor. Josie recognized the set of the squared chin and firm jawline. She had seen it a time or two, whenever Chase had to deal with a particularly distasteful situation…usually with a ranch hand that was about to be terminated or some such. Well, she wasn't a ranch hand, and neither was Dev. She raised her own chin in as much an act of defiance as fortification for her own nerves under the steady glare.

"No one has forgotten about you. You were mentioned a good deal in our conversation today." She didn't elaborate but went back to pouring the last of the grain into the buckets for their mounts' supper. Let him think what he would about that.

"Am I missing something around here?" Dev looked from his brother to Josie and back to the man again.

"There's been some changes around here recently. The most notable being that Josie is engaged to be married."

Dev swung his attention totally on Josie. "To who?"

The words formed and were on the tip of her tongue as she looked at the Braxton brother she idolized for so long. They just seemed to get stuck for some reason.

"To *me*." Chance made the reply for her.

Chapter Ten

"I T REALLY WAS most cosmopolitan of my big brother to give his blessing to our going out to dinner together. I certainly wouldn't be so generous if you were my fiancée."

Dev's remark joined her own thoughts. She had been totally shocked when, instead of Chance being unbending and his stubborn self, he had actually smiled. He had said there was no reason they shouldn't have dinner together when Dev had voiced the invitation he had issued to Josie earlier. He was busy, but he was certain they wouldn't miss him. Chance had practically pushed her at his brother! What was he thinking? She wasn't certain, but she had a feeling there was more to it than just him being nice. Josie looked up into the dark night sky above her head as the sports car flew down the highway.

"Don't you love how you can see so many bright stars above your head in a Texas night sky? There's really nothing like it."

They appeared huge with so little ground light to inter-fere with their brilliance. The lights of Abilene had receded in the distance some time ago, and darkness spread outside the car as they headed back to Braxton and the Monroe ranch.

"I prefer the bright lights of the Strip in Vegas. They're so bright, you can't see any stars in the sky. But you're not there for stargazing, unless you're catching one of the shows. That's my idea of bright lights."

Josie couldn't help but feel a bit sorry for Dev. He seemed to be living in such a fast-paced world that he had no idea what he might be missing around him. But she shook it away. The evening had been nice. In fact, this would be a night to remember. She finally had an actual date with Dev. If she still recorded her thoughts into the diary she kept during her teen years, it would be a red-letter entry. Except it wasn't a date. She was simply having dinner with an old family friend...more than that...the brother of her fiancé. Many things had changed in a very short time.

She couldn't have asked for a more attentive, handsome, charming dinner companion. They had walked into the country club with its linen covered tables and candlelight, and Josie's feet felt as if they barely touched the floor as Dev escorted her across the room. She knew the eyes of several female diners swiveled their direction more than a few times. So that was how it felt...to be the one on his arm? To receive all his attention and smiles? Her imagination was pretty close to the mark of reality. Dev was all polish and knew exactly how to wine and dine a dinner companion.

They talked of many things...or rather *he* talked about his adventures, and she listened, making a comment now and then. Unfortunately, there were some less than pleasant moments. There were too many times during the evening when unbidden comparisons between the two brothers and the two evenings she had spent with each of them crossed her mind.

Chance may not have come with them, but he was there…especially when the light kept catching the brilliance of the stone in the ring on her left hand. It was a constant reminder…a chaperone in its own right. There was something else that had also popped into her mind as they sat at the dining table, being hovered over as if they were special guests. Dev had chosen the classiest place in the city for their dinner out. In his silk suit and Italian shoes, he looked the part of a well-heeled member of the big city gentry.

Her dinner with Chance had been different. Chance gave her the choice of the club or her favorite restaurant. He had made it extra special with the rose and the champagne toast…when he certainly had not needed to do so. The contrasts in the two brothers had become more marked. The rest of the evening went as one would have expected. To her surprise, Josie wasn't that disappointed when the time came to head back to the ranch. And that realization did keep her more thoughtful on the ride homeward. Thankfully, there was little need of conversation on the drive. Each of them seemed content with their own thoughts. When the silence was broken, often by Dev, it was to make some remark about one of the fantastic places he had seen and how she needed to see more of the real world.

The car purred to a standstill in front of the house. She waited as Dev came around, opened her door, and then walked her to the front porch. Josie hadn't thought this far into their evening. That sudden realization surprised her. In her young girl dreams, the moment at the front door was the ultimate high point of the evening. That's when *the kiss* would come. What a different comparison came to mind. Back in those younger days, she would have been so giddy over the prospect of a goodnight kiss from Dev. But reality was different. In fact, it wasn't anticipation she felt. It was uneasiness about the whole situation. She was just being ridiculous, she told herself. It was just a dinner between two longtime friends. Not a date. There could be no date, especially when one was engaged, and one was about to be…or not…married as in Dev's case. Talk about tangled webs.

"I enjoyed this evening, Josie. You have a way of making a person feel relaxed and at ease around you. It's nice to be able to take a breath of fresh air." His tone sounded sincere. The look in those Braxton baby blue eyes definitely was focused only on her.

"I can either see that as a nice way of saying I'm a really dull dinner companion compared to those you're used to, or I can take it as a compliment. I'll choose the latter." She smiled up at him, the semi-circle of light from the single bulb left the rest of the long porch in darkness.

"You should, because it *is* a compliment. Maybe I should have come back to Braxton a lot sooner. Maybe I should think about staying a while longer now that the blinders are off."

"Blinders?" She made the one-word reply, while the look he was giving her definitely played havoc on her ability to

DEBRA HOLT

concentrate on the moment. What was going on?

Two hands reached out, cupped her upper shoulders, and drew her into him. His head lowered towards hers. "I should have seen you coming sooner. Little Josie grew up into quite a desirable woman."

Her eyes closed just as his lips touched hers. *Dev Braxton is kissing me.* Those four words echoed around and around in her brain. The moment had arrived. What was she doing? He wasn't Chance. Her eyes flashed open, and she pushed against his chest, shoving him hard to put distance between them. At the same time, a voice broke into the scene.

"Hate to break up this touching scene, but your *girlfriend* called…twice. You might want to call her." The words were a dash of ice-cold water upon her and the moment. Josie sprang back, her eyes moving in the direction of the speaker.

Chance sat in the corner of the porch, on the railing, arms folded. He wasn't smiling. That was an understatement. His words had dropped like lead weights in the darkness. Slowly, he stood and moved to stand with one shoulder propped against the post at the top of the steps, hands slid into jean pockets. Dark eyes flashed blue sparks from beneath the brim of the hat pulled low over his forehead. He didn't speak, as those eyes slid slowly over Josie's face, pausing on her freshly kissed mouth, before returning to meet her gaze.

"A voice message on my phone would have sufficed. And she is my *ex*-girlfriend…people seem to have a problem remembering that. You didn't need to make a trip over here to tell me that," Dev responded in a controlled voice.

"I didn't make a special trip. I live here, remember?" Chance's remarks were for his brother, but his gaze remained full bore on Josie. "Had to make sure my fiancée got home okay, too. I remember agreeing to the dinner for you two to reminisce but don't recall the part about a goodnight kiss. Or was that a *hello* kiss?"

In spite of the chill of the evening, Josie felt warmth flood over her cheeks and the fire of indignation surged upward, as well. Was Chance trying to make her feel she had done something wrong? She hadn't asked for the kiss. It upset her that it had happened. It only brought more confusing feelings swirling inside her. Why couldn't he trust her?

"You're seriously staying here with Josie?" Dev's frown mirrored his question. He swung his gaze from his brother to her. "Is he really staying here?"

"Yes," Josie replied, sending a less than warm look across to the tall figure still watching them. "In the foreman's old apartment in the barn." She hastened to make that point clear. That finally brought a change to Chance's face...a sarcastic upturn of a corner of his mouth.

"*For now.* That's subject to change very soon." His eyes sent their own message.

Josie tried to ignore the sudden rolling in the pit of her stomach as his words and their real message registered.

"It's cold out here and you have an early morning. I'll see my brother on his way." Chance moved away from the post and gave a direct look at his brother. Josie felt Dev hesitate for a moment. However, he soon thought better of pushing his luck. He flashed a smile at her.

"Chance is right, sweetheart. You get inside and get warm. I'll see you soon. After all…we're going to be family, right?" He was cheeky enough to send a wink at his brother before he added a slow smile for her.

Dev swung his hand out in a gesture that meant for Chance to take the lead, but Chance made it clear that Dev was going first. Chance hesitated for a moment, his brother getting out of earshot. He turned back to Josie.

"Was it everything you imagined all these years?"

Josie looked up at the man watching her with that aggravating way he had of seeing things she didn't need him to see. It confirmed her thoughts.

"You did this on purpose tonight…the dinner…sending us on our own. Was it a test of some sort? So much for the trust that you talk so much about between us."

"I do trust *you*," he replied evenly. "It's my brother I won't turn my back on. I figured this evening might help you lay some ghosts to rest. You always imagined how a date with him would be…and you even got a goodnight kiss thrown in. You should have a lot to dream about tonight."

Chance didn't wait for a reply. He turned and soon joined his brother at his car. A few brief words were exchanged, and Dev headed out, followed by Chance in his truck. Stepping inside the house, she closed the door and slid the deadbolt. She wasn't quite certain what, or who, it was she thought she was locking out.

"IF YOU'RE GOING to lock the front door, you also need to make sure the back door is locked. Otherwise, it doesn't do much good if you're bent on keeping someone out." The words were spoken without much inflection, as she poured herself a cup of coffee the next morning. They came from the man already seated at the kitchen table, in his usual spot, reading the newspaper spread before him. She hadn't spared him a glance since entering the kitchen.

"I'll remember that next time." She picked up her gloves from the counter and headed toward the back door.

"You know better than to skip breakfast, especially on a day like today. The temperature is supposed to drop another twenty degrees by noon." He still had not looked in her direction.

Her hand paused on the doorknob. "Thanks for the weather report." She tossed the words over her shoulder as she stepped outside onto the porch, pulling the door shut none too gently after her. Stomping across the cold ground toward the stables, she fought off the cold from her feet, but that wasn't the real reason. It was to relieve some of the anger that still simmered seeing Chance sitting so calmly at her table when she came downstairs…after she had spent a night of tossing and turning and bad dreams, in all of which Chance, not his brother, had the starring role.

The overhead heaters were working well inside the large barn; however, if the wind decided to gain force, Josie knew they would not chase the entire chill away. She pulled a horse blanket from the side bin and moved into Cookie's stall. Rubbing her hand along the animal's neck and back, she found a smile returning to her face. The horse was her baby and constant companion for the last ten years. They had traveled many a mile together. She felt calm returning. Josie opened the blanket and slid it over the animal's back, buckling the straps that would hold it in place.

"You'll stay warm now. I've got errands to run in town, so you get to have the day off, lucky guy. I'll bring you back some of the apples you like." A soft neigh responded to her words, along with a gentle toss of the animal's head.

"You've spoiled that horse rotten."

Josie realized, much to her regret, that Chance had entered the stable. She kept her eyes on the horse.

"It's bad manners to sneak up on a person without warning."

"I wasn't aware I was sneaking. Maybe if you had eaten something this morning, you wouldn't be in such a bad mood."

She rounded on him at that point. He stood in the opening of the stall, a coil of rope in one hand, and something wrapped in a paper towel in the other. He held that hand out to her.

"You forgot this."

She automatically reached for it. Only then did she notice the paper towel was wrapped around a couple of slices of cinnamon toast…her favorite.

"I didn't ask you…"

"Before you say something that you'll regret later, just say 'thanks' and eat it. There's a thin line between being stubborn and being just plain foolish." He turned away at that point and walked toward the feed bins along the far wall.

Josie started to speak. She opened her mouth. Then she closed it. She hated the way he could be right so much of the time. What she hated even more was the way he had become so good at irritating her almost constantly. Surely, he knew they couldn't go on like they were?

She took a couple of bites of the toast, her mind trying to work out so many things. Why couldn't they find a middle ground? She ventured to find one.

"Are you glad that your brother's home?"

"Probably not as glad as you are."

There he went again. Did he do it on purpose? She left the stall and advanced to where he was reading over the latest feed bills in his hands.

"Do you try to make me angry? Why do you have to be so mean? I was trying to make civil conversation with you." Her eyes shot sparks in his direction.

His head came up, and his steady gaze focused on her. "I was simply making an observation. After all the years you pined over Dev, you have to be overjoyed he has returned, minus a wife, and obviously ready to succumb to your charms. After seeing that kiss last night, I'd say you've got him right where you always wanted him. Congratulations." He moved away from her, turning to rub the large brown and white nose of his own horse that appeared over the neighboring stall door.

"Congratulations? You make it sound like I planned it all, like I set some sort of a trap for him." Tossing the last slice of toast into the nearby trash bin, her hands went to her hips as she planted her feet firmly.

Chance gave her a half smile over his shoulder. "Maybe not consciously. After all, you are still a fairly inexperienced female in comparison to Dev's usual choices. Nevertheless, the combination of those witch eyes and that sexy blue dress you had on last night, were all meant to get him to kiss you. I ask again…was it everything you expected it to be?"

Josie was taken aback by his words, and especially the question. Of course, the way his voice lowered and his eyes grew darker as they zoned in on hers, made strange things happen with her ability to concentrate and maintain a normal rate of breathing.

"I don't know what you mean."

"You dreamed of him kissing you for years. I know, because I heard enough about it. Did your pulse speed up? Have trouble breathing? Feel that hot sensation deep down in the…"

"That's none of your business, Chance Braxton." She cut him off. How dare he speak to her like *that*. How dare he know how she felt when she kissed him! *Dev*, she meant…not *him*, not Chance. *Oh, geez.*

"Want to know what I think? I think you didn't feel any of those things, Josephine Monroe. Only you're just stubborn enough to try and make yourself believe something that wasn't there…was *never* there in fact. If, for no other reason, than to keep from accepting the fact that you felt those things when *you and I* kissed. Maybe, after all these years, your fairytale world finally just got turned right side up and those rose-colored glasses you hid behind are indeed a thing of yesteryear."

"You're partially right about one thing, Chance Braxton. You have turned my world upside *down*," she conceded. "I never had rose-colored glasses…at least where you were concerned."

That got his attention.

"Plus, I never was the center of the town's gossip mill before you came barging into my life. Thanks a lot for that experience," she finished in a tone dry with sarcasm.

Chance's expression changed. "What are you talking about?"

"I'm talking about being informed by Mrs. Ross that my parents would certainly have never approved of you just moving in with me. That I should know better. Seems I am living 'in sin' in the eyes of some of the good townspeople."

Sudden fury lit the blue eyes. "Are you serious, Josie? When did this happen? Who else said such a thing to you?"

"The morning Dev returned. I was picking up some supplies for Tom, and she handed me that bit of news along with them."

"Dammit, Josie! Why didn't you say something sooner? I won't have this happen, and it certainly won't go any further. And what did she think your engagement ring was all about?"

Josie's eyes shot to his. "What do you mean by that? And I didn't have my ring on…I told you before that I keep it in its box when I'm working with stock or whatever."

"I mean that I shouldn't have allowed three weeks to go

by without putting a wedding ring on your hand...for more reasons than one. Against my better judgment, I agreed to delaying the wedding until Reverend Morrison's return. I have a mind to just put you in the truck and drive over to the justice of peace today."

"Not so fast, mister," she spoke up, finding her own ire building at his high-handedness. "I have a say in this, and I don't believe I'll let you tell me what I will or won't do or have you *putting me* anyplace."

"Josie, I'll wager, from the moment you were born, you've been stubborn. However, we have an agreement. You have *my* ring on your hand. You love this ranch, and I want you to keep it. What I will not put up with is anyone in this town daring to smear your family name or your reputation. Eight days Josie...and not one day more. You'll have your wedding with Reverend Morrison like we decided, but I won't be swayed against my better judgment again. The next time you see Mrs. Ross, you'll have a wedding ring on your finger. And it will be a plain one, so you can keep it on your hand at all times."

It was difficult to reply to his last remark, as his long strides took him out of the barn in nothing flat, leaving her staring after him. What was she to do? The bottom line could not be ignored. There was an agreement...a mutually agreed-upon decision.

She had no way to pay back the defaulted loans. As much as she wanted to, and as hard as she could work, it still wouldn't be enough without working capital to get them through the winter and into the spring. Chance's offer was the one way to keep all she had worked so hard for most of her life.

She had been able to keep it running this long only because Mother Nature had cooperated at the right time over a two-year stretch, but now they were into the third year of a long drought, and the only thing draining faster than their stock tanks was her bank account. It was a race to see which would go dry first. She was painted into a corner. The ranch was her birthright. It was all she knew. She hadn't gone to college like so many of her high school classmates had done. What she knew and majored in was the everyday running of a ranch with animals to care for, land to improve, and little money to do it all with. However, she wasn't about to give it up without a fight. Whatever she had to do, she would do it. She knew that for a certainty. *Even if she had to dance with the devil to do it…at their wedding.*

THERE WERE MORE surprises in store for her that very afternoon. Josie quickly had a memory lesson on what happened when Chance got a burr under his saddle about something. Just after lunch, as she was stepping off the porch heading back to the corral area, a silver minivan pulled into the yard, and Marie Ledbetter stepped out. Marie owned Marie's Alterations and Sewing Goods Place in town. From the passenger side stepped Emily Haskins, who, along with her husband Mike, owned and operated Em's Sweetest Things, a bakery and deli combination also in Braxton. They waved at her as she changed her direction and headed toward them, a hand shielding her eyes from the bright sunlight.

"Hi Josie! We were afraid we might have missed you. We came just as soon as we could pack up our stuff and get out here." Marie threw the words over her shoulder as she bent to retrieve items from the van's back end.

"Congratulations, Josie! You must be ecstatic. That bridegroom of yours is quite the man on a mission. We had no idea you two were even engaged until he came into the shop and began booking everything. Eight days...my goodness! Have no fear...we can whip out your perfect wedding in nothing flat. Just leave it to us," Emily chimed in, two large bags clutched in her hands at her sides.

Josie was at a loss but had to quickly recover as it was clear the two women expected to be asked inside her home. They were already heading toward the front door.

"Ecstatic doesn't describe it," she managed to return as she hurried ahead of them. *If they only knew.* "I wasn't really expecting anyone..."

"Now don't you worry about a thing." Marie smiled as she bustled through to the dining room and set her box on the table with Emily close behind her. "We brought everything we need to help you make your choices. Chance was most insistent that you be given anything you choose...of course, given the time constraint we're under and all. We will do our best though."

"I brought along cake samples. I had them on hand for the Flanagan's, because they had scheduled a cake tasting for tomorrow morning, but now that they called the wedding off because..." Emily hushed when she saw the look on Marie's face. "I guess we don't need to talk about such unhappy things when we have a most joyous occasion to focus on instead. I'll just go into your kitchen and plate these up." She hurried through the swinging door with her cake boxes and bags.

"Marisa's wedding was called off?" Josie had gone to high school with Marisa and had been surprised when she announced she was coming back to Braxton to marry a man she had met in Houston while at a convention. The invitation had arrived three weeks back and was still on her refrigerator front. The wedding date was just two weeks away.

Marie shook her head as she continued to unpack her box. "Poor Lila is beside herself. Marisa just walked in the door yesterday at home and announced it was all off. Seems the fellow up and decided to move off to Japan and really didn't seem to care if Marisa went along or not. Poor thing." She looked over at Josie and her smile returned. "But that's something you don't have to worry about. Your Chance won't be going anywhere without you, that's for sure. It's so romantic how things work out sometimes."

Josie was lost. Evidently it showed because Marie hastened to explain. "Everyone knew that one of these days, you'd end up a Braxton. Your mom and dad always set such love, hopes and admiration in Chance over the years. And Chance...well it was plain how he felt about it all."

"Plain?"

"The look in that man's eyes whenever you came around

and wasn't looking. Made even an old heart like mine flutter. Now where's your room? We need to get you into the dress, so I can see what I have ahead of me in alterations."

Josie was still digesting Marie's words about Chance when her mind had to focus on the strange question. "Dress?"

"Chance said he brought it down from the attic and placed it on your bed. It's so wonderful that you decided to wear your mother's dress. She'd be so pleased."

"My room is upstairs." Josie led the way. Walking into the bedroom, she was amazed to find a large box, yellowed around the corners with age, but still tied across the middle with a faded pink ribbon. She recognized it instantly. She had taken a peek inside once as a teenager, when she was looking through some trunks stacked in the corner of the dusty attic, and found it inside a cedar chest. There was no way Chance would have known about its existence or its location unless he had been searching for it. That fact just added to an already strange list of things she couldn't quite wrap her head around in these quickly fleeting few minutes.

The woman undid the box and carefully laid back the tissue paper until the dress was visible. She lifted the material until it was free from the box.

"Oh my, Josie. The workmanship is marvelous on this. It looks like all the beading is intact. I understand this dress was also worn by your grandmother. Amazing how it has withstood the test of time. The candlelight satin has retained its color, and the lace is such a beautiful design. Let's slip it on you."

A few minutes later, Josie stood staring at herself in the full-length mirror in the corner of her bedroom. She didn't recognize the person looking back at her. She looked almost like her mother in the wedding photo of her parents that hung in the dining room. Josie lightly touched the folds of the fabric. Yards of soft candlelight satin made up the skirt that fell from a fitted waist. The sleeves were lace and appliques of the lace covered the bodice. The same lace trimmed the skirt. Miniscule crystal beading and seed pearls decorated the appliques also. Two petticoats made the skirt fuller. The veil was floor-length tulle with the exact lace edging it all the way around.

Both Marie and Emily stood behind her, admiring the garment. "It's amazing, Josie. I need to take it in just a bit in the side seams of the top and shorten a bit on the sleeve length. With the proper shoes, the skirt length will be just right. It could have been made with you in mind."

"That's true," Emily chimed in. "It may have gone through two brides already, but it's timeless. If you tried to find something like this in a store now, you would end up paying thousands for it."

"And the workmanship wouldn't be able to match it if you did," Marie noted. "Wait until your groom sees you in this. That's the moment I want to see."

Emily nodded in agreement. Josie reserved her reply on that one. The mention of Chance brought everything back to the present. In a few short days, she would be wearing this dress and saying vows that were meant to last a lifetime. *What have I done?* Pure panic hit her. She so needed her mother to talk to in that moment.

"I need to get this off. I've got work to do outside." She motioned for the women to undo the buttons of the dress's back. Why was it hard to breathe in her room? The material felt suffocating all of a sudden.

"Careful now," Marie warned. "We don't want to stick you with the pins I have in it. Can't have blood on that satin." The pair of women carried the dress downstairs with them. Marie had moved her items into the sewing room at the back of the house.

Josie redressed in her jeans and work shirt and pulled on her boots in swift time. She took the stairs quickly but was brought up short by Emily standing in the doorway of the dining room.

"Now Josie, you weren't trying to escape, were you?" The baker laughed at the thought. "We're ready for the tasting. You just come sit yourself down." The chair was pulled out and waiting for her.

Josie looked at the chair and then ventured a quick glance at the front door. *So close to freedom…yet so far.* A hand on her arm helped her decision. Emily was probably used to brides with cold feet…or maybe not. At any rate, Josie slid into the chair. On the table in front of her were seven plates with seven different slices of cake on them.

"You want me to eat all of these?"

Another laugh. "Well, not by yourself. I expected Chance might want to take a few bites, too."

"He isn't going to be here, I'm sure. Besides any of these cakes…" Josie didn't finish.

"Sorry I'm running a bit late, ladies. Hope I didn't keep you waiting." The man came through the doorway and dropped into the chair next to Josie's while giving Emily a smile, his hat going onto the post on the back of his chair.

"You're here."

Chance turned the smile on her. "Where else would I be? This is pretty important stuff and one of the fun things a groom can do in all the wedding planning...or so I've been told by those brave men who have gone before me."

"That's the spirit! Josie, you're a very lucky woman to have such a willing groom. Most grooms don't want any part of the planning." Emily beamed at the pair.

Josie looked over at Chance and her gaze was locked by his. The look she saw there made the bottom drop out of the floor, and she subconsciously tightened her grip on the edge of the table top. She could feel the heat rolling over her skin even though she had on warm layers of clothing. But it was the brand of heat generated by the look of desire that brought a response from deep within her core making her forget to breathe.

"A most willing groom, indeed." His words whispered across to her. That was the moment Josie began fighting for her life.

Chapter Eleven

"IS THE COAST clear?" Josie heard the loud whisper before the rest of the body appeared. A few moments later, a smiling Dev stuck his head around the corner of the doorway leading from the mudroom into the kitchen. She responded with a smile.

"If you're asking if your brother is around, the answer is no. I think he went into Abilene early this morning. Want some coffee?"

"That would be wonderful." He moved into the kitchen at that point, drawing out a chair from the table, and making himself comfortable.

She poured two mugs and brought them to the table, taking a seat across from him. "What have you been up to?"

"What do you think? Braxton doesn't exactly have an exciting night life." He took a sip of the hot liquid.

"I guess since I haven't seen you around since our dinner, I just assumed you were busy."

"Well, pretty lady, if I haven't been around it was because my big brother more or less warned me to be on my best behavior around his bride-to-be or *else.*"

Josie hadn't expected that reply. Why would he keep

Dev away from her? Did he not think she could handle herself? Did he not trust her? That made for a not-so-great beginning to any marriage. "I make my own decisions. You're always welcome in my house...anytime."

Dev's grin broadened. "That's *my* Josie. I've really missed you. You can always make me smile. And the fact that you don't bow down to my brother is a breath of fresh air. Seems everywhere I go lately, I'm hearing his praises sung. He's become quite the top dog in this corner of the world. I don't know if they'll nominate him first for sainthood or to public office."

"People do look up to him," Josie conceded. "He works hard to keep improving the ranch. The techniques he's employed in better range management and...what's wrong?" She caught the look on Dev's face and broke off the rest of her comment.

"If I didn't know better, I'd say you've been drinking some of the same Kool-Aid as the rest of the people around here. Or you're just the president of his fan club. But let's talk about something more interesting."

"Such as?"

He set the mug aside and reached out, covering one of her hands as it lay on the table top, leaning toward her as best he could with the table between them. "Such as, you leave Chance waiting at the altar and come away with me. You aren't in love with him. Don't waste the rest of your life on this ranch. You deserve so much more. Let me take you away from here...today."

Josie was speechless. At first, she thought it was just another of his smooth lines. The look in his eyes and the tone of his voice told her soon enough that he wasn't being his usual flirtatious self. Something inside also told her that what she chose to do in the next few seconds would likely impact the rest of her life. Dev Braxton had represented everything she ever wanted…or everything she ever *thought* she wanted. Why didn't she know what she wanted anymore? With dawning clarity, she knew one thing with certainty…and it shocked her. Dev had no place in her future. Somewhere along the way to becoming a grown-up, she had outgrown him. Now she just felt sadness where he was concerned.

"I told you, this ranch is where I want to be…now and forever. It's who I am. But I don't think you ever really knew that or could ever understand it. Just as you know you can't be happy living here in Braxton; you need to be where there are bright lights and lots of people. I know that this is where I was meant to be for all of my life."

"And that sums that up," he replied. "You're a smart lady, Josie. Out of everyone here in Braxton, I think you possibly have been the only one who could see me for what I am. Perhaps understand that I'm wired differently from the other Braxtons. And you still cared." His words were cryptic and, for a moment, Josie thought she saw a glimpse of a man behind a mask. Where that analogy came from, she had no idea. There was an aura of a puzzle when it came to Dev…and perhaps there were one or more pieces that just couldn't be found. But then the old Dev slid back in place.

"So if you won't run away with me, how about dinner?"

"It's a little early for dinner for me. I still have a lot to do that I didn't get around to earlier...seems today was all about unexpected interruptions." First, the ladies from town, and now Dev. She stood up and took both their mugs to the sink, rinsing them and setting them on the drain board.

They parted at his car, and Josie went into the stable to fill Cookie's feed bucket. Josie was emptying the last of the feed into the animal's bucket inside his stall when she heard Chance's truck drive up and park outside. A couple of minutes later, familiar footsteps sounded, heading into the stable. Her pulse picked up in the way that seemed to be the norm whenever Chance came near. And there was little evidence of a sense of dread along with the arrival...it was more along the lines of anticipation that she hadn't recognized before the last few days. She didn't need to turn to know he was standing behind her...too close behind her. The scent of his familiar cologne drifted across her senses, and her gut tightened in response. *Deep breath. Don't let him rattle you.*

"I passed Dev on the road on the way out. Did you two have a nice visit?"

There was a slight edge in the underlying tone. Josie knew she could ignore it, or she could meet it head on. Others might think she preferred to hide her head in the sand at times...and perhaps she did on certain things that were too much to deal with in the moment. But those times were becoming fewer and farther in between. *Bring it on.* She turned to face the waiting cowboy.

"It was brief, but pleasant enough."

"I see. Too bad I missed it. Dare I ask what you two

talked about?"

"Suppose you let me ask my questions first?" She set the empty bucket on the shelf outside the stall. Then she took her time removing her work gloves and stuffing them inside one of her back pockets. All the while, she was aware of Chance standing with arms folded across his chest, leaning against the wall…eyes unreadable.

"Fire away. I sense you've got something you want to say, so let's hear it."

"Why didn't you tell me you had arranged things with Marie and Emily? Don't you think that's something it would have been nice to give your fiancée a heads-up on before it happened?"

Chance gave consideration to her question for a moment or two. He nodded his head. "I should have said something. I guess it slipped my mind amongst all the other things going on around here. I just thought you wouldn't mind them helping to get things together for our wedding. You've got a lot on your own…"

"Yes, I am busy," she spoke up. "But last time I checked, I'm the bride, and I should be taking care of these things. Besides, I thought we agreed to a simple ceremony at your ranch with Reverend Morrison. That doesn't call for a fancy wedding dress and a wedding cake and all that stuff."

He studied the toe of one of his boots for a moment before he responded. "I seem to recall you spent more than a little time one summer with your nose stuck in those bridal magazines. Of course, you were planning a make-believe wedding with a totally different groom in mind. I know your parents would have wanted you to have something nice to remember. That's all I was trying to give you…something they would have wanted for you."

Why did he have to say that? It touched something in the center of her chest. She didn't want him to think she was ungrateful. And why did he have to be so…so *Chance* all the time? "Well, it's the bride's place to pay for those things, so I expect to get the bills."

The breath he drew in sounded suspiciously like a heavy sigh laced with thinly veiled exasperation. "Let's don't even go there, Josie. The bridegroom gives his bride a wedding gift. This wedding is my gift to you. All you need to do is say a polite 'thank you.' Unless you think you could manage something a little more personal, but I leave that up to you."

"Personal?"

"Make it easy on yourself and pretend for a moment I'm Dev. Anything come to mind?"

Her eyes flew to his and found shades of the same look he fixed her with earlier that day at the dining room table when the floor fell out from beneath her. *Danger ahead.* The next thing she knew, Chance had muttered something under his breath, and he closed the gap between them in two strides. Strong hands went to her shoulders and she was fairly lifted off her feet and met the solid wall of his broad chest. The contact was like connecting with an electrical socket while standing in a pool of water. The charge was instantaneous, and she was fairly certain sparks shot out from all her fingertips and toes.

His mouth connected with hers, and a fireworks display

shot off behind her closed eyelids. This kiss was different from any of the previous ones. It wasn't soft and gentle and brief. It meant to make a statement and it did. His lips claimed hers and drew her right inside him. Her bottom lip was teased over by his tongue, which met with no resistance when it dipped into the opening he found. Hands moved from her shoulders to slide around her waist and then lower, bringing her body into contact with his. The discovery she instantly felt of a very aroused male shot up her own blood to the boiling point, especially as she realized there was an answering throb in her womanly core that both shocked and thrilled her at the same time. His kiss had flipped a switch inside her. There had been darkness, and now there was light. Because Chance was kissing her.

On instinct, her arms went upward to encircle his neck, her hands moving into the thick, soft hair. Josie couldn't seem to get close enough to the man who she spent so much time avoiding and fighting each step of the way. Somewhere, her mind was whispering that it was all wrong, but her body and her heart were shouting how right it felt. Deep inside, a spark had been lit that she never knew existed before, and the heat was both comforting and all-consuming. The power of it brought a soft shudder through her.

ON THE EDGES of his drugged mind, Chance registered the change that had come over Josie. With a great deal of effort, he stopped the kisses he was feathering along her soft jawline and slowly drew his head back. The thought clicked for a second in his brain that this change might have occurred with his comment about his brother. That gave him pause. His chin lowered to rest on the top of her head, while he tried to regain some ability to breathe and settle his heart rate down to less than a gallop. He didn't let her out of his arms though. "I've tried hard to be respectful and give you time and some space, but you can wreak havoc on a male's good intentions."

His brain had warned his heart that it was playing with fire and asking to be stomped into the ground. It was the same speech he had given himself daily over the years, while he watched Josie pine over and worship the ground his brother walked upon. He told himself he was doing it out of the goodness of his heart and concern for the girl and her parents. *Right.* Until the day he had found her in the barn's loft, sobbing her eyes out. He had held her in his arms for the first time that day, meaning to just comfort her from whatever slight his brother had done again. That's when a different feeling had hit him like a sledgehammer.

He had wanted to find Dev and beat him senseless for hurting her. Then he realized he wanted to hit him a few times for having a place in her heart that Chance suddenly wanted for himself. The depth of his feelings had scared him, and he had fought to move back behind the wall that he erected between himself and the teenager. After all, he told himself time and again, she was just a girl, barely more than a child.

He was a man and had the weight of running an entire

ranch on his shoulders even though he was barely into his twenties. There was no time to be listening to a teenager's forlorn crush on his self-absorbed brother, who didn't know she existed half the time. However, he told himself he needed to keep an eye on the situation and run interference...help protect Josie's heart. So he watched and waited and listened and consoled.

The inevitable day came when Dev left Texas and Josie behind. And it was Chance's job to pick up the pieces. Except things had changed over the last couple of years. Josie didn't run and confide in him. She tried to take everything on those slim shoulders of hers and would round on him like a tiger if he ventured too close to her territory. He should have left her to it, but he couldn't. She was too much a part of his life...and always would be. Now, all he wanted was to be the one who filled her heart. Only he was afraid her heart wasn't seeing him...it was still too full of his brother.

Slowly, he removed his hands from her and stepped back when he had enough control to do so. "Do me a favor, will ya? If I ever ask you to pretend I'm Dev again, just shoot me. It'll be easier that way." He turned on his heel, grabbed his hat from the hay bale where it had landed, and left her before he made any more of a fool of himself.

JOSIE DIDN'T SEE Chance again until the wedding day. He hadn't come in for his usual breakfast the morning after the kiss in the barn. Josie was both disappointed and relieved at the same time. All night, tossing and turning, and reliving the whole moment. More importantly, trying to sort through the jumble of emotions his touch had brought to the surface. Had they been there all along? For how long? Why now? Why did things have to be so complicated?

And what had Chance meant with his parting words? Did he think she was imagining it was Dev's arms she was held by and Dev she was kissing? Why did it appear to matter so much to him? There was a glimpse of something in those dark eyes before he turned away from her. Was it pain? Why? Chance was always a mystery to her. One moment, he was aloof and stayed at a distance with her. The next, he would do something so unexpected and considerate...how many times had he dried her tears? How many hours had he listened to her adolescent ramblings while he worked and she followed along behind him, whether on foot or horseback? He always had time for her...even when he had to have been so tired from working his ranch all day and helping her father out when he could. He had never turned away from her in those times. Until that moment in the barn. She was left feeling infinitely sad.

The only communication with him since that time had been either in the form of messages passed on to her through Tom or via very brief text messages. And the topics were never personal...just business.

THE DAY OF her wedding dawned bright and clear. It was

supposed to be a good omen, Em pointed that out prior to the ceremony. With the weight of a gold band on her hand, she pondered the wisdom of that.

Chance had kept his word. Mrs. Ross stood in front of her at the moment, admiring the wedding band on her hand.

"Josie Monroe," she beamed. "*Excuse me,* Josie Braxton!" the woman corrected herself. "I just wish your mother could see what a lovely bride you are today."

Josie's head hurt. Her feet hurt, as well, crammed into the pointed toes of the high heels she wore. Even her face hurt from smiling, as she shook hands, received hugs, and responded to well wishes from most of the population of Braxton. Chance had made good on his decision to place a ring on her hand in short order. They had stood together, in front of the large rock fireplace in the main house on the Braxton Ranch, reciting the vows presided over by Reverend Morrison, the pastor having stepped off a jet only hours before the ceremony.

In the final weeks' time, sandwiched between her usual duties on her ranch, she had dress fittings, hair and nail appointments, and fought nerves and an upset stomach along the way. Even at that moment, her stomach was considering revolting again. Her hands smoothed over the soft satin of the wedding dress for the umpteenth time. There was an odd comfort to it.

After her initial surprise, she had come to realize that she was secretly glad Chance had sought out the dress for her to wear. It was yet another insight into the man that she had coupled with the discovery that hit her with quite an impact earlier during the ceremony. That stunning clarity only served to keep her feelings in an uproar.

Catching a glimpse of herself in the large mirror on the wall across the room, she was reminded again of how much she resembled her mother in the dress. Josie felt her loss again as she stood under the large chandelier in the dining room. A strange life was beginning, and an old one was slipping away too quickly. If only she could look up and see a coaxing smile from the woman she had only had for a mere twenty-nine years of life. She needed her infinite words of wisdom. Josie needed to tell her what a fool she had just realized she was over the years. And that her parents had been right after all. But she couldn't do any of that.

Instead of her mother's eyes, she caught Chance's across the room where he stood with a group of fellow ranchers, champagne glass in his hand, looking every inch the pleased bridegroom, smiling and receiving good-natured comments.

As if sensing her, he turned, and the look he sent her way was meant only for her and she felt her cheeks flush and a familiar tingling sensation zinged through her body. Josie wished he didn't look so devastatingly handsome in the black, western-cut tux with black, hand-tooled leather boots, and a bright white dress shirt that set off his deep sapphire eyes and gleaming smile. Her pulse still had not settled from when she came down the stairs and saw him waiting for her at the bottom. She wished for just one-fourth of the confidence he exuded.

His vows sounded sure and strong and echoed throughout the large room, filled with so many people. Chance had made it his mission to seek out the gossip mongers and personally invite them to the nuptials. He also made certain the day was as close to perfect for Josie as he could make it, given the short preparation time. Her favorite pink roses filled vases throughout the house, along with candles giving a romantic glow to the rooms. The aroma of delicious food dishes filling the tables in the dining room wafted through the downstairs. A trio of musicians played for the ceremony and provided music as the guests mingled and ate afterwards.

Josie was amazed at how much Chance had accomplished. She was totally mystified why he would want to go to such lengths for a marriage that was barely more than a business agreement mutually beneficial to them both. It certainly wasn't the hearts and flowers romance everyone attending seemed to think.

Everyone except one person. "You look like you might need another glass of fortification." Dev's voice came from behind her as he stepped up to her side with two glasses in his hands.

"You might say that," she said, smiling in return, taking one of the glasses from him. "I'm sorry we never had time to get together since our evening out. Each time I thought I would have a free moment, it seemed Chance had something that needed to be done for this wedding."

"Almost as if he was keeping you and me apart on purpose," Dev commented, his gaze going in the direction of his brother across the room.

"We'll probably see each other more than before. At least until you leave again for *civilization,* as you refer to it." She hoped to inject some levity into the moment, to keep him in a better mood, and to keep her mind from going off in directions best not traveled. Such as toward the man with the dark, sexy eyes she could feel on her, even as she did her best to ignore the fact.

"Aren't you going to drink the bubbly I brought you?"

Josie looked at the amber liquid in the crystal flute. "I don't think I should drink it. It wouldn't do for the bride to get tipsy."

"That would be a sight to see...Josie Monroe, tipsy." He took a sip of his own champagne, his voice light, but his eyes a deep blue sea color.

"Josie *Braxton*." The correction came from Chance, as he moved quietly to stand between the pair, his hand sliding possessively around Josie's waist, a warm look moving over her, the move obviously meant to stake his claim for all to see.

"I stand corrected, dear brother. I do have to congratulate you. You're one lucky man, marrying the most beautiful woman in the county and gaining even more land for the Braxton ranching empire. Guess that would be the proverbial 'killing two birds with one stone.' Our father would be proud...per usual of his chosen favored son."

The hand at her waist stiffened, and Josie was aware of the hardening of his jawline, as Chance took a moment before he addressed his brother. "Yes, I'm a very lucky man, because Josie is a remarkable woman. You're wrong on the land part, however. Josie's ranch is all hers. Perhaps you shouldn't comment on things of which you have no knowledge."

"I stand corrected…again. It was just a case of true love between you both." Dev's barbs were tipped in sarcasm, but he kept his tone lowered. "No matter what, I do believe, as we are family now, I can kiss the bride to welcome her to the family."

"That's up to my wife."

Both men looked at Josie. She wished to be anywhere but in that spot. Josie was very aware of the guests, as well. She smiled and offered her cheek to Dev. After a moment of hesitation, Dev placed a rather chaste kiss on the proffered cheek.

"Welcome to the family, Josie. I'll be around in case my brother doesn't make you happy."

Josie knew it was time to separate the two men. "I think it's time to cut the cake, isn't it?" She glanced at the tall man beside her. Chance turned his attention away from his brother and back to her. The hard smile softened a bit.

"I believe you're right." He guided her away from Dev, toward the linen-covered table with the three-tier wedding cake.

At the cake tasting, it had been a difficult decision between three flavors. In the end, Chance settled the matter. Each tier of the cake was a different flavor…all iced in buttercream with lots of pink roses trailing down the sides.

"What's it to be? What flavor do you want me to feed you?" Chance grinned down at her as he picked up the cake knife and waited for her to place her hand with his. "Let me guess…the red velvet?"

"Perfect," she replied. "And then it's going to be the chocolate for you."

The photographer was ready, and they cut into the layers. Despite some good-natured teasing from the guests, she refrained from making a mess as she took the small square of cake and popped it between Chance's parted lips. What she wasn't prepared for was Chance's mouth closing and trapping her fingers. A loud hoot went up from the crowd and Chance's eyes gleamed in devilment. His tongue made a slow swirl around her fingertips, and she felt the vibration like a tuning fork, all the way up her arm and into the rest of her body. She took an unsteady breath, and her eyes met his with the gleam of something else shading them. He was well aware of what he was doing to her and enjoying every moment of it. The photographer reminded her that it was her turn and she hastily retrieved her hand.

Josie took the bite of cake from Chance quickly and stepped back so there would be no chance of any repeat of what happened with the last bite. He gave her a look that clearly told her he had labeled her a chicken, but she didn't care.

Toasts came next and Josie held her breath as Dev lifted his glass. To her relief, he kept it very brief and very proper...except for the gleam in his eye as he caught hers before taking a sip of the champagne along with the rest. Josie felt her hand caught in one of Chance's as he drew her through the throng of people to the front porch, where they were met with a barrage of birdseed. They ran the gauntlet and Chance settled her quickly inside his truck. Once he was behind the wheel, they left the farewell waves and guests behind.

For a few minutes, quiet filled the inside of the truck cab and settled around them. Josie's mind searched for something to say but found nothing. What did most couples talk to each other about in these moments?

"Already the bride is no longer smiling. Tell me what's on your mind?"

Trust him to get to the heart of things. She met his quick glance.

"I have no idea how to be married. What do I know about being a wife?"

Chance gave her a smile, his hand capturing hers as it lay on her lap. The warmth was reassuring.

"About the same as I know about being a husband. We'll learn together. That's what everyone else does. Sometimes, we'll get it right. Sometimes, not. But we can do it." He finished with one of those "Chance smiles" that always seemed to make her feel things would turn out okay.

But the bride and groom are usually in love with each other. That was her thought, but she didn't voice it. Her mind switched back to the moment at the altar that had turned her world inside out. Chance had reached for both her hands as the pastor instructed and they stood facing each other. She was certain he could feel her trembling nerves. He gave her hands a slight squeeze as he looked into her eyes with complete confidence in his...as if telling her all would be okay. There was nothing to fear. He was there. *Chance was there.* He had always been there.

And that had been the thunderbolt. As simple—and as

devastating—the truth of the matter was laid plain. It was as if a blindfold had fallen away from her heart. Chance was in her heart and her mind. He had always been there. How did that happen? It wasn't Dev first and foremost in her thoughts; it was Chance. How could she have fallen in love with him? *Why?*

Her eyes had swung to the best man...*Dev.* He had that familiar smile and mocking light in his blue eyes as he watched the two of them. And she felt nothing. The revelation shocked her, and she felt herself going through the motions of everything that followed, with her mind in limbo. That is, until the moment when the kiss came, and Chance had taken her face between his two palms as gently as if he were handling fine china. The kiss he gave her was a solemn vow from him to her. Her heart wanted to leap out of her chest at the fragile beauty of it.

Whatever was she to do? One thing she knew for certain. Chance could not know. This revelation was to be kept to herself until she figured out what it would mean to their arrangement. Falling in love had only been mentioned as it pertained to either of them meeting someone else. Either of them falling in love with each other had never been discussed. Maybe because it was an impossibility as far as he was concerned? It certainly had never entered her head...but her heart never was much good at listening to her brain. What if he found out and then had no such inclinations towards her? He had presented a business deal...not a marriage made in Heaven. What if her heart was the last thing he would ever want? What a fine mess she had made for herself. There was no turning back. Mr. and Mrs. Braxton were heading home.

Chapter Twelve

THE SUN WAS just setting when Chance parked the truck in front of the ranch house. Josie opened her door and slid out before he had an opportunity to come around and help her. The skirts of her dress were a bit heavy, and the coat she had draped around her shoulders earlier against the chill of the early November evening kept sliding off her shoulder. She was also concentrating on trying to not trip and fall off the blasted high heels.

He caught up with her and with his hand under her elbow. Josie managed the steps to the front porch. Chance stepped forward and opened the front door. Instead of stepping back and allowing her to pass into the house, he turned and easily swung her up into his strong arms.

Automatically, Josie's arms encircled his neck to keep her balance. Her protestations didn't stop him. He easily carried her across the threshold and only stopped when they reached the bottom of the staircase. He allowed her to slide down until her feet touched the floor, but his arms did not let go of her.

"Was that really necessary?"

"Of course it was. It would be bad luck to ignore tradition, and in case you haven't figured it out by now, I'm a very traditional kind of guy."

His smile was doing those crazy things to her stomach again. Or maybe it was the fact she only nibbled on the plate of food he tried to get her to eat at the reception. She had been too keyed up to attempt to keep anything down. She was realizing she should have eaten something.

"Well, at least this day is over, and things can get back to normal. That begins with me getting out of this fancy dress and into my regular jeans. Then I'll see what I can find for dinner."

Chance didn't allow her to step away. His arms still held her in place. "I've got dinner covered. I had my housekeeper bring over some food, and it should be warming in the oven for us. And before you change, I just want to say something now that no one is around to interrupt."

Josie had no idea what was coming. Chance paused for a moment, as if choosing the right words really mattered. Was he already regretting what he had just done?

He looked into her eyes, and Josie felt her breath catch in her chest. If she didn't know better, she would think her heart had just turned a somersault in place. Her hands had fallen from his neck to be caught between them, her palms over the center of his chest. The quick thumping of his heart under them seemed to match hers. Of course it would, he had just carried her across the room. *Don't read anything into it.*

"I've always thought you were beautiful, but when you came down the stairs before the ceremony this afternoon, I don't think I've ever seen anyone more perfect. I realize that this might not be the day you dreamed about as a girl, but I hope I was able to make it at least a day you can remember in a good way. I promised your mother I would do my best to always keep you safe and happy. I intend to do that no matter what. You have my solemn oath. You will want for nothing as long as I have breath in my body. Our marriage may not have begun in the usual manner with the usual courtship and all, but it's done, and I promise to do my best to make it work. Just try to remember you aren't alone, Josie."

A mixture of emotions was rising inside her. She was surprised and touched and suddenly emotional. So much so that tears threatened before she could stop them. The last thing she wanted was to feel vulnerable in front of Chance. She had never expected him to be quite so eloquent. She also knew that Chance Braxton never said anything he didn't mean. And he kept his word, no matter what.

But he had not mentioned anything about love. He had made a promise to her mother. He had made an agreement with Josie. Chance was simply keeping his word to both of them. *Doing his duty as he saw it.*

"I hope those are tears of happiness I see in your eyes, little one." He reached inside his jacket and withdrew a white handkerchief, offering it to her.

Josie took it and dabbed at the corner of an eye. "It's just been an emotional day and an emotional few weeks. I guess it's just a bunch of things all finally hitting at once."

With a gentle movement, Chance brushed a few strands

of hair away from the side of her face, his fingers touching her skin and sending immediate shivers across her nerve endings. If he noted the reaction, he didn't comment on it. "I think there was a time or two today when you were really missing your mom. I felt helpless because I knew I couldn't find any words to make it better for you. But I have a feeling that Mama Dianne and your dad were not far away from us today."

His words were her undoing, and it was as if a dam burst. Strong arms gathered her against the warmth of his chest and held her tightly as Josie finally felt the release of so many emotions coming forth. Even as she tried to control the soft sobs, she felt a wave of relief filtering through her body.

"Let it out, Josie," Chance whispered against the top of her head, one hand moving slowly up and down along her back, the other softly smoothing over her hair as it lay around her shoulders. "You've tried to keep things together for a long time…even before your mom's death. Just let it all go. I've got you."

The sobs increased, just as another thought came to her. "Oh, Chance! Your suit. It's wet, and I'm ruining it." She tried to step back, but he wouldn't allow it.

"Nonsense. It's just a piece of cloth, and it doesn't matter." He pulled her back against his chest and she went willingly.

For several long minutes, they stood in that spot. Josie's sniffles became less, and the tears slowly subsided. In their place was a quiet, relaxed feeling of being emotionally released. There was also another sensation filtering across her mind and through her body. It was a sensation she hadn't felt in a very long time, at least not since the days when her family was still all together, and the world was right and made sense. It gave her pause to realize she found it again inside Chance's embrace. *Home.* It would be so good just to stay inside his arms and lose herself in the wonder of it all. That thought frightened her, and she stiffened, managing to take a step back.

Chance didn't stop her.

"Go on and change your clothes. I'll see about our dinner." He stepped away, sliding his hands into his trouser pockets.

"I won't be long." Josie turned and climbed the stairs, gathering her long skirts up in order to not trip. Reaching the top, she walked into her darkened bedroom, let the coat slip from her shoulders and land on a chair in the corner before she reached out and switched on the bedside lamp. Her eyes blinked a time or two as her brain registered the change in her bedroom. At least she thought it was her bedroom. When she had left earlier that morning, her single bed had been in its usual place between the two windows. It was no longer there. There could only be one answer.

Turning on her heel, she marched directly out of the room and stopped at the head of the stairs. It wasn't a surprise to see that Chance stood in much the same place at the bottom of the staircase, his arms folded on top of the newel post and one foot resting on the bottom step. He looked as though he had not a concern in the world.

"Where the hell is my bed?"

Chance grinned up at her. "Yep, the Josie I know is back. I assume you refer to your previous bed. It was donated to the thrift store in town."

Josie opened and closed her mouth a couple of times, the words not coming out. At least, not the words that ran through her mind at the conclusion of his reply. When she did find her voice, the words were bit out through gritted teeth. "I did not ask for a new bed. I liked my old bed just fine."

"That might be the case, but it wasn't feasible."

"Feasible?"

"It wasn't big enough for the both of us." The words hung suspended in the quiet of the hall.

"That's *my* room."

"It is now *our* room."

"You aren't serious," she muttered before she thought better of it.

The grin faded. His gaze honed in on hers.

"Josie, I'm very serious. We're married, and we *will* share a bedroom. What we do in that bedroom will be strictly up to you." With that said, Chance turned and disappeared in the direction of the kitchen.

Josie had two alternatives. Follow him and waste her breath arguing with him. Or return to her room...*their* room...and change her clothing. Once she was back to herself again, then she could join him downstairs and figure out how to deal with this new situation. The latter was the wisest course of action. Of course she wasn't so naïve to think married couples did not share rooms and the same bed. She just hadn't sat down and actually thought things through to their logical conclusion. But she was faced with the facts of it now.

As she moved around the bedroom, her eyes kept falling on the wide expanse of bed with its swirls of browns and blues and creams on the plush bedding and pillows. The king-sized bed seemed to dwarf the room.

Shedding the wedding finery, she packed it away in the large box it originally came from. Josie would deal with the rest of it on another day. It would need to be cleaned and stored in a different way. Someday, maybe she would have a daughter that she could pass it on to. It would be a link to the grandmother the child would never know. Just as quickly as that thought came, a more frightening one came along. *Children. Heirs.* The legacy Chance wanted and the reason he had agreed to help her out. She was going to get something from their bargain and so was he. If they stayed together after that year mark.

It would be impossible to keep her feelings hidden from Chance if he didn't keep to what he said downstairs...about letting her make the decision. She was fairly certain that most brides didn't find themselves in such a quandary on their wedding night. *No,* their thoughts would be of a more intimate and exciting nature. They wouldn't be dreading sharing a bed with their new husband. She opened the second closet door and slid the box onto the shelf. That's when she became aware of something different about the contents.

Not only had Chance managed to add a new bed to her room, but he had wasted no time in moving a fair amount of his clothing into the closet space. Slamming the closet door, Josie gathered her jeans and a soft red turtleneck sweater. She combed out her long hair and left it to fall around her shoulders. Adding a light pink lip gloss, she decided her makeup was fine the way it was. She reasoned there was no real excuse to dress up for dinner with Chance.

There was no reason, yet, she reached for a pair of gold loops for her ears and a gold locket on a chain that she often wore due to its sentimental value. It was her mother's, given to her by Josie on their last Mother's Day together. With a final, quick glance over her shoulder at the newest addition to her room, she took in a deep breath and returned downstairs.

Josie came to a halt just inside the archway leading to the formal, yet seldom-used dining room. The dark oak table was covered with a cream linen cloth and set with china and even crystal stemware. A bouquet of more pink and cream roses sat in the center of the table between two tall candles.

Slowly, she became aware that Chance stood in the doorway across from her, leading to the kitchen. He seemed to be waiting for her to say something.

"When did you manage all this?"

He stepped forward to rest his hands on the back of the chair, pulling it out for her. He waited until she eased into the chair. "I didn't. It's called delegation."

Tossing a swath of hair over her shoulder, Josie withdrew the napkin from her plate and placed it on her lap, in order to do something with her hands and calm her racing nerves. "People always do what you say."

She noted the lift of the corner of his well-chiseled mouth as he settled into his own chair. "Most of them do. With the exception of one stubborn female."

"Get used to it. I'm my own person and I won't be changing for anyone."

"I'm well aware of that and I don't want to change you. I would like you to be more cautious perhaps. Also, I hope you'll come to realize that you don't have to do everything alone. We're partners. My shoulders are broad and I'm here to share the load. It's okay to relax once in a while."

She noted how Chance looked even sexier as he sat there with the candlelight playing off the planes and shadows of his face. Gone was the jacket and tie, but he still looked far more dressed for a fancy meal than she was. Josie wished she had perhaps taken a bit more care and chosen a pair of slacks instead of her serviceable jeans. Maybe a pair of flats instead of the leather boots.

Chance moved his hand to pick up his water glass and take a sip. The light caught the bright gold of the band on his hand. She remembered her surprise when she saw the pair of wedding rings he handed to the officiant prior to the start of the ceremony.

"I wasn't aware you wanted to wear a ring. Sorry I didn't think to get you one."

"That's okay. Things haven't exactly gone by the usual etiquette book on this wedding. Perhaps we should have a toast right now." He lifted his wine glass and waited for her to do the same. "To us and to a future that's ours to make." His eyes rested on hers as he took a sip of the burgundy wine.

"The future," she echoed barely above a whisper before she took her sip and brought her gaze away from his.

The meal was delicious. Stuffed chicken breasts and a rich sauce, steamed vegetables and homemade rolls were a far cry from the usual dinner fare in the ranch's kitchen. Josie was only sorry she couldn't enjoy the food more. Nerves were rolling around in her stomach too much at the moment. It had a lot to do with the nearness of the man beside her and uncertainty of what was still to come.

"This meal was certainly one of your better delegations."

"It was indeed. Juanita is responsible for the meal and for coming over and preparing the rooms and food."

Josie found a smile curving her mouth at the mention of the woman's name. The housekeeper and her husband had worked for the Braxton family for as long as Josie could remember. "I have fond memories of her. I remember sneaking into the kitchen at your ranch, and she would feed me beans and freshly made tortillas. I would come home, stuffed, and my mom would worry I was coming down with something when I was too full to eat the supper she had cooked. It took a while, but she finally figured it out."

Chance laced his fingers together over his plate and responded with a smile of his own. "There are a lot of good memories that we share."

"Yes, I suppose we do."

"After our mother died, I don't know what would have

become of Devlin and me if Mama Dianne hadn't stepped in now and then, smoothed out a bit of the sharp edges on us."

"I'm sure your father did the best he could."

"He did what he knew best…running cattle and making money." Chance didn't say more.

Josie had vague memories of the tall, quiet man always with a ramrod stiff back and a stern look on his face. She had wondered a time or two if the man ever smiled at all. Josie supposed neither son had felt much warmth from the man, particularly after their mother had died suddenly of a brain aneurism (replace with "aneurysm") while standing in her kitchen one morning, fixing the boys their breakfast. Dev had been eight and Chance was eleven. Overnight, Chance had to step in and try to raise his brother and handle his ever-increasing ranch duties at the same time. His father had expected and demanded no less.

"I want you to know that I asked Chadwick at the bank to set up an account for you, besides the main ranch account. You can use it for whatever you need or want."

Josie immediately bristled, her eyes flashing to his. "Why would you do that? I don't need charity. The Monroe Ranch may not be the almighty Braxton Ranch, but we can take care of ourselves. As long as the ranch has what it needs to get it back on its feet, that's more than enough."

"It's not charity, Josie. It's what married people do. They share things. This ranch is yours to run. As my wife, you'll share in what's mine, too."

"I don't need anything."

"Or anyone?"

"I run a ranch," she responded, attempting to ignore the stirring within her at his last question. "I better be able to handle things on my own."

"There's another pair of hands now, and there's a shoulder to lean on when you need it. You used to need it a lot."

"I grew up."

"Josie, it's not a sign of weakness to need someone. We all need someone."

She gave him a long look. "Even you? I've never seen you need anyone."

His eyes darkened, and he moved them from hers to rest on the last bit of liquid in his glass. "Maybe that's because you've never looked." Returning his glass to the table, he pushed his chair back and stood. Whatever his eyes held was shielded when he looked in her direction next.

"It's late. Sunup comes early. You know, we could still fly down to San Antonio or over to Dallas for a couple of days if you want. Most brides want some type of honeymoon."

Josie stood up at that point. "I'm not most brides. Besides, that stuff is for real couples."

A muscle twitched along his jawline. "We're as real as it gets, honey. Why don't you go on up? I'll clear and be up in a few minutes."

"Look, I can help…"

He stopped her. "No, *you* look. I know you didn't want me here. You didn't want this marriage. But it's done. The sooner you find a way to deal with it, the better. And it starts with you getting used to the fact that we will be sharing a bed and a bedroom." Chance moved to stand within easy reach of her, yet he didn't touch her. He didn't have to. His blue gaze eased over her in heated flickers.

"I said that I don't intend to force you to do anything you don't want to do. I think you know what I want. However, I won't push you. You'll have to make the decision on your own."

"What decision?" Did he detect the hint of breathlessness in her tone? She was certainly finding it difficult to breathe normally or keep her eyes from falling on the pair of magnetic male lips.

"To let me be your husband…in every sense of the word."

Subconsciously, her lips parted a bit to form a response, but none came, and that was just as well. His mouth claimed hers in an easy conquest. His tongue met no resistance as it slid in to meet hers. One strong hand slid around her neck and under her hair to capture and hold her still as his lips drew upon the softness of hers. The fact that Chance could kiss like no one she had ever been kissed by before, and the fact that she could feel it to the very tip of her toes, registered in a foggy brain. It was lulled by an instant fever that sprang alive as his tongue danced with hers and his kiss became more demanding.

Josie was drugged by sensations she never experienced before, except for the last time they shared a mind-numbing kiss. Her hands, fingers splayed, met the hard, muscular chest, and she stepped closer, under the spell cast by his touch.

Chance's free hand moved to her hip and slowly upward, the long fingers easily sliding underneath the hem of her sweater and finding the warm flesh of her back. His touch upon her skin sent a shock wave of tingles up her spine and sparked through her brain, enough to bring her to reality. Her eyes flew wide, her body stiffening. She stepped away, and Chance did not stop her. She fought to keep her mind clear and her breathing under enough control to speak. However, she didn't get her chance.

"Sweet dreams, Josie." Chance walked away first, disappearing into the kitchen.

Chapter Thirteen

THE BED WAS huge and seemed to have grown since the first time she saw it. Josie changed quickly into a soft pink flannel gown and swiftly slid under the covers, pulling them up under her chin, turning onto her side, facing away from the empty pillows beside her. The lights were off, and she was profoundly glad for the darkness.

Her cheeks felt on fire still as she tried to block the scene from the dining room from her thoughts. What had come over her? She responded so eagerly when Chance kissed her. She had participated in it from beginning to the abrupt end. It would be ridiculous to believe otherwise. She was already in a precarious spot where Chance was concerned. Because her heart was fully involved, it made her vulnerable, and that was a feeling that frightened her. Her ears were tuned in to every sound, real and imagined, in the darkened room and the hall beyond.

A half hour later, there was a roll of thunder in the distance beyond the windows. In a few minutes, light raindrops could be heard on the metal roof overhead. The sound worked to soothe her nerves, until her eyelids became too heavy to remain open. Josie slept soundly, and she was not aware when Chance entered the room an hour later, moving silently across the bedroom, stopping to adjust the covers over her shoulder, before he turned and stepped away.

IT WAS A while later that Chance entered the bedroom. Part of him hoped to find an eager bride waiting in their bed for him. What he found was an exhausted Josie fast asleep, curled on her side, her breathing slow and deep. He approached the bed with soft footsteps and bent to adjust the covers higher on her shoulder. With the softest of touches, he placed a light kiss on her forehead and then left the room.

The night air was needed to clear his mind and took a deep breath of it as he stepped outside. Not for the first time in the last couple of weeks, Chance knew what it was to second-guess himself. He had it planned out...or so he thought. It wasn't going to be easy, he realized that. But he might have underestimated his self-control and patience level in some recent situations.

He was a married man. Josie was his wife. And it was their wedding day. He had tried his best to make it memorable for her. Now, he was sitting on the front porch, a full moon rising in the east after the storm clouds had dissipated. A romantic setting and he was alone. His bride was upstairs in their new big bed, having fallen asleep...upset with him. He tried not to move too fast...lose the ground they had gained in their relationship. Such as it was.

If his brother hadn't shown up when he did, things

might have been a lot better. But then, maybe it had worked out in his favor. He had taken a gamble with allowing Dev to take Josie out to dinner. He hadn't bargained on the kiss, and it had taken everything in him not to put him on the floor. But Josie's reaction had been interesting…and hopeful. It was all part of a gamble. He knew he had to go all in once and for all. If he hoped for a future for him and Josie, he had to put his heart on the line. He counted on the fact Josie knew what it was to keep her word once she gave it. She'd do her best to live up to her part of their "deal." Only he hoped she would see that there were far more positives involved, and she could learn to truly trust herself and him.

There was hope. Kissing Josie had been more than he had ever imagined it would be. Her response gave him the impetus to remain hopeful…she couldn't be indifferent to him if she could respond to him as she did. One day at a time. He had committed his heart a long time ago. Josie held it in the palm of her hands…hopefully, one day, she could find room in her heart for him. He had to pray for a lot more patience to get him through whatever was to come.

🌿

JOSIE'S EYES OPENED slowly. The first thing she was aware of was the fact she had slept deeper and more soundly than she had in years. She marked it up to the combination of champagne and other wine from the previous day's events. The second thought was that she slept in a new bed, and she was probably not alone in it. Her hearing did not pick up any sounds nor did she feel any movement.

Glancing at the clock on the bedside table, she saw the alarm would be sounding in the next ten minutes. Carefully, she reached out and switched it off. Just as slowly, she eased from the covers and reached for the robe on the chair beside the bed. She hastily donned it and stood. Only then did she venture a look at the opposite side of the bed.

Empty. The only hint that someone might have been there, was a slight indentation in the top pillow. The covers were in place and seemingly undisturbed. There was an ambivalent mixture of feeling…both relief, and also disappointment. They blended to add to her confusion. Perhaps Chance had changed his mind about sharing a room? *Don't count on it.* Josie ventured toward the bathroom and found it empty as well. She wasted little time in taking her shower and dressing in jeans, green work shirt, and brown boots for the day ahead. Pulling her hair back into a ponytail, she grabbed a heavy work jacket and headed downstairs.

The smell of coffee met her as she stepped into the kitchen. However, the room was empty. Her eyes went to the pegs beside the mudroom door, and she saw that Chance's hat and jacket were gone. He evidently got an early jump on the day ahead. *Just as well.* It was to be business as usual. What did she expect? *Nothing.* As long as she kept that in mind, the less likely her heart would be hurt.

She was grateful for the additional time to prepare to face the man after the events of the last twenty-four hours and, in particular, the shared kisses. Grabbing a quick bowl of oatmeal and some toast, Josie downed a second cup of coffee and then bundled up against the cold of the morning. She stepped outside, pulling her hat onto her head, and sliding heavy gloves on her hands. The simple gold band still shone brightly and, while the engagement ring rested in its box upstairs, she had kept the band on her hand. She didn't identify why it was important to her to keep it there. It just felt...right. Her breath was frosted in the early morning as the sun was just coloring the sky a brilliant pink in the east. A thin layer of dewy frost colored the ground a pale white around the buildings.

Once saddled, she and Cookie headed in the direction of the holding pens less than a mile from the main ranch compound. There was a good deal of activity. The men were penning the heifers that would be palpated that morning. Doc McGrew stood at the gate to the chute where each one would be placed. He was suited up and ready for the messy job ahead...his arm in a long plastic sleeve that reached almost to the top of his shoulder.

Palpating of heifers was a necessary part of their business. Doc would reach his arm inside the cow and feel for the presence of a calf. The heifers that had been successfully bred would be culled from those who were not. Josie's eyes did a quick sweep of the area and found that Chance was nowhere to be seen. She moved her horse forward. The next hour was spent in the culling process, so she had to concentrate harder than usual to keep her mind from wandering in directions it shouldn't. Such as where was her new husband? Maybe he was bored with his new role already?

"We're still short a couple of cows. Chance went off to

locate them earlier." This bit of news came from Tom as he rode up to join her. She had her answer. When, a half hour later, Chance had still not made an appearance, Josie swung into her saddle and told the men she would take a look for the cows herself. The rain the night before had left the ground a bit soggy in some places but nothing to impede her progress too much.

The sun was climbing in the blue sky, and the brisk morning air was losing some of its bite. She paused long enough to remove her heavy jacket and place it under the straps at the back of her saddle. Ten minutes later, Josie topped a rise and saw one of the cows. She was in the draw below and was evidently mired in a mud hole.

Reining in Cookie as close as possible to the site, Josie removed her coil of rope from the saddle horn and attempted to place the noose over the cow's head. Twice, the cow flipped its head and the rope slithered off. On the third attempt, the rope caught and held. Quickly, Josie wound the rope around the saddle horn and tapped Cookie's side to ease back, tightening the rope and drawing the cow toward the edge of the hole. Things were going fine until the animal decided to be stubborn and came to a standstill within a couple of feet from the edge.

Josie, exasperated with the cow, dismounted and moved along the taut rope. There was nothing for it but to ease toward the animal and hope to entice it a few steps more. The mud was just above her ankle when she stopped and grabbed for a better grip on the line. The animal steadfastly refused to budge.

"Come on, you stupid side of beef. I'm trying to help you."

"Seems you've met your match."

Josie's head jerked toward the sound of the voice. Chance sat on his horse, a few yards away, watching with clear amusement on his face.

Naturally, he would choose to make an appearance when she was in a situation that was both maddening and embarrassing. How could she be taken seriously in running the ranch if she couldn't control one stubborn cow? Josie shot him a look that should have wiped the amusement off his face. It didn't.

"Did you find the other heifer?"

"Yes, I did," he responded. "When I got her back to the pens, Tom told me you had taken off in this direction, so I thought I would see if you had any luck." He still did not move from his horse.

Josie's mouth thinned, and she counted in silence to ten. When she spoke, she tried to maintain an evenness that she was far from feeling. Her feet were slipping a little and she tightened her grip on the rope. "Do you think you might possibly help me out here?"

"I can't believe it." He straightened in the saddle.

"Can't believe what?"

"You're actually asking for help. See…it's not that hard at all."

"Forget it. I'll do it myself." She turned back toward the cow, but before she could take more than a couple of steps, a rope snaked through the air and landed perfectly over the animal's head. Josie stopped and turned.

"Well? What are you waiting for?" Chance grinned at her.

Josie stomped back toward her horse and soon was in the saddle. This time, with two ropes around the errant animal's head, their horses backing slowly, the reluctant cow emerged to stand at the edge of the hole. Josie and Chance both dismounted at the same time, moving toward the animal to retrieve their ropes. He removed his and then went to do the same for her.

"I can get my own rope, thank you."

Chance stepped back and waited for her to do so. Josie had just cleared the animal's head when the now-freed animal decided to exercise its freedom. With a toss of its head in Josie's direction, it caught her off balance as she took a step forward. In a split second, Josie found herself flat on her backside in the mud hole. The cow went trotting away.

Chance stood on the bank, his shoulders shaking visibly beneath the heavy coat. The brim of his hat was pulled low, but the uptilt of the corners of his mouth was a giveaway. He was laughing at her!

"You think this is funny?"

That only added fuel to Josie's discomfort and growing anger at both the cow and the man. She moved to hoist herself up and immediately found her hand slipping. She ended up making a muddy splash.

There was no control now, as Chance could contain his laughter no more. He did step forward and, with an arm and hand outstretched toward her, he managed to speak, "Grab my hand."

Josie looked at him and then at his hand. She gave a brief smile and took his hand with one of her mud-covered ones. Taking a good grip, she leveraged herself up and took a step forward as she pulled swiftly on the hand she still held. There was a muttered oath. Then Chance took the place she had just vacated when his foot slipped in the mud. Josie had perfect timing to take advantage of it. From her stance on the dry land, she was the one who stood laughing at the site before her. The mighty Chance Braxton, with a priceless expression on his face, looked at her with a definite gleam of anger.

"Now, *that* is funny."

"Laugh while you can. Payback will be mine."

Josie was in her saddle before Chance made firm land. She gave him a smart wave and headed to round up the cow and complete the job. Chance was not far behind.

IT WAS ANOTHER two hours before Josie was able to head Cookie toward the barn and home. She finally gave in when Chance threatened to haul her off her horse and put her in a truck and have one of the hands drive her back to the house. Neither of them had taken time to do anything about the mud-covered clothing because all hands were needed when they reached the others.

It wasn't the first time either of them had worked in such conditions. However, the moment things slacked up, Chance told her to go to the house and change. Making a scene in front of the ranch hands was not something she wanted to engage in. Although they didn't appear interested in the tableau playing out between her and Chance, she knew they couldn't help but hear it. She gave him a final look that told him she was not at all happy with his high handedness, but she would suck it up this time and do as he ordered.

As she entered the welcome warmth of the house, she realized it might not have been such a bad idea after all…coming in out of the cold, where a light drizzle had begun to fall just as she made the house. Her clothing was caked in dried mud, and she stopped in her tracks when she caught sight of herself in the mirror in the small half bath downstairs. She had streaks of mud on her face and even in her hair. She looked worse than something a cat would drag in. No wonder Chance found her amusing.

Her jacket, hat, gloves, and boots were left in the mudroom. By the time she reached her bedroom, she had the shirt off, and the jeans soon followed. The dirty clothing went into the clothes hamper as she passed into the bathroom. Within a few minutes, she stood under a hot stream of water in the glass-tiled shower. Her chilled limbs began to warm, and renewed circulation began to return to them. She shampooed her hair and stood for a while longer under the showerhead.

With reluctance, she shut off the water and reached for the fluffy blue towel hanging on the rod next to the door. Drying off, she wrapped the towel around her and stepped out of the shower. Just as she reached for a hand towel to wipe the steam off the mirror, the door opened behind her and she swung toward it, her hand automatically going to the folds where the towel was tucked in to secure it.

"What are you doing? Can't you knock?"

Chance seemed totally nonplussed at her presence or her obvious discomfort. He acted as though a half-naked woman in his bathroom was a perfectly normal occurrence. He moved into the room, causing Josie to back up until she couldn't go any further due to the vanity behind her.

"It should be obvious what I'm doing. Since I'm coated in mud, I thought a shower would be appropriate before I have to leave to attend a meeting in town. I had hoped to get here sooner, in order to conserve water." He began removing his shirt as he spoke.

Josie tried to keep her focus on his face and what he was saying. It was becoming increasingly difficult to concentrate, given the fact that his broad-shouldered, muscular chest, with its light smattering of fine hair tapering down to disappear below the button at the waist of his jeans, kept drawing her eyes downward like a pull from a magnet. It was definitely steamier in the room by the time he reached for and undid the belt and drew the zipper downward.

"Conserve water? Can't you wait until I'm done in here?" Did her voice end on a squeaky note? She licked her lips in nervousness.

"Conservation of water in a drought season is very good, haven't you heard? I thought we could share the shower. Only you were faster than I anticipated. But don't let me stop whatever you were doing."

With that, the jeans went to the floor, leaving him clad only in dark navy briefs that definitely caused her blood pressure to shoot through the roof and impeded her breathing. Chance stepped closer to where she stood, his arm reaching above her for a towel from the shelf behind her. His arm touched her bare skin, and she felt as if a live wire had flicked over her. A shiver went down her back.

"Are you cold?" he asked, his eyes falling on hers, and letting her know that he already knew the answer to the question.

"I prefer to have my bathroom to myself."

"Which you would have if you hadn't pulled me into that mud hole. Guess you brought this on yourself. Little girls who play with fire can get burned."

"If this is your idea of a payback, then you've made your point. You can leave now." She tried to sound a lot braver than she was feeling at the moment, clad only in a towel that was way too short. There were all sorts of feelings swirling through her body at the nearness of the almost naked man, and anger was not high on the list.

Chance's dark sapphire blue gaze slid over her face and fell lower, very slowly, across the expanse of skin and swells of her breasts that were barely concealed by the material. The fact that what he saw met with his approval was very apparent in the gleam in his eyes and the increase in his own breathing pattern as evidenced by the taut muscles of his chest. Josie felt a flash of womanly pleasure in the fact that he obviously found her appealing.

It was becoming increasingly difficult for her to keep in

mind all the reasons why she should remember that giving in to any sexual desires with Chance would be most unwise in their present situation. It was practically impossible when he placed both hands on the vanity on either side of her hips, effectively blocking her from escape…if escape was to enter her mind.

His face, particularly his lips, was no more than an inch from hers. Warm breath fanned her chin as he spoke in lowered, velvet-lined tones. "I could use some help making sure I get all the mud off my back…and other places."

It would be so very easy for her to give in to her feelings at that moment. That realization was very clear. Her hands itched to roam over the broad expanse of tanned skin and muscle and beyond. The temptation was causing her body to react in ways she had never experienced before. He was tempting her. He was also paying her back. She had tweaked his male ego back at the mud pond. That sobering thought came at just the right moment. Josie latched on to it as a lifeline back to sanity and reason.

"That seems to be the least I could do. Of course, I'll help you out. Step into the shower and get the water nice and hot." The smile she gave him matched the sultry quality of her voice. She worked to stifle the sudden urge to laugh out loud when she saw the look of sheer surprise that crossed Chance's face at her reply. He didn't say anything, but a wide grin split his face. He stepped to the shower door, opened it, and with a quick movement, the briefs came off.

Josie averted her eyes, but not before catching a glimpse of a very firm, sexy male butt. She caught her bottom lip to steady her thoughts and enable her to move forward. If Chance thought he was going to win this round, he was about to get his comeuppance. Two could play the game he had started.

"Come on in, the water's fine," Chance called out, moving to stand under the spray.

"Here you go," Josie replied, stepping quickly to the opening and tossing in a long-handled scrub brush. "You wanted help to scrub your back. This should do." She paused as she was about to turn away. She tossed the surprised man a wide smile over her shoulder. The towel she wore came off in her hand. She tossed that in as well. "I'll even help you out with a towel, too. Enjoy!" She shut the door between them and ran from the room, laughing. The sound of some very colorful words from the man in the shower followed behind her.

Chapter Fourteen

"I T'S NICE TO finally get some time alone with you without big brother watching over us." Dev had arrived about twenty minutes after Chance left for his meeting in town. Josie had made herself scarce until she saw Chance pull away in his truck after he had showered and dressed. After the stunt in the bathroom, she had dressed in record time and made her getaway to the stables to discuss some things with Tom in order to not have to deal with the man she had played her shower trick on.

Josie's cheeks still burned as she remembered her sudden and totally uncharacteristic decision to drop her towel and tease Chance with a quick view of her derriere. She wasn't sure she would ever be ready to face him again. What had possessed her?

"Is it by design or coincidence that your arrival comes right after your brother left the ranch?" She handed Dev the glass of tea, as he lounged with one shoulder against the fireplace in the living room. Taking her own drink in both hands, she tucked her legs underneath her as she settled into a corner of the couch across from him.

Dev gave her a blue-eyed wink as he took a sip. "You

have me figured out."

"You know you could come over for a visit anytime. Whether Chance is here or not."

"You and I need to have an opportunity to talk without him around. I need your help with something and I don't need him interrupting us." Dev came to sit beside her on the couch.

"Sounds important."

"It is. It could make quite a difference in my life. You just may be the key to making things much better."

"I'm glad to help if I can. So tell me what it is you think I can do." She settled against the cushions and prepared to listen.

Dev set his drink on the coffee table in front of him. He gave her the smile she remembered so well. The one that always used to make the butterflies take flight in the pit of her stomach. Now, she could see that it was devoid of that magical power over her. The dark navy corduroy jacket over a white turtleneck sweater and the dark slacks all served to heighten his blonde good looks. Only Josie had to admit that, as much as she searched, none of the stirrings she once felt for the man beside her were present any longer. Somewhere along the way, she had actually outgrown her girlhood crush on Dev. It was a time to be remembered fondly but never to be revisited.

"I need you to talk to Chance and get him to see the light. If he'll agree and petition the trust for a change in the terms, they'll do it. With the extra funds each month, I'll be able to invest in the future and settle down. Maybe I'll even come back to Braxton and build a house here. I do have quite a few acres of the Braxton Ranch in my name."

"I can't quite see you coming back here after the glamor of Las Vegas and being content to watch the grass grow. You always said the only cattle you wanted anything to do with was the steak on your plate."

"My dear Josie." He smiled, one hand reaching to take the tea from her hands and setting it on the table next to his. "There are other things besides cows around here to keep my attention. My brother isn't the only one who can appreciate the charms to be found in our next-door neighbor." His hand moved to rest in a far too familiar way on Josie's thigh.

Josie felt a strange sensation at the touch. It wasn't a welcome one, and she moved her leg from under his hand. "What makes you think I can persuade Chance to do anything?"

"My brother is besotted with his lovely wife. That's why he sees the green-eyed monster each time I come around. Of course, I don't blame him. I'd feel the same way if you were mine." The words were definitely a smooth line. And he had no idea what Chance felt about her because, if he did, he would certainly not say he was jealous.

Chance jealous? It was preposterous. *Right?* Of course, it was. Not self-sufficient, cool-no-matter-what, tough-as-nails Chance. Why did her heart speed up at the thought? Maybe because she wished that could be the case? What would it be like to have Chance's heart? The woman who managed that would be very lucky. Why hadn't she seen the real man sooner? Because she had been blinded by glitter and overlooked the real gold right in front of her.

"Earth to Josie," Dev cut in, his eyes searching hers. "I need you with me on this, sweetheart. You know that you and I have a connection that Chance will never hope to have with you. I'm the one you should be with. You've always wanted me, and now we can be together." His hand moved to rest on her thigh, and she found herself tensing at his touch. She was given no time to react.

"In the old days, I could either call you out for a duel or simply shoot you on sight for poaching my territory."

The steel-honed low tones of Chance's voice broke them apart, and both pairs of eyes met the dark look fastened on them from where the man stood in the doorway from the hall. For a split second, Josie saw Dev's eyes spark with frustration, but it quickly subsided and eased into the shadows as the docile, charming smile reappeared. He nonchalantly drew a hand over his neatly groomed head.

"Bloodshed won't be necessary. I was just chatting with my favorite sister-in-law. No harm in that, is there?" Dev stood from the couch as he spoke.

Chance ignored his comment. His gaze fell to Josie, still seated on the couch. She could feel the heat rising in her cheeks. His gaze shuttered as he moved into the room to stand with his back to the fireplace, his hands sliding into his pant pockets. Silence stretched as tight as a guitar string. Any moment, it would break.

Dev made the first move. "I'll just leave you two alone. I'm sure honeymooners don't want a third wheel around." He paused in the doorway, giving Josie a smile that was meant to be another jab at his brother. "I'll give you a call tomorrow."

Josie rose and followed behind him to the front door. Just as she was about to close the door, Dev turned and paused in the doorway, his voice just above a whisper. "Work your magic on the man, babe. I need you. I'm counting on you." He gave a wink and left the porch.

Slowly, Josie closed and latched the front door. There was nothing to it but to go back into the living room and face Chance. She turned and came up short. Chance had moved, silent as a stalking cat, to stand, leaning with his back against the newel post of the staircase, arms folded across his chest, his gaze thoughtful as he fixed it on her.

"I could offer an apology for interrupting the touching scene on the couch, but it wouldn't be sincere."

She moistened her dry lips and smoothed her sweater over her hips. Why did she feel guilty when she hadn't done anything to be guilty about? "You didn't interrupt anything. I had no idea he was coming over here."

"Yet, you weren't protesting."

"I have no intention of apologizing for something that I neither expected nor wanted. And I don't intend to stand here and debate it with you." Josie went to move rigidly by the man, but a strong arm snaked out, and his hand caught her wrist, bringing her to a standstill less than a foot from his side.

"After all the years you pined away for the man, that's quite a change of heart…you not wanting his kiss or even his touch."

"People grow up. Why do you seem to find it so hard to believe me? Dev was a crush and a foolish one at that."

"Maybe it's hard to believe because of all the times I dried your tears because of him," Chance responded. His expression did change some. His eyes darkened, and there was a hint of softening in his expression, along with a tinge of something close to regret. "Maybe because I've waited a long time for you to see my brother as he is. And to realize there are other things you might be overlooking."

"There aren't any blinders. What is it that I need to see?"

"That's for you to figure out," he replied, a smile softening the corners of his mouth. "Here's a hint." His head lowered to hers. His hand still held her wrist, but even if it didn't, Josie wasn't going anywhere. Chance was kissing her. Each kiss from the first time, which had been swift and playful, to the second that had been probing and a challenge, to the last couple that were mind-blowing and sensuous…each one only left her craving more. This one was long and asked both a question and supplied an answer.

Josie responded in kind. She had her own questions. Why could the slightest touch of Chance's lips on hers blot out all reason and everything else from her mind? Why did Dev's kisses leave her emotionless and Chance's leave her wanting so much more? A determination fueled the desires licking along the brittle nerve endings throughout her body. Instead of stepping away, she stepped forward, her body fitting itself against the hard-male length of his, sending thrills along her spine and bringing a fever to her mind.

"I want to make love to you, Josie." The words were

whispered against her mouth as his lips loosened their hold on hers for a few moments. A pair of strong hands moved to cradle her head, giving him unfettered access to the plains and contours of her face where his mouth trailed hot kisses. "It's your decision. Say yes."

A low moan sounded faint from within her. Her fingers itched to touch the heated flesh she could feel even through the material of his shirt. With determined movements, it wasn't long before her fingertips bunched the material just above his belt and found the access they sought, the warmth of his skin.

Chance's hands moved then, gliding slowly over her shoulders, bringing her against him until there wasn't an inch of space between them. His palms smoothed down her back until they cupped her bottom, and he shifted, bringing his lower body into hard contact with hers. His tongue darted inside the opening of her lips as she sucked in a quick breath at the primal movement. Hers met his in a timeless dance. The hard length of him pressing against her made it perfectly clear that he was more than ready to take what he wanted, needed.

Josie was lost. Yet, she felt strangely *found* at the same time. Her arms went upward to entwine around Chance's neck, her fingers luxuriating in the silken feel of his hair as it met his collar. The scent of him filled her. His taste became her new craving. His mouth moved to nip at the soft flesh of her earlobe, sending a wave of goose bumps along her flesh.

"Say it, Josie," the whisper came again. "Say yes."

"Yes, yes," she hissed in a breathless reply. There wasn't

any need for more. Strong arms lifted her easily and swung her against his chest as he managed the stairs. Somewhere her brain managed to telegraph the fact to the rest of her body that something extraordinary was about to happen. There was no time to dwell upon it, however, as the feel of the comforter beneath her registered the fact they had made it to the big bed in record time.

Chance followed her down onto the bed, keeping his weight off her by resting it on his forearms along either side of her, his mouth continuing to draw upon hers. Her hands were not idle. Having drawn his shirttail from his pants earlier, it was easy for her to divest him of the heavy sweater. Her hands then glided over the broad shoulders and taut muscles of his upper back. The actuality of touching him was so much better than she could have imagined. It was a hypnotic sensation.

With equal fervor, Chance's hands moved deftly, easily unbuttoning her sweater and then sliding her jeans over her hips. In a swift movement, he stood beside the bed, and his jeans and boots joined hers. Through lowered lashes, Josie gazed upon the toned, hard body of her husband. A fever brushed her skin. Her breathing increased along with each wild beat of her heart as anticipation and longing filled her body. Deep within her, she felt an incredible surge of desire spilling into a molten pool in her lower regions. The fire became a blaze as a blatantly sensual look warmed Chance's sapphire gaze, as he slowly removed his briefs and stood in all his virile glory, before lowering himself to her side.

His hand moved to claim one lace-covered breast, while

his mouth rained hot kisses down her throat and over one mound, to the lacy edge. Her hands balled into the covers at her sides as she tried to remain still under the heated touches. For a moment, he lifted his head and a slow smile curved his lips as he trailed a couple of fingers along the frilled edge of lace over one breast.

"I'm very turned on by you in your sexy black lace. Who would have guessed what was under the work shirt and jeans?" Then his gaze grew more focused. A finger slowly traced along her bottom lip. "One important part of any marriage is that a husband and wife be open and trust each other to be able to do that." He hesitated for a moment, and Josie kept her gaze on his. "I like to think I know most everything about you, since we've shared a good amount of time together over the years. I can recall most of the boys who came around. It just dawned on me I may have been wrong in assuming something. Are you still a virgin, Josie?"

Oh great. Now for the ultimate embarrassment. No getting around the fact, because he was going to find out the answer for himself soon enough. "I wasn't interested enough in anyone to have sex just for the sake of having it. Sorry to…" The finger now lay against her lips, stopping her next words.

"Hold on, sweetheart. Don't be sorry for anything. And sex is just a part of what's going on here tonight. I'm honored that you said yes to me and give me your trust. I'll do my best to make this special." His lips replaced the finger on her mouth, and the embarrassment soon vanished, along with any other coherent thought.

Steady fingers reached beneath her, and her bra was no

longer between them. A fire flared in the gaze that hungrily looked over the exposed mounds of flesh as they stiffened and ached to know his touch. Chance did not keep her waiting long. His tongue reached out and flicked over first one point and then the other, before drawing them in, one at a time. At the same time, his fingers slid downward and edged under the lace panties, searching and then finding the sweet spot they sought. At his touch, a quick intake of breath and a soft moan erupted from within her. The mouth at her breast began suckling in rhythm to the movements of his fingers as they lost themselves deeper into her heated moistness.

Josie was consumed by strange new sensations that had her body moving of its own will, as her need for the deep ache in her core to be fulfilled doubled and tripled with each touch of Chance's body. Soft sounds escaped her lips as the ache inside her built toward an incredible pitch. Her hands, body, and mouth met his, kiss for kiss, touch for touch. He led, and she followed. He was an incredible guide on their first journey together.

Chance's lips whispered her name time and again as his movements were near worshipful at moments as he stroked her, intent on giving her as much pleasure as he could. She sensed he fought to maintain control over his own desires in order to heighten her pleasure longer. Sensing they were both almost at the point of no control, Josie was aware of movement and heard a drawer opening by the bed. The crackle of foil came next, and Chance quickly applied protection before returning to her. Everything intensified until she thought she would explode if he didn't give her what her body was craving.

When his leg moved between hers, his knee making room, she welcomed him, trying to not stiffen as she felt his length make an entrance. "That's it, sweetheart," the words were whispered hot and heavy against her ear. Her palms increased their hold on his shoulders. "Just relax a bit." He filled her slowly and completely. Josie reveled in the feeling of having him inside her. The small amount of pain involved registered only for a second.

With her name whispered as both a prayer and a soft plea, he began to move inside her, her hips joined in natural response. Nails dug into the flesh along his upper back as he took them both on a mounting race to an incredible and frenzied climax. Her soft cry muffled against his shoulder as shudder upon shudder rocked from his body to hers and back. His mouth claimed hers in a kiss that sealed their last breath together. Just when she thought her lungs would burst, Chance rolled them both to their sides, his arms gathering her close, his lips continuing to place light kisses into the top of her hair, as her cheek came to rest on his solid chest. Beneath her ear, his fast-beating heart could only be matched by her own. A sheen of fine moisture on the hard planes of his chest and stomach resulted from the fevered pitch of their lovemaking. They lay spent for several long moments, each trying to regain control of breathing and emotions.

"Are you okay?" Chance's whispered inquiry seeped into her foggy brain.

She didn't trust her voice, so she simply nodded her head against his chest.

"I'm sorry, Josie. I hadn't planned on this happening quite like this. I didn't want to take advantage of …"

Josie didn't want to hear any more. Chance was sorry it had happened…he had been disappointed. After all, she was a virgin. Or had been. What did she know about pleasing any man? She just didn't want to hear him say what she knew to be true. Moving from his side, she rolled away and managed to grab the throw at the bottom of the bed, wrapping it around her body as she stood. "There's no need to dissect what happened. You're sorry and so am I. We just got carried away. Just let it be."

She made it to the safety of the bathroom and finally took a breath as she leaned against the locked door at her back. Biting her lip, she moved to the shower and turned it on full blast. Only after she stepped inside and closed the door, did she finally allow the tears to flow.

There were two reasons that she stood crying under the hot spray. Chance had apologized, when it had clearly been her own inadequacy that had disappointed. Of course, she hadn't satisfied him. The second reason brought the true pain. She had given her heart to Chance and now he had her body as well. Yet she had nothing of his. Not really. The joke was on her. She was in love with the man she married. How much worse could things get?

Chapter Fifteen

LEAVING THE RANCH and the crew behind, Chance finally headed his horse toward the open range. He figured it was the best course of action for everyone's sake within a mile of him. He was in no mood to talk to anyone, let alone have patience for the myriad of problems waiting for him as the day began. Tired of the looks cast his way by the foreman and the questioning gazes of the hands as they steered a wide path around him, he knew it was best for him to distance himself.

Reaching a stock tank, its windmill cranking in the breeze, Chance drew his horse up, pushed his hat back on his forehead, and took a deep breath of the chilled morning air. After spending a sleepless night, he had risen and left the house long before daybreak. He was used to being in charge, to knowing what needed to be done and how to resolve problems. However, he had no idea how to solve the mess he had apparently made of things with Josie and their situation.

It had started when he walked in to the house and found his brother making a pass at his wife. He saw red and he wanted to throw Dev off the ranch, after beating him senseless. Yet, he hadn't done either. Proud of his being able to control his desire to inflict bodily harm on his sibling, he had not, however, been able to control the urge to kiss Josie, and things suddenly had really gotten out of control.

With long hours on his horse and cold showers over the days since they had become engaged, he had managed to keep himself in control and not act upon the desire to force things intimately between him and Josie. He had told her he would not do that. But he should have known better that such a promise couldn't last. Not given how he felt about her. The fact that he did ask her if she wanted to make love with him last night and she had said yes, did nothing to salve his conscience or alleviate his self-loathing.

The fact that Josie had still been a virgin was something he should have kept in mind, and he had done so, until her responses drove him beyond the point of all sane thought. At least he had enough control to think to use a condom. He wanted children…a legacy…with Josie. But only when Josie was ready…and was able to give him her heart completely.

Chance wanted to do nothing but give them both incredible pleasures once he realized he was far from the point of calling a halt to things. Afterwards, he tried to apologize for his behavior, but she brushed it aside and admitted that she was sorry it had happened at all. The fact that Josie regretted their lovemaking was a gut blow. It felt like a cold knife going through his insides, and he had no clue what to do to make it better. So he did nothing.

When she had finally emerged from the bathroom, he pretended to be asleep. Nothing was further from the truth. When she slid beneath the sheets, turned her back to him, and then stayed glued to the far edge of their bed, the knife twisted more.

Chance wished he had never agreed to her mother's wishes. As much as he wanted to help and to stay close to Josie, it was turning into a mess. How could he possibly have thought he could make Josie see him as anything other than a problem to be endured for the sake of saving what she really loved…her family's ranch? All he had managed to do was to scare her off and make things worse.

He had done everything possible to let her see his feelings. Except coming right out and telling her that he was in love with her. That he wanted nothing more than to live the rest of his days with her. He could have added that he had probably loved her since she was the scraggly kid following after him and acting like a silly fool over his brother. He was the boss. He was the man who led, and others followed, and he never looked back or second-guessed his decisions. *Until Josie.*

He could admit it to his horse and to the wide-open spaces, but when it came to saying the words to the woman herself, he always held back. Chance knew he was afraid…afraid of losing her altogether, of scaring her off for good…of possibly sending her flying into his brother's arms.

Now he had managed to do that with a thoughtless loss of control. He had made matters worse. He had scared her off, but he had also made his need of her worse. If he allowed himself to dwell on how she had looked and felt and tasted the night before, the ache deep inside him would only grow more painful. Somehow, he had to keep his feelings in check and find a way to continue to get through each day with Josie. Chance had no idea how to accomplish that. No problem had ever gotten the best of him, but it would take considerably more thought how to solve this one.

"Aren't you looking pretty today?" Myrna Davis made the comment as she accepted the package handed to her across the post office counter.

The comment threw Josie's concentration off for a moment. So much so, she had to erase what she had written on the ticket and begin again. "Thank you, Myrna." She had no idea what else to say. She was dressed in her usual ranch work clothes and heavy jacket. Her hair was pulled back in a ponytail with her hat jammed on top.

"Must be that marriage agrees with you," the woman continued. "You have that new bride glow about you." Then Myrna gave a wink along with a wide grin. "And you're blushing, too."

Josie quickly pushed the paperwork toward the woman, wanting to be away from her. She was aware that others in line behind her were smiling and turning attention in her direction. She might as well have a huge neon sign above her head or something. "*Josie had great sex last night.*" Quickly, she bid the woman good afternoon and did not venture any further glances in anyone else's direction as she made her exit from the post office.

Her next stop was the bank. Hopefully, she wouldn't be

subjected to any further comments of a personal nature. Ted Vickers, the assistant bank manager, stepped up to the counter as she approached.

"How are you today, Mrs. Braxton?"

Josie stopped for a moment, her mind having to quickly grasp the fact that this was the first time anyone in a professional capacity had actually addressed her by her married name. It caused a flurry of butterflies in the pit of her stomach. She thought it was a rather strange reaction to something so mundane. Except it wasn't mundane; it was all part of her very surreal new life. A new life in which she had no clue how to adjust.

"I'm fine, Mr. Vickers. I wanted to deposit this check into my account, please." She handed the paper over to the man.

"Certainly. Which account would you like it in?"

"Which account?" Josie blinked a moment, her mind wrapping around his question.

"Yes…your personal account or the ranch account?"

"My personal account?"

"The account that was opened last week."

Josie had forgotten what Chance had said about opening an account for her at the bank. "Just place it in the ranch account, please."

The man completed the transaction within a couple of minutes. He handed the deposit slip back to her. "I jotted down the new account and its balance on the back of this ticket for you, in case you haven't received your new card yet."

Josie took the paper and thanked him. As she reached the sidewalk, she opened her bag and went to slip the paper inside. She paused and flipped the deposit slip over and noted the account number, along with what had to be a huge mistake. She turned immediately and retraced her steps to the counter. The man looked at her and smiled.

"Another transaction so quickly?"

"I'm afraid there has to be a mistake on the amount you wrote on the ticket for the new account. Could you please verify that?"

The man punched in some numbers on his computer screen and read the information. He looked at the written amount and back to the screen. He nodded his head. "That balance is correct."

Josie slowly withdrew the slip from the counter, thanking him for his time. She turned and left the bank. Not until she was seated inside the ranch truck did she look at the deposit ticket again. The amount was more than they had ever made in an entire year of ranching. Chance had simply deposited it in the bank for her. She knew the Braxtons were well off, but until that moment, she had never been faced with the enormity of it all.

Of course, she had no intention of ever touching the money in that account. She had never been a female who needed much. A pair of good boots, sturdy coat, a few pairs of jeans and work shirts. Then again, as Chance's wife, she might have to dress up a few times. No matter what, the money would sit there. She'd get by on what was left after the ranch bills were paid.

At the outskirts of town, Josie slowed the truck and pulled off the highway into the parking lot of the church. Passing the building, she pulled in and parked next to the stone wall which encircled the cemetery. The tall pecan trees were stark skeletons without their leaves now that winter was upon them. As she stepped from the truck cab, she was met by an immense sense of peacefulness with the breeze rustling across the dry leaves under her feet causing the only sound heard. Now and then, a vehicle passed by on the highway on the other side of the buildings, but, other than that, it was quiet in this spot, with limitless views of the surrounding ranch lands and the distant mesas.

Josie carried the small bouquet of yellow and orange chrysanthemums toward the newest headstone in the cemetery. Seeing her mother's name carved next to her father's still gave her a jolt. She wondered how long that reaction would continue. Josie withdrew the withered bouquet from the metal vase holder on the stone and replaced it with the fresh flowers. The spot of color was pronounced against the grayness of the surroundings. Brushing away leaf debris from the marker, she finally stood and looked around her.

"It's an awfully quiet spot here, Momma. You always did like it, though. It's strange talking to you like this, but it feels right, too. You probably know that the ranch is going okay. We have a nice herd of pregnant cows for the spring. There will be lots of newborns to fuss over." Josie smiled as she said that, remembering how her mother always enjoyed seeing the first calves of the season. How many weak ones had she and her mother nursed on a bottle, often in front of the stove in the kitchen on cold nights, trying to save each little one? Too many to remember.

The smile left her face. How she wished her mother could give her the advice she sought. "I don't know what to do about Chance. I so wish you were here to tell me. I agreed to this arrangement to save the ranch. I know you and daddy always wanted us to get together, but it's not going to work. It's just a mess. You knew what it took me so long to figure out? I love him, Momma. And it's all a mess." Her voice broke on the last words and her throat burned all of a sudden. She blinked hard to keep tears from falling.

"He doesn't love me; not like I want him to. How could he? All I ever talked to him about was how much I loved his brother. But I didn't…not really. I see that now. I'm just a responsibility, and Chance feels he needs to watch out for me. What happens when he wakes up and realizes that he wants someone a lot prettier and smarter than me to spend the rest of his life with? What if he decides he can't do it and wants out? I've been really mean to him so many times, so I can't blame him."

Josie wished she could close her eyes tight enough and listen close enough, and maybe some divine intervention would allow an answer to cross her heart. There was only silence. She drew in a deep breath and then slowly expelled it. She was on her own.

"I'll leave you and Dad in peace now. I'm a grown woman and I'll handle whatever comes. You taught me to do that. I miss you so much and love you both."

Slowly, she walked back to the truck. With a final look

toward the graves, she turned on the engine and headed toward the highway. Taking things one day at a time, one foot in front of the other, was the only option she had. She could do that. Someday, maybe it all wouldn't hurt so much.

>✥<

TOM WAS COMING out of the barn as Josie pulled into the drive and parked. He paused at the corner of his own truck as Josie stepped out of hers.

"We completed the replacement of the wellhead on tank three. The boys also managed to get the last part of the roof replaced on the hay barn that blew off in the rainstorm the other night."

"Good. Thanks for the hard work today. I know Mary probably has a hot supper ready for you, so go enjoy."

"I plan to do just that," Tom replied, opening the door of the truck. He stopped for a moment. "Almost forgot. Chance said to give you the message that he had some things to take care of over at his place, and then he would just grab something to eat over there. He might be late."

Josie kept her smile even and nodded her head. "Thanks for letting me know. 'Night!"

Tom tossed his hand in the air in parting, and she headed toward the house. Once inside, she turned on a couple of lamps in the living room before going upstairs to change clothes. She tried to not look too closely at the fact that Chance was obviously intent on putting some distance between them. After the events of the night before, his absence only punctuated the words she recalled him saying—he was sorry they had made love.

That was fine. She was a big girl. She could handle the rejection. Although, as naïve as she might be in the ways of intimacy between a man and woman, she could have sworn that Chance felt *something* for her. At least, something more than just responsibility. Looking in her vanity mirror, as she combed her hair, gathered it up, and secured it on top of her head, she wished she possessed the confidence other girls had in relationships. While other girls spent their time discussing boys and getting their hair and nails done, she had been following along behind Chance or learning how to run a ranch from her father.

It was useless to try to be something she wasn't. There wasn't any need to try and look nicer. Chance wasn't going to be home. She pulled on a pair of comfy blue and white checked sweatpants, topped with a soft navy sweatshirt.

Padding downstairs in thick socks, she moved about the kitchen, finally opening a can of chicken noodle soup. Once the soup was heated, she poured it into a bowl and added a glass of cold milk. A TV tray in the living room served as a dining table. Josie ate her meal and half listened to the newscaster on her television, realizing this would be her daily routine in the years ahead. That thought chased her appetite away. Josie turned the channels, trying to find a program that would keep such thoughts away. Borrowing trouble from tomorrow never did anyone any good. That had been another pearl of wisdom from her mom. It was true. Tomorrow would come no matter what, and she would face it. *Alone.*

Chapter Sixteen

THE SMELL OF bacon drifted up the staircase and met Josie as she stopped at the top of the stairs. Evidently, Chance had come in late last night, after she had gone to bed and fallen asleep. The last time she had looked at the alarm clock, it had read just a little after one in the morning. He had not woken her when he came to bed. The only evidence she saw that he had appeared at all was the fact that his dirty clothing was in the clothes hamper in the corner of the bathroom.

Josie ran a quick hand over her hair, securing a loose strand into the barrette that held the soft mass away from her face. To bolster herself, she had applied a light bit of makeup and some lip gloss, along with the soft green sweater and newer jeans. It was a feeble attempt to boost her confidence. She knew that Chance probably wouldn't even notice, but it was time she took notice of her attire and other feminine things. If she hoped to ever attract a potential partner in life, such things would be necessary evils. By the time she reached the kitchen doorway, she had a smile on her face and hoped she looked a lot more natural than she felt.

She stepped into the room and then stopped. The first

person she saw was Tom, seated at the table, a cup of coffee in his hand.

"Good morning, Josie. Chance invited me in for a cup of coffee this morning. Then he twisted my arm to stay for some breakfast. I just finished up."

Josie's eyes caught sight of the tall man standing at the stove with his back to the room. His attention was on the frying pan in front of him. She moved toward the cabinet, taking a mug off the shelf and poured herself coffee. Turning to the table, she sat down across from Tom. "Morning, Tom. You know you're always welcome at this table."

"Perfect timing," Chance threw the words over his shoulder, lifting the eggs from the pan and sliding them onto a plate. "Your eggs are ready." He stepped to the table and Josie kept her eyes on the plate he slid in front of her. The food looked as good as it smelled, and her stomach stirred.

Of course, she wasn't certain if it was the food causing the disturbance or the fact that Chance stood so close beside her...close enough that she caught a whiff of the expensive cologne he often wore. Then she noticed that he wasn't dressed in the normal work attire this morning but had on dark brown slacks and a cream button-down shirt. No matter what he wore, he was far too sexy for her peace of mind. She murmured a quick "thanks" and focused on Tom.

"I was just telling Chance that one of the boys came across a fresh kill late last night on his way back along the north road fence line. Looks like the coyotes are getting bolder coming in so close. Couple of men are going out tracking this morning."

"Good. We can't afford to lose cattle if we can help it. If we had the time and funds, I'd rather try to catch and release on park land, but we have to do what we can right now."

"I'll leave you to your breakfast now. You don't pay me to sit around drinking coffee all morning," he finished with a grin. Rising, he set his cup next to the sink and then left them alone.

Josie kept her attention on the food in front of her. It smelled good and looked appetizing, but it had no taste because her nerves were on edge. She could feel Chance's gaze on her bent head. The silence stretched, even though she was aware he poured himself another cup of coffee and then eased into the vacated chair across from her.

"Would you like some juice with that?"

"No, thanks, this is fine." She took another bite of egg.

"Hope I didn't disturb you last night when I came in. It was really late."

"You didn't disturb me. I must have been dead to the world. I didn't hear a thing." She took another sip of coffee.

"I suppose we could talk about the weather next."

"The weather?" Her head popped up from her breakfast. "Has the forecast changed? Is there a storm coming in?"

Chance's mouth lifted at the corner in mild amusement. "A true rancher. The weather topic gets your attention when nothing else will."

Josie knew he was aware of what she had been doing in trying to ignore him. There wasn't much anyone could ever put over on Chance. She knew that better than most. She had certainly tried often enough growing up. With his sixth sense, eyes in the back of his head, and hearing like a bat, he was always one step ahead.

"No, there's not a problem with the weather. I have to fly down to Austin this morning. Something's come up with the paperwork for the wind field application, and it would be easier for me to be there in person to handle it."

Josie experienced feelings of disappointment that darkened the start of the day. On one hand, it would certainly not be as nerve wracking for her if Chance were gone, but the fact he would be gone for longer than a few hours gave her pause. The fact that she would even miss him hit her with bald clarity.

"How long do you think you'll be gone?" She asked the question as nonchalantly as possible while gathering dirty dishes and carrying them to the cabinet next to the sink.

"I hope to be back in two or three days' time," he replied, joining her at the sink, reaching for the plates as she scraped them and then he placed them in the dishwasher.

"You don't have to help with this. I'm sure you want to get on your way."

He didn't step away but continued to help. "You know; you could come with me. Maybe do some shopping while I'm taking care of my business. It would do you good to get away from the ranch for a little while. Tom has everything under control. How about it?"

Chance asked her to go with him. The whole idea made her stop and think. Away from the ranch, she'd be out of her element. And she would be alone with Chance, in a hotel. A fight waged inside her. Part of her wanted to take the offer of the trip and spend time with Chance in another place, away from the ranch and Dev and everything else that colored their world almost every moment. While the other part...the *sensible* part...warned her it would be tempting an unknown fate. Besides, there was work to be done, and it was her ranch to run. Her lack of a reply gave Chance his answer before she could say the words.

"Forget I said anything. At any rate, I'll be back to take you to the Winter Festival Dance on Friday night. So have your dancing shoes dusted off."

Chance obviously took her lengthy time in replying to his invitation as automatically being a negative sign. She would leave it at that. Drying her hands on a dish towel, she gave a slight shake of her head. "You know I haven't danced in ages, not since high school." Even as she shook her head, a thrill went through her at the thought Chance would want to be there to take her to the annual dance.

Without warning, Chance's hand secured one of hers and whirled her around, his other hand sliding smoothly around her waist, drawing her into a two-step around the kitchen. The grin on his face was reflected in the gleam of his blue eyes smiling down at the look of surprise in her eyes.

"Chance! What are you doing? I have work, and you have to leave." She clutched his shoulder with her free hand and tried not to step on his feet. His hold on her tightened, only sending her pulse into instant overdrive.

"Just getting in a little practice. See, it's coming back to you."

Josie hated to admit it, but she supposed it was like riding a bicycle, as she remembered the repetitive steps. It also helped that Chance was an excellent dancer.

"If anyone comes in and sees us, they would think we've lost our minds. We don't even have music."

"Who needs music when I have you in my arms?"

That definitely made Josie trip over a step and end on top of Chance's left foot. She looked up and saw him fight to conceal a quick wince before his gaze returned to hers.

"Sorry," she said, as she dropped her hand from his shoulder and tried to extricate her hand from his. "I did warn you I was rusty. You should have listened."

"It's not that you're rusty at dancing. You just shy away from me whenever I try to pay you a compliment," he observed, still holding her hand.

"That makes no sense."

"It does if it's because you aren't sure of your own feelings."

His surprising words brought her to a standstill in trying to gain freedom of her hand. "I think it's time we stop this foolishness and get…" Her words were cut off when Chance brought her up against him and captured her lips with his. It was a swift movement, but he took his sweet time after that. The kiss drew her quite naturally to fold herself against him, a place that seemed to be made just for her.

"I agree, Josie," he whispered against her mouth, before drawing her bottom lip into his for a quick nibble. "It's time to stop being foolish and sidestepping the fact that there is something between us besides friendship and responsibility and a business agreement. And while I thought about apologizing again for making love to you the other night, I must confess that I can't do that. Because I plan to make love with you again. Only next time, you'll have to be the one to want *me.* So think about it, Josie. I took a step. Now, it's up to you to do the same. I'll be home as soon as I can."

He dropped another kiss on her upturned mouth before walking out of the room. She listened to his strides click down the polished hallway, and the opening and closing of the front door. Slowly, Josie moved to the window over the sink. She watched as Chance slid his arms into his suit jacket, adjusted the brown Stetson on his head, and then climbed into his truck. She still watched until the truck disappeared from sight.

Totally confused by his words, and totally blown away by his goodbye kiss, Josie knew she had a lot of thinking to do before Chance pulled back into the drive in three days' time.

AT FIRST, JOSIE thought the three days would drag by. However, life on a ranch is always full of surprises, and each day is a new day. That was certainly the case. Not two hours after Chance left, the call came in from Tom that, evidently, a group of hot-rodding teenagers missed the last curve before the intersection on Highway 118 and flew off the road and through a good slice of pasture fencing. That had allowed a small herd of cow ponies to escape to the tall grass along the highway, and the sheriff and his deputies were none too pleased with having to herd the animals away from their accident scene.

Josie grabbed hat and coat, and she and Cookie were kept busy. She didn't return to the house until after dark. Tom and Mary had invited her to join them for supper at their house, which sat about two miles east of the main ranch house. Not looking forward to a quiet house on her own, she accepted.

Not that she was expecting a phone call from Chance while he was gone, but the fact there was none served to nag her on the second day as she tried to concentrate on her work. She searched out more things to keep busy with so that doubts wouldn't start playing their games with her mind. By the third day, she was both peeved and hurt that there had been no word from him. However, Tom did mention at lunch on the third day that Chance had evidently been keeping in contact with him, checking on the ranch, but Tom never mentioned if he said anything about her, and she certainly wasn't going to ask. So she just nodded her head and moved on to other subjects. Josie could only assume Chance still planned to return in time for the dance…an event she looked forward to with both trepidation and anticipation.

She knew that the anticipation part had a lot to do with seeing the man again and nothing to do with dancing. The feelings she had for Chance were so new and so jumbled up inside her, at times in a mass like Christmas lights tangled into one of those huge balls after being stored for a year. Sorting it all out was almost impossible.

The doorbell chimed just as the hall clock struck the last beat of six on Friday evening. Josie almost didn't recognize the sound. Very few people actually used the doorbell to announce their arrival. It was either a few brief knocks or someone just sticking their head in the door and calling out to see if anyone was home. She exited the living room and approached the door. Through the cut glass work of the door's oval center, she could make out the familiar form and her pulse quickened. *He was home!*

"Chance, why are you ringing the doorbell?" she asked as she opened the door wide, and then found her heartbeat pounding in her ears. Chance had evidently showered and changed clothes at his ranch before coming to pick her up. He was the epitome of tall, dark, and definitely dangerous to her self-control.

The black western-cut jacket fit his broad shoulders perfectly, while the crimson shirt set off his dark blue eyes and hair. She tried not to venture much below his waist, as his long legs were encased in a pair of black jeans that only caused stirrings in the lower regions of her body that were best ignored at the present time. His cologne stirred her pulse rate, and the look in his eyes caused her stomach to somersault against her ribs. The man was much too sexy for her peace of mind.

"That's what people normally do on dates, Josie. The man arrives, flowers in hand, and rings the doorbell." His words brought her eyes to rest on the beautiful roses he held, their crimson and deep pink petals lush in a full bouquet.

Her eyes went back to his, and she was speechless for a

few moments. When she did speak, her words only managed to state the obvious. "You live here. You don't need to ring the bell."

"Josie, just take the flowers. Then get your coat and let's be on our way. I don't want to waste a moment of dancing with you." Was there a hint of exasperation in his voice? Or was he just teasing her as usual? She was having trouble reading this new and strange-acting Chance. Had something happened on his trip? Whatever it was, she wasn't exactly unhappy with the turn of events.

Quickly, she took the flowers and went in search of a vase in the kitchen cabinets. Finding one, she filled it, and quickly placed the flowers inside, drawing a quick breath of their scent before grabbing her coat off the back of the couch. Chance stood in much the same place she had left him, in front of the door, his hands resting in the pockets of his jeans, thumbs hooked at the corners. His expression looked thoughtful, until he sensed her presence, and then it was gone, replaced by a smile that caused her pulse rate to soar again.

He took the coat from her fingers and held it while she slipped her arms into it. "You look very beautiful this evening, Josie. Every man will want to dance with you tonight. Just remember who brought you to the dance."

She felt the flush creep over her cheeks at his compliment. If only he knew that she had tried on at least a dozen outfits at the boutique in town two days before. She had settled on the poinsettia red-colored sweater with squared neck and long sleeves worn over a black full suede skirt with a slit cut up the side to show more than a fair amount of leg. The leather boots, with their slim, high heels, made her feel taller and sexy…which was definitely a new feeling for her.

Josie wanted to look her best for her first dance with Chance…in their new grown-up versions. Josie knew she was probably being silly. It wouldn't mean the same thing to him as it did to her. *Because she was in love with him.*

His feelings were nowhere close to that. She pushed the sad realization from her mind as she was determined to enjoy the evening. His hands rested a trifle longer than necessary on her shoulders. Her back was to him, so she couldn't see his expression. "Thank you, Chance. I doubt that though. Once they see my dancing, they'll likely run the other direction." She pulled the coat around her and turned to face him. She shouldn't have, because the look in those cobalt eyes told her he was dead serious in his compliment.

"Just say, *Thank you, Chance.*"

"Thank you, Chance. For the flowers and the compliment."

"That's enough," he broke in. "Never overdo a thank you. I can see you're a little rusty in the art of dating. I have my work cut out for me this evening."

His words were very strange and made little sense. She wasn't given time to comment. His hand slid under her elbow and she was propelled out of the door and to the black luxury car sitting at the end of the sidewalk. She knew Chance had this car, but she had only seen him drive it once before. He opened the door and held it while she slid onto the leather seat. Once she was situated, he closed the door and went around the hood of the car to the driver's side. Shortly, they were headed toward the town hall where the festival was being held.

Chance slipped a George Strait CD into the car's system, and the music filled the space around them, making the need for conversation a moot point. Josie settled into her seat and allowed a smile to form on her lips. She would live in the moment and not think too far ahead or look back over the past. Tonight, she was determined to take it one step at a time. She would just be content to follow Chance's lead…in more ways than one.

The town hall was festooned in decorations of red, green, gold, and silver. Lanterns were glowing on the gold linen-covered tables. Hay bales sat around the corners of the dance floor, and a local band was in the middle of a country tune when they entered. Twinkling strands of multi-colored lights hung from the rafters, and the smell of baked goods and country cooking mixed with the cool night air filtering through the open windows of the loft ceiling.

As they entered, she and Chance were greeted by people they knew, and they found themselves invited to share a table with three other couples. Josie didn't get to sit, though. Removing their coats, Chance took hers and draped it over her chair back. Then he took hold of her hand, intent on heading toward the dance floor.

"Can't we have something to eat or drink first?"

"No stalling, Josie. I have waited all I intend to wait to dance with you." Chance drew her into his arms and tightened her up against his body, quickly shoving every other thought or word from her mind. "Just relax. It'll come back to you. Close your eyes and remember what I taught you that day in the barn…before the prom."

How could he expect her to remember that when all she could think of at the moment was how her body felt every inch of the way along where his body touched hers? They fit like two pieces of a jigsaw puzzle…her angles and his planes became one…moving to the slow tune. She became so lost in the feelings that she had no time to think about the fact that she was actually dancing.

When Chance moved his chin beside her head, his warm breath tickling the top of her ear, only then did she exhale a sigh of contentment.

"I told you that you could dance. You're a natural in the way you move."

"You're a good teacher. That's why you were in such a hurry to dance with me. You were fishing for another compliment." Josie gave a smile against his shoulder.

"Wrong. I was just in a hurry to get you in my arms. I figured this was the surest way to do it. The three days away felt more like three weeks."

That caused Josie to miss a step, but Chance easily smoothed it over and sent a chuckle into the soft hair at the top of her head. "Don't *think,* Josie. Just relax and enjoy."

She did just that. His words tumbled over and over within her the rest of the evening. Coupled with the smiles and the way his dark blue gaze would catch hers and hold it, sending a message that definitely heated up her insides and promised things still to come, she was lost between hope and desire. Dare she believe that all of this could be real? And not just for the benefit of their neighbors and fellow partygoers? Josie decided that, for just a little while, she would allow herself to believe that all things were possible…including Chance actually coming to care for her.

The night was going by too quickly. Josie found herself enjoying it all and smiling and laughing far more easily than she had in months. Chance's attentiveness and his open flirting buoyed her spirits even more. Maybe dressing like a grown-up woman and realizing that just maybe she might be able to ignite a spark of interest in Chance…and, with a spark, a fire could grow into a full-blown blaze. Maybe she was getting ahead of herself a bit…but nothing ventured, nothing gained. And he did say it was up to her to make the next move…if there was one.

When Chance led her off the dance floor before the end of the last dance and passed their table, stopping only long enough to say brief goodnights and grab her coat, she didn't object. She was more than ready to be alone with Chance. Her heart pounded at the expectation, and butterflies took flight in her stomach. When he slid behind the wheel of the sedan, put the car in gear, and then raised his hand to her, she read the invitation in his eyes. Grateful that nothing impeded the way in this expensive classic model, she slid across the seat. Josie nestled her side against his, the heat from their bodies fairly sizzling even through the layers of clothing between them.

Josie allowed a sigh to escape her lips as she settled her head against the strong shoulder, and he situated her even more comfortably in the crook of his arm. There was definitely something to be said for vehicles without the hindrance of consoles in the front seating area. His fingers drifted across the sensitive skin of the column of her throat and drew lazy circles along her shoulders, beneath the heavy coat. She allowed her hand to rest lightly on the muscular upper thigh beside her.

Was he as affected by the evening as she? She closed her eyes and breathed in the heavenly scent of him and pushed every thought away which did not end with them happily ever after. She chose to delude herself for just one evening. If she had one wish, it would be to stay just as they were in that moment in time forever.

The night was chilly, but there was a myriad of stars in the black sky, and a silver moon rose in the eastern sky. There were very few cars on the road at the late hour. Chance slowed the car and eventually pulled onto the road leading to the ranch, and Josie's pulse skipped a couple of beats when the car slowed even more and finally came to a stop on the side of the road.

Raising her head from the warmth of his shoulder, she lifted her eyes to his, a question forming on her lips but quickly forgotten when she saw and felt the fiery gleam return.

"I tried but I can't wait any longer for this." His words were smothered against her mouth as he drew her into his arms, his lips hot against hers, his tongue searching and quickly finding the warm welcome he sought.

Josie returned his kiss with equal need, her hands sliding

upward and looping around his neck, her body turned into his and strained to find the contact she craved. His hand slid between them, finding the release of her seat belt and then his own. The same hand hit a button and the seat whispered back, giving him room to move away from the steering column.

Once that was done, she felt strong hands sliding around her back to lift her against him. She used the moment to slide her coat off her shoulders and hastily pushed it away from her body. The windows of the automobile were already steaming over with the heat from the inside meeting the cold from outside. They were lost in a dark cocoon of total silence in the middle of nowhere.

Lips continued to draw upon each other, Josie's soft mews becoming deeper moans in her throat as she gave in to a whirl of new desires. When Chance's hands moved from her back and slipped under the front of her sweater, she caught her breath. Sure fingers grasped the hem and she raised her arms automatically as the material left her body and was tossed onto the dashboard.

The movement liberated something inside her, and she moved her hands over his broad chest, yanking the shirt material from inside his pants, her deft fingers trying to rid the buttons of their holes faster than she could manage. Once the material parted, she allowed her palms to feast on the solid flesh beneath them. Her mouth moved along the whipcord length of his neck, her teeth nipping lightly at the hollow of his throat, which brought his hands to tightly cup her bottom.

Her knees straddled his hips as his hands moved to find the clip at the back of her red lace bra. The sudden cool air hitting her bare skin caused her sensitized nipples to tighten into hard, aching nubs. His tongue flicked over each, causing sparks to shoot off behind her eyelids. Josie buried her fingers into the rich, silky hair at the back of his head, holding him tighter against her as he suckled her, drawing heated moans from deep within her. Her hips shoved against his, and his hot shaft answered against the zipper of his tight jeans.

"I don't think I can wait to get you home into that big bed," his mouth whispered against the slope of her breast.

"Beds are overrated," she replied through clenched teeth, her fingers finding his zipper. Carefully, she drew the metal downward and felt his shaft respond under her fingertips, straining to be set free.

"I like how you think." Chance's eyes gleamed under lowered lashes as he fixed hers with his gaze while his hand easily arranged the jeans. Then his fingers slid under her skirt to quickly and easily move the wisp of silken material aside and allow the hot tip to seek her damp opening. At its touch, her head fell back on her shoulders, as her hips moved to take his entire length inside her, slowly and exquisitely, until he filled her.

His hands on her hips moved their bodies into a slow, syncopated rhythm, each one intent on giving the other total fulfillment. Slowly at first, then, as the fever pitch raced to a crescendo, Chance's mouth caught a taut nipple between his lips, his tongue whipping it, as his hands at her waist held her against his thrusting hips. His guttural moan combined with hers until they exploded together, her cries echoing in the dark and his muffled against her skin. For long moments, their bodies shuddered in after-quakes, as they clung together, their breathing adding to the clouded windows.

They collapsed against each other, slowly readjusting clothing, Josie slipping her arms into the sleeves of her coat, not bothering to completely redress. Chance said it would save time once they got to their bedroom, ending with a wink, and then placing a long kiss on her lips. He put the car in gear and didn't waste time getting them home.

Josie couldn't keep the smile from her face or the blush from her cheeks as she remembered her wanton behavior. Totally out of character and not something she ever imagined herself doing. She was smugly pleased with Chance's response. There was a euphoric feeling emanating from within her as if she could feel the glow's warmth. The warmth was still on her cheeks and in her eyes as they came to a halt in front of the house. They had just made it to the front of the car when the sudden appearance of someone coming out of the shadows from the porch halted them. It was Dev. Only then did Josie note the sports car parked in the shadows at the far side of the house.

To say his appearance was like a blast of cold water on the sizzling passion would be an understatement. Josie bundled her coat around her more tightly and tried not to think how undressed she was underneath its folds. A quick glance over at Chance told her he had his jaw set into that familiar hard line, and the scowl on his forehead should have been a warning to their late-night visitor.

"What are you doing here, Dev? It's late."

"Hello to you, too, Chance. I had stopped by to say hi and find out the latest news since I had to be up in Lubbock for the last few days. I just about gave up when I saw the car lights coming down the road. Looks like you two have been out on the town. Celebrating?"

"Tonight was the dance at the…" she began.

"I suggest you stop by tomorrow or the next day…during daylight hours." Chance was short on manners at the moment.

"I see," Dev replied and the look he moved over Josie made her feel the heat rise in her cheeks. She was certain he had a good idea what they were about to do inside the house. *Ridiculous.* It had to be her guilty conscience coloring her perception. *Guilty conscience?* Why should she feel guilty about anything? They were married for Pete's sake. Still, it was awkward.

"I'll stop by tomorrow sometime. You two have a really good night. Don't do anything I wouldn't do." With a wink, he turned and headed toward his car.

Chapter Seventeen

CHANCE DIDN'T BOTHER to turn on the lights as they stepped inside the house. He secured Josie's hand inside his and pulled her into the entryway. He paused long enough to lock the front door behind them. "Just in case anyone else wants to drop by uninvited tonight. I'll invest in a 'Do Not Disturb' sign tomorrow." He didn't wait for any response from her but headed toward the stairway, and Josie didn't hesitate to follow.

Once they reached their bedroom, he let go of her hand, and set about ridding himself of his jacket, then shirt. Josie gave him a slow smile and headed into the bathroom.

"Hurry back."

She paused in the doorway, giving him a slow grin over her shoulder. "Five minutes." Once the door closed behind her, she shed the coat and made swift work of the rest of her outfit. Inside the closet, she opened one of the drawers and withdrew a couple of items she had purchased at the same time she bought her outfit for the dance.

At the time, she thought she was an idiot to do so. Josie never thought she would ever have the guts to buy such garments...much less actually wear them. But something had come over her in the car, and the new Josie was ready to throw caution and the rule book to the wind. Chance had said it would be up to her what happened when he returned home. Well, she would say that what happened in the car had definitely been a good start. Now it was time to heat things up and see where they might end up next.

When she was done, she finally faced the full-length mirror. She was both shocked and amazed at the woman staring back at her. The fitted black lace bustier pushed her breasts upwards, and the frill of black lace ruffle around the top barely concealed the tips of mounds already aching to burst forth. The wisp of a matching thong was scandalous and coupled with the black and red satin garter belt, the black lace hose, and red satin, super-high heels…well, the word vixen was probably the nicest word that went through her mind as she turned first one way and then another to give herself time to back out.

Only she wasn't going to do that. There was a determination inside her that had grown since she opened the door earlier that evening and saw Chance standing there with the flowers in hand making her insides melt in an inferno of desire.

"Five minutes are up in thirty seconds." The male voice filtered through the closed door. "You aren't planning to stand me up, are you?"

Now or never. Josie shook her long mane of hair loose from the barrette that had held it back from her face at the dance. She wished she had more experience to pull off what seemed so easy in her mind…before Chance had arrived.

There was nothing left but to let the chips fall where they may…she would follow her instincts. *Don't fail me now.*

Opening the door, she paused on the threshold, hands on her hips, her head cocked to the side and a slow smile curved her lips. Chance hadn't wasted his time alone. The trio of candles on the dresser had been lit and flickered shadows on the walls. The man reclined against the pillows of the bed, clad only in black briefs, and there was no mistake he was more than ready and waiting.

His grin faded. At the same time, the gleam in his eyes changed into a hot fire, as he fixed his very surprised gaze upon the sight before him. Chance sat up slowly, swinging his long legs over the side of the bed. Silence stretched as Josie watched and almost felt the gaze touch each part of her body as it raked her from head to toe and back again.

"Cat got your tongue?" She tried to hide her nervousness with a bit of wit.

A slow shake of his head accompanied his reply. "Just wondering what you did with the Josie I left three days ago."

"Well, you did say I needed to do some thinking and then it would be up to me to make things happen next time. So I guess I did my thinking, and now I'm doing something to make things happen. Any objections?"

A slow grin began to form on his mouth, and a devilish gleam set those blue eyes on fire. "Absolutely *none.* I can't wait to see what's on your mind. You have my undivided attention."

"Well, I do want your undivided attention *and* your participation. I figure you're a lot more experienced…in certain areas…than I am. You might need to give me some pointers along the way." As she said the words, she moved slowly toward him, stopping a couple of inches from where he sat. One hand raised, and her fingers trailed lightly along his upper arm, across his shoulder, and then a couple of fingers lightly played with the lobe of his ear.

Muscles tensed across his chest, and she noted his breathing became more contained. *So far so good.* "I should be upset with you."

"Upset with me? What did I do?" His gaze stayed on hers, even as she felt his fingers begin to lightly tap dance their way up the sides of her thighs, to play along the tops of her hose…something that was increasing her pulse rate exponentially.

"For three days, not one word. Guess you didn't miss me all that much."

Fingers curled around the snaps of her front garters and then they were open. "I gave you time to think about us. It wasn't because I wasn't thinking about you every second."

"What were you thinking?"

"Surprisingly, a lot of it was along these same lines…what I want to do with you in our big bed."

A rush of heat sprang from her core, and her stomach clenched. His voice was deep and slow, and he used it, along with his hands, in perfect unison. The garter belt was easily slid down her thighs to pool at her feet, where she stepped out of it and kicked it to the side. Her hands rubbed over the muscles of his shoulders as she stepped forward, and his legs easily parted to situate her between his knees, his fingers moving upward over her bottom and then hooking themselves into the waistband of her thong.

"I hope I'm not overdressed for the occasion."

In a surprise movement, she felt his warm tongue flick out and circle around her belly button, sending goose bumps across her skin, catching her breath in her throat. At the same time, his fingers lowered the thong over her hips, and it soon ended up much the same as the garter belt before it. His hands cupped her bottom to hold her steady, as his tongue moved downward, very slowly, his intent being allowed to soak into her fevered mind. The anticipation overwhelmed her. Fingers automatically dug into the smooth flesh of his back as his breath blew warm across her feminine opening, and her breath caught in her chest at the exquisite torture that he began to rain upon her, as his tongue touched and tickled and brought her hot and wet within moments…a low moan escaped her and only served to fuel his intent to bring her to a complete, blissful orgasm, which he did.

Josie's legs went limp, yet he held her steady and supported her body, as the waves of intense pleasure subsided, along with her soft cries. "That's my beauty. Now that you mention it, you might be just a bit overdressed. Allow me to fix that. But the red stilettos have to stay. They are just too sexy."

Slowly, the black ribbon front closure of the bustier was dealt with. His fingers worked to rid her of the garment in a way that was super sexy in itself. Soon she was left with only the lace stockings and red high heels.

Josie sank onto his lap and then he drew them both back onto the bed, his hands at her waist. Those same hands lifted her and moved her to slide forward until his mouth was able to capture a throbbing nipple, and he worked sensual magic on her body once more, awakening feelings she never knew she possessed. She wanted more and knew she needed to go for it.

Rising away from his touch for a moment, she slowly slid her body downward along his, allowing their skin to have contact, until her hands found what they sought.

"You're the one who is way overdressed now. But not for long." Her fingers captured the waistband of his briefs and they joined her clothing on the floor next to the bed. He lay in all his male glory, watching her enjoy the view. She didn't waste a lot of time in claiming the prize she sought. Slowly, yet determinedly, her warm wet opening took possession of his hard cock and slid him inside her as far as she possibly could. Then she followed her womanly instincts, giving him pleasure as she took hers at her own pace. Reaching climax together, their cries intermingled with each other. He rolled her beneath him and claimed her mouth.

Twice more, they pleasured each other, Chance being the teacher and Josie proving a most apt pupil. They stayed locked in their dark, safe cocoon until, finally exhausted, they fell asleep….Josie cuddled against his side and his arm around her.

Josie slept so soundly that she opened her eyes after the sun was filtering into the room and the bed beside her was empty. She lay for a long time, her mind running over the previous night's memories, which both shocked and excited her at the same time. The one fact she was certain of in that moment…she had no idea what to expect when she next would see Chance.

She had only one thing that was still a secret from him…she hoped. The fact that she had fallen in love with him. It was as if something inside her knew that would be the ultimate power to hand him and, in their current predicament with the "agreement" …that was something she needed to hold onto…for her own peace of mind. Walking into the bathroom, her eyes fell on a piece of paper propped next to her makeup case. She picked it up and saw Chance's familiar handwriting. Her heart took flight at just the simple sight.

> *"Good morning, beautiful. I'm sorry that I forgot to tell you earlier. I have to go to Amarillo today. However, we did get sidetracked last night. Forgive me if I got carried away. We need to talk later. Chance."*

Josie's heart did a nose dive. She had an odd feeling that reality was about to set in.

"THAT ABOUT DOES it, Josie. Is there anything else we can get for you today?" Hank Honeycutt tossed the last fifty-pound bag of oats into the back of the ranch truck, then raised and secured the tailgate. He stepped back onto the loading dock of the H & H Feed Store.

"That should do it for this trip, Hank. Sorry I didn't get to see Leslie when she was home last weekend. Maybe we can catch up at Christmas."

Hank's daughter, Leslie, and Josie had gone through all twelve grades of school together. Then Leslie had left for Dallas and college and medical school. They kept in touch via infrequent emails and grabbed a cup of coffee whenever Leslie made one of her few and far between visits to her hometown. She was in the middle of her residency, so the communication between them had been limited at best. Josie missed the girl talk, but she wasn't surprised Leslie had moved on. She had a career, and they didn't have all that much in common any longer. Still, it would be nice to see her again.

"I hope we'll get to see her, too. She's so busy finishing up her residency, her mother and I are lucky to hear from her every other week, and then maybe only for about three minutes on the phone," Hank replied with a sad shake of his head.

"It must be hard, but soon she'll have achieved her dream of being the best cardiologist in the state." Josie sent him a smile and tried to brighten him.

"That's true. That's the best a parent can hope for their child, that they reach their dreams and are happy."

Josie thought over his words even after she pulled away from the feed store. Her parents had been the same. They never tried to force their thinking or their dreams onto her shoulders. That's not to say they didn't hint broadly a time or two, but they had always been supportive in whatever she chose. When she had told them that she wasn't going to college but staying on the ranch, she sensed their disappointment on one level but felt quiet approval on another.

She had told them what she learned daily working on the ranch itself was more valuable to her than sitting for four years in a classroom, reading out of a textbook. They hadn't argued with her. They had simply loved her. She hoped she could be the same kind of parent one day.

That thought opened up a whole other train of images. For a few minutes, she allowed herself to dwell in a place where all dreams could come true. In that place, she and Chance would live happily ever after, surrounded by three or four sons and daughters, and live out their days on the land they loved. That dream ended with them rocking away in rockers on a wide front porch with grandchildren and great grandchildren coming to visit. A blast from a nearby car horn brought her quickly back to reality. Her eyes caught sight of the familiar figure behind the wheel of the silver Corvette.

Devlin Braxton. He was waving at her and motioning for her to follow him. *Now what*? A small voice inside her head told her that it might not be the best thing to do, but how often did she listen when she should? What harm could there be in broad daylight in downtown Braxton? Both vehicles pulled into two vacant spots across from Pete's Pizza Pie Place.

Dev was out of his vehicle and had his hand on her door, opening it for her before she could do the same. A wide grin brightened his sassy blue eyes as he slid the dark shades off and hooked them into the vee of his shirt. The deep blue pullover was probably chosen for what it did to enhance his looks, along with the snug-fitting designer jeans and fancy leather boots. He was way too sexy for his own good. No way could he be mistaken for a local rancher…maybe the city slicker variety. Josie slid out of the truck, and he shut the door behind her.

"This is a pleasant surprise. I was just on my way out to the ranch to see if I could steal you away and here you are. That's a sign."

"A sign of what?" She returned his smile with one of her own simply because it was always easy to smile at Dev. A fleeting question came to mind. Did he ever have a serious bone in his body? She wasn't given time to dwell upon an answer. His hand slid easily under her elbow, and he maneuvered her toward the pizzeria across the street.

"A sign that you and I are destined to have lunch together today. I admit that I would much prefer it to be dinner, but I will take this opportunity for what it is. Besides, dinner can come later."

"You're certainly one smooth operator, Dev. You could probably charm the barnacles off a boat if you put your mind to it."

He threw back his head and let out a full-throated laugh. "Josie, you never cease to amuse me. *Barnacles and boats.* You do have a colorful way with words." He pushed the door of the small eatery open and allowed her to enter ahead of him. They were soon seated in a booth, had placed an order and received their drinks.

"I really need to make this a quick lunch," Josie said. "I need to get the supplies back to the ranch."

"You shouldn't have to do that. With all the men Chance has on the payroll, you'd think he would make certain his wife wasn't doing manual labor."

"I do manual labor because I run a ranch, and I choose to work *my* land, not just sit on it and watch others do it." His words had definitely caused her to bristle. "What about you, Dev? Haven't you ever wanted to actually *do* something, *build* something with your own hands?"

A scowl chased away his bright smile. "There you go again, sounding like my brother and dear, departed dad. Neither of them cared to find out that there is more to the world than the Braxton Ranch. It seems I'm to be treated like a turncoat for daring to want something else than to be stuck watching grass grow and cattle eat it."

"As I recall, both your father and Chance went out into the world. They both served in the military. Yet they came back to Braxton as soon as they possibly could. I don't think Chance holds it against you that you don't want life here in your hometown. I think he wants to see you happy and settled in your life, regardless of how it might seem to you."

"You've certainly changed, little Josie. You used to be a lot quieter and kept your thoughts to yourself. How did my brother get you to change your mind? Or should I ask?"

"You can ask, but it doesn't mean I'll answer you. You sound like you might wish I still was that shy girl with the huge crush on you. The one content to follow quietly in your immense shadow." Josie caught herself as she said the words. She spent years trying to keep her "secret" crush just that…a secret, and especially so from the object of that crush. However, that seemed like a silly notion now. So much had changed in her life and most of it very recently.

Their conversation was interrupted with the arrival of the pizza. The soft drinks were refreshed and then they were left alone again.

"Let's get back to what you just said a few minutes ago," Dev spoke up, a gleam in his eyes. "So you admit you have a crush on me."

Josie finished the bite of cheese pizza in her mouth before she corrected him. "*Had* is the operative word. I'm sure it had to do with the fact that you did leave the ranch and, each time you returned, you seemed to be more worldly and mysterious. You were almost secretive at times and larger than life in comparison to everyone else in Braxton." Josie laughed at her own silliness in those days. "Thank heavens I had calmer heads to keep my feet grounded in reality."

Dev frowned at that turn of phrase. "Calmer heads, as in my big brother, I'm sure. He isn't my biggest fan. He used his being here with you to his advantage while I was gone."

Josie finished off the slice of pizza on her plate and contemplated the man across from her. It was amazing how clearly she could see him now. Those rose-colored glasses had certainly been taken off and thrown away. She slowly shook her head. "You could have returned anytime. You didn't. That was *your* choice. And that is the past, and I prefer to think about the here and now."

Dev covered her hand with one of his as it lay on the table beside her plate. "Yes, the here and now. That's the thing that's really important. First off, please accept my apology for barging in last night. I have the feeling I interrupted at the most inopportune time."

He did know what they were about to do. Josie squelched any feeling of embarrassment. They were all consenting adults, and she wasn't a naïve young girl. *Certainly not after last evening.* She wasn't about to allow the memory of what happened once she and Chance did make it to their big bed bring on the heat of a blush across her cheekbones. Lucky for her, Dev changed the subject.

"Have you spoken to Chance about changing the terms of the trust for me? I really want to get started with the plans I told you about the other evening, before we were interrupted. As I explained, my future lies in your hands, Josie. Your very capable and beautiful hands." He lifted the hand he caressed and actually placed a light kiss on it, along with a slow wink in her direction.

Josie became aware there were interested glances being sent their way by the few other diners during the late lunch hour. She didn't care for the way his words and his touch affected her. She never cared for shallow people and insincerity, and she had just seen and heard both. Josie pulled her hand away and it joined her other one in her lap under the table.

"I haven't spoken to him. It really isn't my place. I'm afraid you'll have to handle this on your own. Chance isn't a monster. It's how you approach him. Now, I really have to get back to the ranch." She went to move, and Dev quickly changed his tone and the look on his face. She hadn't seen such a serious intent in his features before. A shiver went down her spine. His next words froze her in place.

"If you won't help me, Josie, you should do it for Chance. If you want to keep him healthy."

Chapter Eighteen

J OSIE FELT THE blood drain from her head to her feet as the implication of Dev's words sank into her brain. The look on his face then told her he was not making some sick joke. He was dead serious.

"Sorry I had to put it so bluntly, Josie. But this situation has gone beyond serious, and the clock is ticking down."

"Then you better explain exactly what it is you're talking about, and make it quick." Her words were weighted stones as they fell across the table. The look in her eyes warned him to make it fast.

"It's all very involved, but putting it into condensed form, it began when I broke off my engagement with Mariah, the latest fiancée. I met her because her family owns one of the casinos I liked to spend my time in. I was on a hot streak and winning big. As they often do with high rollers, they began to wine and dine me and put me up in the biggest, fanciest suite, and Mariah more or less devoted all her time to making certain I was shown a good time.

Well, Lady Luck has a fickle way about her. She began to reverse course on me. The casino was more than happy to increase my line of credit. I ended up owing them quite a bit for my markers. A few months passed. Since I was 'family,' they didn't care about the money at that moment. That is, until I split with Mariah; then they demanded every penny on the spot. Money that I don't have at the moment."

"That explains why you want the trust amended, but it doesn't explain why the remark about Chance's health." Josie felt another cold chill go through her even as she said the words.

"These people are business-minded. They don't like to lose…especially lots of money. Mariah had told them about the trust fund. These people aren't known for their patience. They figure that it could be just as easy for me to gain the money to pay them back by inheritance as by amending the trust. In fact, it would be faster and easier maybe."

By inheritance. Those words and the implication stopped her heart. Dev inherited if his brother was out of the picture. Chance was in danger, and he didn't even know it. They had to be stopped.

"What have you done, Dev? Why haven't you told Chance? He has no idea he could be in danger! We've got to call him right now."

Dev's grip was solid as he stalled her hand on her phone. His face no longer held any hint of a smile. In fact, it was a whole different tone. A strange change was visible in the man across from her. At first, it looked like there was an apology and a shadow of sorrow. But then it disappeared like smoke and a hardness was in its place. "Listen to me, Josie. Nothing is going to stop these guys until they have their money. And they don't intend to wait much longer. I came here to try and persuade Chance to amend the trust.

"However, I had no idea about the changes happening around here…between the two of you. I know it would be easier to get him to cooperate if you talked him into it. Last time I tried to talk to him about the trust, he shut me down fast and said he didn't want to hear another word about it. You seem to have a way with my brother. I don't think he'll turn you down."

Josie's mind was going a mile a minute. There had to be a solution. She didn't care about the thinly veiled insinuation Dev just made about her having "a way" with Chance. There were more important matters at hand.

"How much do you owe them?" The amount he replied with made the situation seem hopeless…at first. Until the gears in her brain kicked in and the practical business-side of her got back on track. "How much money do you have?"

"Not much…four or five thousand maybe. It takes a lot to live on."

"Particularly if you want to live in all those hot spots you love so much."

"Guess I might have fallen down a bit in your hero worship of me."

Hero worship? Dev? If there had ever been any hero worship, or anyone remotely worthy of that, it would have been Chance. The man who never had the opportunity to be a carefree kid, but grew up fast to shoulder more responsibility than he should have…given the fact he had an equally able-bodied brother in the same house. But then Dev had always behaved as if he were special. Why not? People always seemed to forgive him for anything and moved too quickly to make excuses for him. And Josie had been as blind as anyone when it came to him…overlooking far too easily things that might have given her an insight into the real person behind the perfect smile and dazzling blue eyes.

"Whether anyone worships you or not shouldn't be your main concern right now. You should be worried about your brother and how you can stop this mess and protect him from the low-lifes you evidently thought so much better to be around than people like the ones who live in Braxton." She felt an anger rising in her that she couldn't stop. "You certainly hightailed it back here fast enough when you got yourself in trouble, though. Well, I have to say that I wouldn't care what those people want to do about getting their money from you, except it involves Chance and that's my only concern now."

"Marriage has certainly changed you in more ways than one. I haven't seen you so riled up before." He did have the decency to look taken back and even apologetic. "And you know that I can't just go to Chance and tell him about this…he is stubborn, and he'd end up doing something to make these guys a lot madder. And they don't play nice, Josie."

Josie wasn't buying any part of his being contrite or sorry any longer. Standing up, she held Dev's gaze with her own. "I have a couple of things to do right now. You need to go to the bank and withdraw your money in the form of a five-thousand-dollar cashier's check. I'll call you tomorrow morning."

"Are you going to get the money from Chance?"

"I haven't thought it all out yet, but we need to get this debt paid fast. You need to call those people and tell them they'll have their money within the next two days."

"I'll wait for your call. Are you going to tell Chance about all of this?"

"I don't know what I'll say to him. You just do your part. I've got to get busy."

Josie didn't wait for him to follow. In fact, she was glad when he didn't. Anger seethed inside her at Dev for placing Chance in danger…for placing them all in a bad situation. All because he acted irresponsibly with little thought to consequences. She couldn't let herself get bogged down in anger and the blame game. At the moment, she was going to have to use her wits and some believable acting.

JOSIE TOOK SEVERAL deep breaths before she got out of the truck after she parked in front of the bank. She replayed the idea in her head more than a few times as she drove from the pizzeria across town to the bank. The special account Chance had set up for her instantly popped into her mind when Dev had spoken the amount needed. Withdrawing the funds and placing Dev's small amount with it, there would be enough to settle the debt. Of course, she had to hope that Mr. Chadwick, the president of the bank and a friend of the Braxton family would not ask too many questions or alert Chance to what she had done…if she could manage it at all.

Josie knew she simply had to try. From the moment Dev had told her about the danger Chance could be in, she had thought of nothing else. She had experienced an intense anger at Dev for being so thoughtless and cavalier with the fact that his recklessness had endangered his brother. And she also felt intensely sick each time she thought of the possibility of anything happening to Chance. Chance was worth a hundred of his brother, and she had been so blinded to that over the years. No matter what she had to do, she would do it to try to keep Chance safe. And Dev was right about not being able to let Chance in on any of this mess. He would take the bull by the horns, and that might not be the best course of action for these type of people. Her goal was to protect Chance first and foremost.

Being a Braxton had its advantages, and Josie found she experienced little resistance as she completed the paperwork for withdrawal of the funds. It went smoothly until the woman behind the desk reappeared from behind the office door with the bank's president in tow. He stepped forward and shook Josie's hand.

"Josie, it's good to see you again. I want to say again how much my wife and I enjoyed the festivities at the ranch for your wedding."

"Thank you," she responded, keeping her smile as even as possible, even though her nerves were anything but as she shook his hand. "Chance and I were so pleased you could join us."

"I see you wish to withdraw almost all the funds in the special account. Is there a problem? If there is an issue with the bank in any…"

She hastened to assure him. "There's no problem. I just want to do something special for Chance for his birthday…it being the first together as a married couple and all…and it's going to take a bit more funds than I expected but, then again, you'd probably do the same for your spouse, I'm sure."

A smile that was both understanding and relieved lit the man's face. "Well, I suppose I can certainly understand that. Even though you're both still in your honeymoon stage, Chance is one lucky man to have such a caring and generous wife. I'll have the teller take care of this right away. Give my best to Chance."

Twenty minutes later, Josie was on her way home. Only when she had shut the door behind her and walked into the living room, did she allow herself to slow down. It was amazing how quickly what she thought would be a normal day of ranch work had gone so completely off track since the moment Dev had told her the news over lunch.

Her stomach was rolling with nerves, and she knew she couldn't eat dinner. There was no use going into the kitchen. She went into her small office and seated herself behind the desk. The quiet loneliness of the house settled around her. Chance's presence had changed things in just a few short weeks. Now, his absence made her painfully aware of just how much she had come to rely on his company, in some strange way that had infiltrated her life when she wasn't looking. He had walked right in and staked his place and his claim on her heart.

She knew he saw her differently than he had the gangly girl following him around, talking incessantly about her silly feelings for his brother. He was attracted to her. He said he wanted her, and he had made love to her. Her face warmed with the recollection of her responses to him. Surely, he had to have known how she felt about him. But wanting wasn't loving.

His response after the first time had been to apologize to her. That pretty well summed up the fact his heart wasn't involved. The second time, there had been no apology, just a man totally into the heat of the moment…and no words of love or other closely-related emotion had been spoken. It couldn't matter. All that did matter at the moment was that she could do something to somehow make things right and keep both Chance and his brother safe. She was never going to touch all the funds Chance had placed in her account anyway. It could be used to help Dev and keep Chance safe. Once she had made certain there was no more danger to Chance, she would tell him what she had done.

The ringing of her cell phone broke the silence of the room. She didn't look at the caller ID before she answered. It was bound to be Dev.

"Did you make the arrangements?"

"Arrangements?" The voice did not belong to Dev. It was Chance. "Guess you found the note that I had to run up to Amarillo for that replacement gear on the pump house at the foaling barn. There wasn't anyone extra to be spared today, so I'm on the way. I should be back tomorrow afternoon. I'm also going to swing by and look at the mare Chuck

Donovan has for sale while I'm in the area. Will you miss me?"

The unexpected sound of his voice on the other end of the line shocked her and her mind had to run to switch gears. "Hi. Yes…I did read the note. Thanks. I hope your arrangements all go as planned," she replied, grasping to remember what Chance had just told her about his trip and the reason for it. "Of course, I'll miss you. Just be careful and take your time coming back. Drive safely."

There was a long moment of silence on the other end of the line. "Josie…you sound a little strange. Is everything okay?"

He couldn't get suspicious. She needed him to believe all was well. "I've just walked in the door from town, and I need to get over to the stables before Tom leaves. My mind is on my long list of things to do…as usual."

"Well, I won't keep you on the phone, then. I realize we didn't have much time for talking last night, but we'll make time when I get back. Try not to miss me too much."

Chance's voice felt as if it came through the phone and melted over her bones. She already missed him far too much.

"I'll try not to. Have a safe trip."

"I'll call later." That was it. Nothing remotely close to *I love you and miss you*. But what did she really expect? It was all just a nice fantasy. However, there was a dark reality pressing in and she needed to concentrate on that.

THE ROAD WAS flat with few bends in it from Lubbock to Amarillo. It gave Chance's mind room to wander back over the conversation with Josie that just kept gnawing at him. It had been short, but there was something in her tone he couldn't put his finger on. Or was it in what she wasn't saying more than what she did say? His gut told him that something wasn't right back at home. Had he come on too strong? Overplayed his hand? Taken things too far between them, too fast?

Chance had tried to put brakes on his feelings and hold back on his actions in order to not scare her off. He had planned to woo her. Give her time to get used to him and the idea of caring for him. If he gave her time, surely, she might start seeing him as more than the friendly shoulder he had been for so many years. Things might have progressed further and sooner if Dev hadn't unexpectedly come back into the picture.

His brother kept popping up at the most inopportune moments, and Josie certainly seemed to not mind…until last night. *Last night.* His mind kept trying to reconcile the Josie he knew with the Josie who took matters into her own hands…in more ways than one. She had lit a fire that turned into an inferno.

Dev's sudden appearance tampered it down a bit, but once they were alone again, in their bedroom, the new and definitely improved Josie had returned in her sexy black lace undies and no holding back. They had finally fallen asleep, exhausted, in each other's arms in the early morning hours. He had hated to leave her alone in that big bed when he had crawled out of it, knowing he needed to be on the road, so he could take care of things and get back to her side. He felt hope inside him that they were on the right track toward making a life together.

His cell phone rang, and he reached for the button on the steering column to connect. "Braxton." He answered, eyes still on the road, his mind trying to will itself away from Josie.

"Hey there, Chance. It's Mike over at the bank. Hope I'm not calling at a bad time?"

"Mike…this is a surprise. You caught me on the road to Amarillo. What can I do for you?"

"Well, I might be overstepping here, but I had a feeling that I needed to give you a call on this. I sure hope Josie will forgive me if I'm wrong and have spoiled her surprise for you."

Chance's mind was instantly on alert. "What's the problem?"

"Well, Josie came into the bank this morning, and she withdrew everything from the account you set up for her…except for a hundred dollars. She said it was for a surprise for your birthday. However, after she left, I got to thinking on it and looked it up and sure enough…your birthday was four months ago. I'm sure sorry if I blew whatever the surprise is for you."

A sinking feeling began to form in Chance's stomach. He had had a feeling something wasn't right with Josie when he spoke to her on the phone. What was she doing taking that much money out of the account? There could be no "surprise" worth that. Unless it had something to do with his brother.

"Say, Chance," the banker continued, "there's something else, and I only tell you this as a family friend and nothing against your brother or anything…"

Knew it. "What is it, Mike?" Chance knew his tone sounded abrupt, but at the mention of his brother, a feeling fairly close to fear hit him. Had his brother persuaded Josie into something?

"Some of us were having an early lunch over at Pete's, and I was surprised to see Josie and Dev there. They seemed to be in a pretty deep conversation. One minute it looked like they were pretty friendly…and the next, Josie looked upset…as in *mad*…when she left him. Then she shows up at the bank, and you know the rest."

Chance's grip increased on the steering wheel. "Thanks for letting me know, Mike. I do need to check into some things. Give my best to Anita."

"Sure thing and hope all is okay."

Chance's mind was moving a mile a minute. What the hell was going on? He couldn't come up with any valid reason for Josie to need all of the money from her account…not when she had vowed she'd never touch it when he told her about it. But now, Dev was in the mix. When Dev came around, she wasn't the same Josie that she was with him.

What had their lunch meeting been about? Why didn't she mention it during their call earlier? There was a thought that came into his mind and was immediately tossed away.

Only it wouldn't stay away. What if she needed the money to go away with Dev? Dev was always in need of money. She had access to more than he did. His mind replayed all the times he had walked in to the house or the stables and there was Dev…and Josie. Once during a kiss…actually there were two kisses they had shared. Three, if he counted the one on the cheek at the wedding.

Had he been played for a fool? Josie had agreed to the marriage *before* Dev had returned. Surely, she could have stopped the marriage at any time up to the wedding itself if she wanted his brother? Or did she want the ranch more? Maybe she was trying to have both of them…the ranch *and* Dev? Whatever the excuse, she was hiding something from him. It was time to find out what the hell Josie and his brother were up to.

Chapter Nineteen

THE LIGHTS TWINKLED on across the city as dusk settled. Chance's room looked over the mostly flat vista from the top floor of the hotel. He looked due south, his mind flying across the darkening miles to the house where Josie would be...*should* be. Was she there? Or had she already left with his brother for the bright lights of some big city? His mind couldn't wrap around that scenario.

He would stake his life on the fact that Josie would never leave the land she was born and raised on and was so much a part of her fabric. But then, he had little experience with what a woman in love would do for the man she wanted. That reminded him what a fool he had been to believe in a happily-ever-after with the woman he married.

He had gotten to the machine shop earlier and picked up the part that was needed. He'd take a chance the mare would still be available once he got to the bottom of what was going on at home. The plane he chartered would be ready to leave at six in the morning. He could have turned around and driven back the six hours, but he might put himself in a ditch if he did that, and then where would he be but in another mess. For two hours, he had talked himself out of calling Josie. He had called his ranch and found out from Juanita that his brother had finished his dinner and was in the den making some phone calls. He'd bet one of those would probably be to Josie.

Chance could stand it no longer. He set the glass of whiskey down on the table and reached for his cell phone. He took a deep breath and listened to the ringing of the phone, fully expecting to go straight to her voice mail.

"Hello?"

The sound of her actual voice threw him off for a moment. "It's me…Chance. Didn't know if I'd catch you in or not."

"Where else would I be at this hour of the day? I'm just finishing up a bowl of stew. I didn't feel like eating earlier."

"That sounds good. I haven't decided on anything to eat yet."

There was a stretch of silence. "You should take advantage of one of the good steakhouses up there and go out," she suggested.

"I'm really not in the mood for being out in a crowded restaurant. I'll probably just order something from room service. How did your day go today? Tell me about it."

"Nothing out of the ordinary. I picked up supplies in town and ran a few other errands to the dry cleaners and post office. Then back to the ranch." There were a few moments of hesitation on the line. "Are you still planning to be back sometime tomorrow afternoon?"

"I hope to be back then. That'll give me time to shower and change and make the monthly cattlemen's meeting.

What are your plans for tomorrow?"

"Just another typical day."

Conversation waned between them. Josie finally spoke.

"Are you feeling okay?"

"Why do you ask that?"

"I don't know. You seem a little preoccupied or something."

"Guess I do have some things on my mind," Chance admitted with a sigh.

"Is something wrong?"

"No…not really. Just have some things to sort out. Don't worry about it. I better let you go and find something to eat and then hit the sack. I'll see you tomorrow afternoon. Sweet dreams."

Josie didn't want to let him go. She realized how much she missed him and the depth of it had shocked her.

"Is there something else on your mind?" He spoke up when she was silent for so long.

"A girl has to have some secrets."

"You *used* to tell me your secrets. Remember?"

"I remember. However, I told you *most* of them, but never all."

"Should I be worried about the ones you don't tell me?"

His voice lowered, and he held his breath…hoping that she would trust him one more time.

"Tom is here, and I need to talk to him. Have a safe trip back tomorrow."

There was another long pause on the line. "Okay, Josie. I'll let you run away one last time. Bye."

"Good night, Chance."

Chance sat looking at the phone in his hand for several long seconds. He had asked her what was wrong. She had every opportunity to tell him. She chose not to say anything. She had also left out the part where she had lunch with Dev and her trip to the bank. He ended up not ordering room service. He had another drink instead. The morning couldn't come fast enough. He needed to get back to Josie.

"DO YOU HAVE your money?" Those were the first words Josie spoke as she met Dev on the sidewalk outside the house at the planned time next morning. It was almost ten. Tom and the rest of the ranch hands were in a far pasture working, and everything was quiet around the ranch house…just as she planned. She didn't want anyone to see Dev arrive or her hand him anything.

"I have mine," he said, patting the breast pocket of his suit jacket. "What about the money from Chance?"

"I have the money here." Josie reached inside her jacket pocket and withdrew the white envelope. Inside the envelope, was the cashier's check for almost the entire amount Chance had placed in an account for her to use at her discretion. She knew this wouldn't be the usage Chance had in his mind when he had made those provisions, but he did say it was up to her how it was spent. If she chose to use it to keep Chance safe and Dev out of trouble, then so be it. When all was said and done, she would explain to Chance what she had done and why.

"I knew I could count on you getting Chance to help out."

"Chance doesn't know anything about this, Dev. This money isn't exactly from him. But that doesn't matter right now. What matters is that you have the money to pay back your debt to those people, so they won't make good on their threats. The sooner you do it, the better." Josie was glad to be rid of the envelope. Dev took it with a swift eagerness and added it to what was already in his pocket. He flashed the smile that used to always make her day brighter. It no longer had the same attraction.

"Well, it makes no difference where it came from. You're an angel for helping me out. I'll be on the next plane to Vegas and get this all straightened out."

"Don't bother. We can get it straightened out right now." The voice surprised them both. Josie caught sight of Dev's face before she quickly turned to look at the two men standing at the corner of the house. There was a strange mixture of surprise and perhaps a moment of fear in his eyes. That immediately put her body on alert. The stark reality of how alone they were at the moment hit her.

"Looks like we get to save you the cost of that plane ticket, Devlin. Shouldn't you be thanking us?" The taller man of the pair, dressed in a gray silk suit and too much gold jewelry, advanced to stand just a couple of feet from them both. The shorter one hung back a few steps, his eyes watchful and cold. "Unless, of course, you were actually planning to disappear on us again, with all that money? Like you did when we found you in Atlantic City, last June?"

Josie swung her gaze to Dev. He had grown pale under his tan.

"Who are these men, Dev? And what about Atlantic City?" She was beginning to get a really sick feeling in the pit of her stomach.

"Devlin's forgotten his manners," the man spoke up. He turned his smarmy smile on Josie, extending a manicured hand in her direction. "Allow me to make the introductions, sweetheart. I'm Caesar Marin, one of the brothers of Devlin's heartbroken ex-fiancée, Mariah. This other quiet visitor is Jaime…a cousin of ours. And, being a gambling man, I'd wager you'd be Devlin's latest conquest."

"You'd lose that one." Dev finally found his voice and edged closer to Josie's side, placing his body more between her and the man whose outstretched palm was ignored. "She's none of your business. I told you I would have your money today. We agreed to meet in town. We'll leave here and meet as planned."

"Well, I think this is a fine place for a meeting." The man's eyes took in the quietness and the obvious fact no one else was around to cause problems. "You just hand over the money, and I'll keep this beautiful lady company in the meantime."

His gaze made Josie's blood run cold in her veins. What mess had Dev gotten them both into?

"The only people going anywhere will be you and your friend…off this ranch and out of Braxton."

Josie's breath caught in her throat as her eyes swung with

everyone else's in the direction where Chance stood at the edge of the porch, his face half concealed by his hat low on his forehead, his mouth set in a grim line. His stance indicated he was ready for a fight. She had never been so glad to see anyone in her life. It was hard not to run straight into his arms. That thought was quickly followed by the one reminding her that these men were the ones who threatened Chance's life in the first place. His being there at all put him directly in harm's way.

"This is getting to be some party," the man named Jaime spoke up. "I'm not in the mood for parties. Give us the money now, or we'll take a ride with the little lady instead."

"As I said, you won't be taking my wife anywhere. You, on the other hand, will take what money is owed to you, and get off our land…and stay off. Hand them over the money, Devlin." Chance's voice sounded as if it were edged with cold steel. It even sent a chill through Josie. His eyes never moved from the unwanted pair.

"What makes you think they'll leave then? You don't know them, Chance. These guys are armed," Dev spoke up.

"They'll leave because I've arranged for an escort for them."

"What escort?" Dev asked.

"Us. And we're armed, too."

Where had Sheriff Waller and three of his deputies come from? Josie could only watch in wide-eyed surprise as the two men from Vegas quickly calculated the new odds and found the house stacked against them.

"Give them what they came for." Chance repeated the

order.

Dev slowly withdrew the two cashier's checks from his pocket and handed them over to the man called Caesar.

"You've got what you came for," Chance spoke up. "Get off our property."

Dev didn't even try to look apologetic. "You heard my brother."

The two men from Las Vegas looked at each other, and then Caesar smiled at Chance. "It was a pleasure doing business with you." He looked at Dev. "I'm sure we'll see you again in our city. You won't be able to stay away." He gave a brief nod in Josie's direction and then the two took their leave. Evidently, they had parked their car at the rear of the house. They pulled out, and a couple of deputy sheriffs' cars weren't far behind them. There would be no chance for them to change their mind about leaving. The sheriff stepped up and shook hands with Chance, then tipped his hat in Josie's direction and wished her good day. That left the three of them on the porch.

"I'll follow you to our ranch," Chance said to Dev, his voice still hard and flat, his eyes dark.

Dev looked about to say something but saw something in his brother's face that kept him quiet. He looked in Josie's direction next.

"Save the goodbye for later. Get moving." Chance took a step that moved him between Josie and his brother.

Dev didn't argue. He headed for his car and was pulling away in a matter of a few short minutes. That left Chance and Josie alone.

"How did…"

Josie didn't have a chance to finish the question. Chance turned in her direction and spoke to her for the first time since arriving with the cavalry.

"The bank called me. Mike was a bit concerned that you might be in trouble of some sort…especially since he saw you two locked in a 'pretty friendly discussion' to use his words prior to cleaning out your account. Plus, he knew my birthday was four months ago…he and I had breakfast to celebrate it before a meeting of the trustees."

"It's a good thing he did call, but he got the wrong…"

"Yes, at least *he* did call and let me know what was going on behind my back," he said, cutting her off. "I've got some things to discuss with Dev. You and I will need to talk later. I suggest you be ready with the truth when we do."

"That sounds like a command, and I don't do well with those." His attitude was beginning to grate on her raw nerves and his implication she was a liar hurt.

"It's time you started listening to them. If you had done so sooner, we wouldn't have had another of Dev's messes to clean up today. If I hadn't arrived when I did, along with the sheriff, just what do you think might have happened? Do you think my brother would have been able to protect you from his low-life acquaintances?"

"I have had all I want to hear about this battle between you and your brother. I have a command of my own. Both of you need to stay away from me until you settle your family feud once and for all."

She punctuated her words by slamming the door behind

her and sliding the deadbolt.

A few minutes later, Josie was totally alone, having watched Chance's truck as it disappeared down the road. Only then did she finally release the breath she felt as if she had been holding for quite a while. And she realized the truth of Chance's words…if Chance hadn't arrived when he did, she couldn't imagine what would have happened. Those men could have taken her with them. And then what? A shiver went through her.

Instead of explaining what and why she had done what she did, she had lost her temper. Chance was upset with her and she knew he had every right to be, but his whole demeanor and his coldness was her undoing. *Don't borrow trouble from tomorrow.* It was sage advice. Josie just wished she was better at heeding it.

Chapter Twenty

"I TOOK THE liberty of pouring me one," Dev said, holding up a small glass with ice cubes and scotch in it. "Want me to pour you one as well?"

Chance walked across the carpeted floor of his study, shrugging out of his coat as he did so, and then tossing it and his hat onto the chair next to his desk. He ran a hand through the thick hair on his head as he moved toward his brother, who held out a glass for Chance. Dev didn't see the fist coming his way. He ended up on his back on the other side of the coffee table, the contents of the glass pooling on the carpet. He slowly sat up, his hand at his jaw. "Geez, brother. Take it easy on the face. Did that make you feel better?"

Chance fixed Dev with a long look, while he tried to marshal his thoughts and control his temper. He had lost it with Josie and made a bigger mess of things with her, but he would deal with all that later. At the moment, he had some long overdue business to take care of with his brother.

"It's a start. And you don't need any more to drink. You need a clear head to participate in this discussion."

Dev hesitated and then finally rose to his feet. "Guess I

do need to keep my wits about me. I suppose this is where I need to fall on my knees in abject apology for bringing my messy business to your doorstep."

"Save your breath. I've heard this song before. What I want to know is what the hell you thought you were doing putting Josie in such danger? Why didn't you come to me and leave her out of it?" Chance locked his gaze with Devs.

"That didn't work too well in the past. I thought, given the way you feel about her, that you'd not turn her down when she asked you to have the trust revised. I had no idea the Marins would go to such lengths and threaten her, too. But it all worked out. She's okay, and they have their money."

"And what do you plan to do tomorrow? I suppose you and she ride off into the sunset? You came back here, and you turned her head with more of your smooth lines. You don't love her. It's just a salve for that ego of yours…gives it a boost when you need it. It stops *now.* You aren't going to hurt her ever again."

"Maybe the lady has something different to say about that. Let's ask her if…"

Dev didn't get to finish what he was saying, because Chance's fist made certain of that when it connected once again with his jaw and sent him flying backwards over the edge of the couch to end up on the floor, shaking his head. "Damn, Chance! I don't want to fight you over this. But I'm not going to be a punching bag." He got to his feet again.

"I probably should have done that a hell of a long time ago." Chance's eyes darkened even more as he regarded the man who was related to him by blood but little else. Their father had known early on that Dev was the weak link, the son who would always have the wanderlust and never be settled for long. Chance had done his best to clean up his messes in the beginning…first because they were related. Then, later, it was because Josie cared so much about him. It was time for Chance to cut the cord once and for all.

"It's time for you to move on. And to leave Josie alone, *for good.*"

"What if I don't want to leave without her?"

"There are two problems with that scenario. One is that she emptied her account, so there's no money to fund your next gambling binge. Two is the fact she is a married woman, and I don't plan to just step aside."

Dev scratched his chin while considering the situation and Chance's words. "Well, here's a newsflash for you, brother. I hadn't planned on taking her with me. She seems to be too stuck in this damn ranch mentality."

"Josie would never be happy anyplace else. This land and this way of life are in her blood. She's a totally different breed of woman than what you have any experience with."

Dev gave him a half-smile, half-grimace as he rubbed his jawbone again. "It's all she's ever known. If she got away from it and saw something of the world away from here, she might not look back. Why don't you let her decide? Or are you afraid?"

"Tread carefully," Chance warned him. "You don't know the first thing about Josie. You toyed with her and passed time with her when you were bored. If you truly cared, you'd never have left here to begin with."

"I still say that you're too scared to set her free and see what she really wants. You'll keep her tied to this land and to you because you can't let her go. Does she know how you feel about her?"

"My marriage is none of your business. There is something that you *can* understand…I've instructed Phillip Banks to revise the restrictions and give you access to your entire trust…with one provision."

Dev's full attention was on Chance. "Which is?"

"You take the money, and it is a buyout of any and all claims you have on Braxton Ranch. There will be a monthly stipend paid into your account as usual from the oil and gas holdings. But that is it. There will be nothing left for you here on this ranch…*nothing.*" It only took to the count of ten for Dev to respond to the offer.

"You have a deal."

EVIDENTLY, BOTH MEN took her request to heart. Over the next week, Josie didn't see either Dev or Chance. She did know that Chance called to confer with Tom on some things during the week because Tom mentioned he had in their morning conversations each day. Josie had been aware of the look Tom gave her as he reiterated the conversations, which involved daily issues with the ranch and nothing more.

People had to be aware of the fact that she and Chance were no longer sharing the ranch house, but none of the hands gave any indication of it when she was around. She was glad of that. The last thing she needed was anyone showing pity for her. It was her own fault that she had dared to believe in fairytales and love like those silly romance books touted. Served her right for thinking she was anything but Josie Monroe, broke rancher and spinster-to-be.

On Thursday evening, Josie was brushing down Cookie after a long day in the saddle. The sound of a vehicle pulling into the yard caused her pulse to begin to race. Her first thought was that Chance had finally decided to make an appearance. She tossed the brush onto the workbench and sent a quick hand over her hair in a nervous gesture. Stepping to the open doorway, she halted. Biting her lower lip, she hastened to place a noncommittal look on her face and keep the surge of disappointment from showing. She stuffed her hands into the back pockets of her jeans and waited.

Dev walked from the sports car to stand a few feet from her, a look of sheepish apology on his face. When it was clear she expected him to speak first, he cleared his throat and gave a brief smile. "I guess it's a good sign that you haven't called someone to throw me off your land by now."

"I wouldn't need to summon anyone to do that. If I wanted you gone, you would be. I keep a loaded gun on a shelf very close at hand."

That did bring a grin to his face. It didn't last long when he noted she didn't smile. "I'm on my way to Dallas. I wanted to stop by first and apologize."

"Dallas and not Las Vegas?"

"I think I've had enough of the bright lights. Besides, I

agreed with Chance that perhaps the west was not for me...at least for a while. He signed the trust papers. My money is all mine. I can go pretty much anyplace. I figure I might like to see Florida, maybe invest some money in a resort. I find I have a way with people and it might be a good fit for me. Anyway, you always said I needed to have a plan for my future. By the way, I returned all the money you withdrew for me. It's back in your account at the bank."

"Thank you for that. I'm glad for you, Dev. I think you might be very good at that sort of thing. People tend to like you right away. I wish you luck."

"I also want to apologize for being such a pompous, uncaring ass to you these last few weeks. My only excuse is that I behaved like a jealous idiot. I guess I sort of liked you having a crush on me. It was good for my ego. I'm sorry for saying those things to you the other night. It was ridiculous to think there was ever anyone else for you or Chance. Although it took me a while to figure that one out. But I want you to know that you and your family always meant a great deal to me. And I will always be right here if you ever need me. I mean that."

Josie didn't want to discuss Chance with Dev. She certainly didn't want to hear that she and Chance belonged together. Nothing was further from the truth. "People grow up; feelings do the same. I will always care about what happens to you, Dev. You've been a large part of my life. That won't change no matter where you go."

Dev gave her possibly the first heartfelt, genuine smile in a very long time. It reminded her of a more carefree time, now long gone. She responded with one of her own. Taking a step, she met his hug. It was brief but spoke volumes.

She stepped back first. "Have a safe journey and keep in touch. Don't forget to invite me to your next wedding...if you ever actually get to the altar, of course." Her attempt at a joke brought a smile from him.

He shook his head at her. "I think the bachelor life is for me, at least for the foreseeable future. I can't say the same for my brother. When are you going to put him out of his misery?"

Josie lost her smile. "There are some things that are mistakes from the beginning. We want different things, see things differently. Don't worry about us. We'll do what we must."

"Well, I think you're in for a surprise. Mr. Banks was at the ranch today handing me the copy of my trust papers. I overheard some of the conversation he had with Chance, and I think you're about to get your freedom sooner than you think. Anyway, give Chance the opportunity to talk to you, Josie. You know he isn't very communicative at times, so you may have to help him out. He always had to be the tough one after Mom died. I don't think he felt he could actually enjoy himself, he was so busy making sure Dad was pleased, and the ranch ran right, and his kid brother stayed in school and out of trouble. He's so busy taking care of everything and everyone else; he doesn't know what it's like to have someone care for him and him alone. Lord knows, neither Dad nor I ever gave much thought to it. But now, he has you to teach him those things."

"You best be on the road before it gets dark. Don't want you taking the wrong turn and heading west, instead of east." She forestalled the rest of his words with a smile.

"Funny one. See you later, Josie. Be happy." His finger tapped the end of her nose, and he gave her a wink and a wave before he climbed behind the wheel of the Corvette.

Josie waved a final time as the car disappeared from the yard. Slowly, she walked toward the house, Dev's words replaying in her head. What was Chance up to with Phillip Banks? Whatever it was, she would find out sooner or later, she supposed. The words that troubled the most were when Dev spoke of Chance needing someone. She had to admit that she had never given that a thought before. He always seemed to be *Chance*...as solid and steady as the Rock of Gibraltar. Someone who always remained calm no matter what, someone always there to soothe every hurt or pain away. *Just Chance.* Did he ever *need* anyone?

"I'M GLAD YOU could stop by today, Josie. I wanted to get out your way before now, but one thing after another conspired to keep me tied to my desk." Phillip Banks smiled his apologies as he held out his hand indicating the chair in front of his desk.

Seating herself, Josie smiled in return. "I understand. It worked out that I needed to stop by the bank, and there were also some other errands I needed to handle."

"Good. I won't keep you long. I'm sure you'll be happy

when I tell you why I asked to speak with you."

Josie sat on the edge of the chair, not sure what to expect.

"Chance came to see me a few days ago. As you know, Chance had asked me earlier to do whatever was needed to allow him to relinquish his position as executor in your mother's will. The court has approved the change, and all is well. He further stipulated to me and to Chadwick at the bank that both notes for the loans against your ranch and its holdings are forgiven. I presume that is quite agreeable to you."

She sat speechless for a long while. Chance had done what he said he could not do. And without telling her his intentions. He was going back on his word to her mother. She never would have guessed he would do that. Chance always set such high bars at keeping his word. *Maybe to everyone else, but not to her.* Instead of feeling relief, she realized she was feeling a growing anger. What right did he have to change things now? And the loans? What did he think he was doing? She wasn't a charity case. They had an agreement, and it wasn't just up to him to change things in a blink of an eye. Josie stood up. Mr. Banks, caught off guard, was slower to do the same, a quizzical lift to his gray brows.

"You presume wrong, Mr. Banks. I'll take up this matter with Chance. You don't need to bother him with it. Have a good day!" She left the office and went to her truck.

Her first thought was to go straight to the Braxton Ranch to confront Chance. However, as she drove from town toward the country, a calmer head prevailed. She needed time to absorb what Chance had done and figure out exactly how she would deal with it. Instead of taking the turnoff to his ranch, she continued toward her own.

THREE DAYS LATER, the first real winter blast hit them. Snow began falling just after noon. As the day progressed, so did the wind and the weatherman's forecast of a potential "white out" looked to be on target. Josie and Tom made sure that the generator was working and ready if needed. She made one more trip to the barn to ensure that Cookie and the other horses were fed and secured. Sliding the large door shut behind her, she had to lean into the wind to make any headway back to the porch, the snowflakes whipping around her, coating her clothing. She had made it to the porch steps when the sound of an engine carried to her, and she turned to see one of the Braxton Ranch work trucks pull into the drive. She assumed it would be one of the hands sent by Chance to check on things. She was wrong. It was the man himself. Unfortunately, she had little time to prepare herself for this first meeting after so much had happened the last time they were together.

He made it up the sidewalk, his hat pulled tight on his head and the heavy sheepskin collar of his jacket turned up against the wind. As he got closer, she could see the stubble on his chin, as if he hadn't bothered with a razor in a couple of days. She stepped to the front door and opened it, leaving him to follow her or not. Josie didn't stop until she stood in front of the fireplace with its warm flames.

Shedding her jacket and gloves, she bent to unzip her all-weather boots and set them on the corner of the hearth. The bits of snow which had fallen off her clothing were making little puddles on the floor. She would clean them up once she dealt with her unexpected visitor.

"What were you doing out in this mess?" His voice was gruff and caught her off guard. It also irked her. He hadn't bothered to speak to her in almost two weeks, and that was the best he could come up with?

"Not that it is any business of yours, but I was checking on Cookie and the others one more time before the weather worsened. What are *you* doing here?"

He swept the hat off his head and unbuttoned his jacket, the warmth of the room making the outer clothing a bit much. Withdrawing the gloves from his hands, he stuck them in his side pocket. "Checking on you. I tried to call, but the call failed. I guess the weather has downed the tower."

"You really didn't need to come over. This isn't the first storm I've been through. It won't be the last. You should be on your way before the drifts get too high on the road."

"What are you still doing here?"

She blinked at the unexpected and odd question. Looking closer, she could see there were fine lines at the corner of his eyes and he looked tired. Was he not well? She had never known Chance Braxton to have one sick day in his life. A sharp feeling of worry shot through her. She ignored it as best she could. Yet a strange compulsion engulfed her, and she felt the need to be more understanding.

"I don't know what you're referring to. Where else would I be? And I have a pot of chili on the stove right now that I need to check on." She didn't wait for a reply but headed in the direction of the kitchen.

A few minutes later, she replaced the lid on the pot and turned, only to stop short when she found him leaning against the doorway. He lingered there, hands shoved in his pockets, appearing almost hesitant about stepping any further into the room.

"I was just going to have a bowl. Would you like to join me?"

He seemed about to reply in the negative, but he changed his mind at the last moment. "I never could refuse your mother's chili recipe."

"Have a seat and I'll dish it up." She kept her mind on the matter at hand, no easy task, as she was acutely aware of his eyes following her around the room. She wished her jeans and the burgundy sweatshirt she wore were less faded. Her hair must be a mess, escaping from the ponytail in the wind of the morning. She couldn't worry about such things now. Besides, Chance had seen her in a lot worse shape. Such as covered head to toe in mud after the cow incident.

Setting the steaming bowls on the table, along with a loaf of homemade bread and two mugs of coffee, she drew out her chair and sat down.

Chance took a bite, then a second one. "This is good, Josie. It hits the spot on a day like today."

"Thank you. Now why don't you explain what you

meant by your question?"

He took another bite, before wiping his mouth with his napkin and laying it beside his bowl. "I figured once Dev got his trust fund money, and decided to head to Florida, he'd be able to talk you into joining him. You have Tom to keep an eye on the ranch. You deserve to take some time and get away from here."

Things were coming into clarity for Josie. And her frustration was also on the rise again. She fought to keep it under control. "By any chance, would that also be the reason you took it upon yourself to wipe out the debt of the loans? The ones we had agreed I would have time to pay off?"

He looked at her then and, for the first time since coming into the house, he met her gaze straight on. Josie had to grip her hands underneath the table top to keep breathing as normally as possible. The man could cause her stomach to flip flop and her heart to race with one look. She doubted she would ever be immune to it. She waited for his reply.

"I removed every excuse you could have about not following your heart. The last one will be removed as soon as the courthouse opens on Monday."

She knitted her brow, trying to decipher what he meant.

"You can't very well go after my brother while married to me. I signed the papers, and all they need is your signature." He reached into his coat pocket and withdrew a small packet. He laid it on the table between them.

Josie never expected this. She drew back into her chair, as far from the packet as possible. A month ago, she would have grabbed for the nearest pen and signed on the dotted line.

That was before she had realized Chance had her heart all along. Only now it was apparent that he didn't want it.

"I see. So you worked all this out in your mind and decided for me what was best?"

"It isn't exactly the way you make it sound, but the outcome is the same. You'll have your freedom as soon as I can give it to you."

"You'll be free as well. That's what this is really about, isn't it? Although, I never figured you were one to ever go back on your word to anyone, especially to my mother." She scored a direct hit as she saw the fire that lit the dark eyes. A muscle twitched at the corner of his implacable jaw line.

"I've tried to honor your mother's request, but I'm only human. Above all else, she asked me to make sure you were taken care of and happy. I released Dev's trust to him, and that should be more than enough to keep you both taken care of for a very long time…as long as you keep an eye on the funds yourself. And if you decide that you never want to come back here to Braxton after you've gotten a taste of the world outside this ranch, then I'll make sure you get top dollar for it. In that respect, I'm keeping my word to her. However, it's up to Dev to make you happy, not me." He bit out the last as if it left a bad taste in his mouth, rising from his chair, and grabbing his hat and coat from the one beside him.

"Thanks for the chili." Chance jammed the hat on his head and was shrugging into his coat as he headed down the hallway toward the front door, apparently bent on getting away from her and the discussion as soon as he could.

"Why are you determined to push me toward Dev? I told him goodbye and good luck with his new life in Florida. I'm still here. I will still be here fifty years from now. So you can just get used to that, Chance Braxton." Josie's voice rose on the last sentence. Her hands on her hips and feet planted slightly apart only underlined the fact that she had had it with his whole attitude and the subject itself.

Chance turned from the front door and gave her a long look. There was a hint of skepticism still lurking in the dark sapphire eyes. "Until Dev shows up again and needs you to feel sorry for him or bail him out of another mess."

Her eyes narrowed, but she held to her stance. "It's the money, isn't it? You're angry about me giving him all the money in the bank account you set up for me. I don't want to split hairs, but you did tell me that I could use it in any way I saw fit. I did just that."

"Yes, you did. Dev turned on the blue-eyed charm and you fell for it all over again."

Josie advanced to stand a few feet from him. Her chin lifted to dare him to argue the point. "I did *not* fall for any charms. I didn't give him the blasted money for himself. It would have served him right to have to get himself out of his own mess for once. I did it to keep those men from coming after *you*, you big idiot." She immediately wished she could take back that last little bit. The look on Chance's face quickly turned to disbelief.

"Coming after *me*? What are you talking about?"

"Dev said that it made no difference to those men if they got the money from a trust or from inheritance. In fact, inheritance might be preferable. They were making threats against *you*, and I knew I could stop it by handing him over the money. So I did it."

Chance took a step closer to her, his fingers pushing the brim of his hat back from his forehead as if he needed to get a good look at her. "You gave him the money to keep *me* from getting hurt?"

"I don't know how many times I have to repeat it for you...but *yes*!"

The frown left his face as he slowly turned the words over in his mind. His hand reached out toward her, just as the front door blew open and Tom stepped in, bringing a lot of snowflakes with him. Chance's hand dropped back to his side and the moment changed.

"Sorry about not knocking, but I saw Chance's truck, and we have a situation and not a lot of time." The man tried to catch his breath at the same time he was explaining. Josie and Chance both stepped forward.

"Stock?" Josie asked before Chance could. She was already reaching for her heavy jacket from the hall closet.

"No, one of the deputies stopped by because they couldn't get us on the phone. They have a report of a family stranded on the blacktop to the south, just past Cutter's Creek. The road is pretty well drifted over. We're saddling up and trying to hit it by going across pastures. You know the area around the arroyo better than most of us, Chance. The last communication they had from them indicated the father might have had an attack of some sort before the phone went dead."

"I'll need a horse." Chance was already moving to the door.

"We have one saddled for you...figured you'd join us." Tom nodded.

"Did you saddle Cookie?"

Tom remained silent, and his eyes flew to Chance, who had stopped and turned to face Josie. "If he did, he can unsaddle him. You need to stay put. Once we find the family, we may need to bring them here."

"I am as able as any of you..."

"It isn't about whether you're tough enough. You're staying put and not wasting our time in argument. Listen for the radio. I'll have mine and so will Tom. Find as many blankets as you can and get the first aid supplies ready."

Josie wanted to argue and stamp her foot and make him see reason, but she knew that a large part of what he was saying was for the best. So she held back what she wanted to say. Instead, she simply said, "Check in every fifteen minutes and let me know what's going on. Be careful out there, *all* of you."

Tom nodded and disappeared out the door. Chance buttoned his coat and then dug into its pockets. Josie remembered something and opened the drawer of the hall table. She found what she sought and turned to face the man. "You'll need these heavier gloves. You left them on the table a while back."

Chance reached to take them from her, and their hands touched briefly. The electric shock was felt by both, and their eyes met. "Static caused by the storm," he mumbled, drawing the lined gloves on his hands. Turning to the door, he paused and glanced back at her.

"I mean it, Josie. Stay inside and don't even think of going anywhere in this mess. I don't want to have to worry about you, too."

"I heard you the first time, Chance. Just make sure you bring my horse back okay." She said the words, but all she wanted to do in that moment was throw her arms around his neck and beg him to stay safe. She didn't move.

His mouth turned up at one corner indicating his amusement at her words. He didn't say anything but stepped through the door and quickly shut it behind him to keep the snow and cold from blowing inside. The house was eerily quiet once he left. Josie moved to the window in the living room and was shocked at the change in the weather in just the last hour. The barn's dark outline was barely discernible in the blowing whiteness. Drifts had piled up halfway on the stone fence at the edge of the yard, and Chance's footprints were barely visible along the walkway, the snow was falling so fast.

Her gaze stayed on the barn and on the blurry figures that emerged on horseback a few moments later, small lights attached to stirrups to help keep each other in sight. Josie watched until they were lost in the curtain of white. Even though she could no longer see anyone, Josie didn't move from the window for a few minutes. There was a strange feeling growing inside her, and she couldn't shake it. Hopefully, news would come soon, and everyone would be okay and back home safely. She needed to see Chance walk through that front door once again.

Chapter Twenty-One

THE HOUR PASSED, then a second one. The radio had remained silent after the first forty-five minutes or so of the search. Josie kept checking it to make sure it still had power. As much as she wanted to call out to Tom or to Chance, she kept herself from doing so. They needed to concentrate on what they were doing. She traced and retraced her steps from the rear-kitchen window to the window in the living room too many times. An attempt to try and catch up on some paperwork on her desk failed after adding and re-adding the same column of figures for the fifth time, making her toss the pencil down and give up. She hated feeling helpless.

At the end of the third hour, Josie's stomach began knotting. Not only was the storm increasing in snowfall and wind velocity, but darkness was creeping in too quickly. Surely, the men would be returning soon, unable to continue the search after dark. When they did return, they would be cold and hungry. She kept her mind occupied with making a second batch of the chili, along with a couple of loaves of homemade bread. Josie turned her attention to the kitchen and decided it was as good a time as any to scrub the oven.

With that deed done, she poured herself a mug of steaming hot chocolate and curled up into the deep chair she had pulled closer to the fire.

Luckily, the electricity was still holding its own. Her eyes kept moving to the face of the grandfather clock in the corner of the room. The hands seemed to progress at a snail's pace. Her fingers went to rub her neck. The muscles were tense, and she couldn't keep from feeling something was not right. Something's *off*. It scared her because she recognized it as the same feeling she had just before the call came from the hospital telling her she needed to return quickly, her mother had taken a turn for the worse.

Josie wouldn't let her mind dwell on such things. *Think of positives*. Chance was smart. He was strong, and he never took chances with the lives of his men or the animals. However, he would never be out in such weather unless there was an emergency, and this was certainly not the typical emergency. People's lives were at stake.

She hoped they found the family, and everyone was okay. More than that, she hoped it would soon be over because she didn't know if she could stand much more of the waiting and silence. Once they did return, she would make sure she gave Chance a piece of her mind about not checking in with her like he promised. Of course, that would come after she thanked God for bringing him back safe and sound.

Just after the clock chimed out the final count of five, her ears detected another sound. She flew out of her chair and reached the hallway just as the outer door opened and Tom blew in with the wind. He shut the door behind him. *That wasn't right.*

"Where's Chance? Did you find the family? Is everyone alright? Why didn't you check in on the radio?" Even as she said the words, she knew that all wasn't right. It was in the lines of his body and the eyes that didn't want to meet hers but had no choice.

"The radios wouldn't transmit. I guess it had to do with the weather. But the family's okay. We were able to get them to where the second ambulance could transport them on the main highway by using one of the Sampson's tractors to cut across the Ridgeway pasture."

"Second ambulance. You said *second.* There was a first one?" She walked up to the man, her eyes pinning him to the spot.

"There was a problem getting to the car. It went off the road right at the Cutter's Creek bridge. It caught half on and half off the bridge." Josie could tell Tom was choosing his words carefully.

Josie felt a coldness seep around her heart that had nothing to do with the weather. She *knew.* "It's Chance. Something happened to Chance, didn't it? He's dead…" Her voice cracked on the word, and Tom took hold of her shoulders. His face moved close to hers, wanting to reassure her and keep her focused on what he was saying.

"No, Josie. He isn't dead. He's unconscious and on his way to the hospital. We've got the grader out front, and we're going to get you down to the main highway. Sheriff Waller has a truck waiting for you there. It'll be slow going, but we'll get you to Chance."

Josie didn't wait to hear the last part; she was grabbing her jacket and gloves. She only slowed when she almost landed at the bottom of the porch steps when her boot hit an icy spot. Luckily, Tom was right behind her and caught her. She never slowed down. The minutes were ticking like seconds, and her one thought was that she had to get to Chance.

The road grader was cumbersome, and the snow drifts made it slow going. What normally would take only ten minutes to travel to the main highway took them almost thirty. Josie thought she would lose her mind, even though she knew Tom and the hands were doing their best to get her to the hospital. She and Tom transferred to the snowcat with the deputy behind the wheel. Only then did Josie ask the questions swarming in her mind. Tom did his best to answer. Josie sensed he was giving her the abbreviated version on a lot of it.

"What happened when you reached the bridge?"

"Chance was afraid the car would slide on over the edge in the high wind. The others were trying to get to the spot, but they had to clear the roads as they went. So we set about trying to get some rope and lines on its bumpers and around the back. Chance had us tie a rope around him, and he made it to the back door of the car and busted out the window.

"He managed to get the two kids out and pass them along to us. The woman was fairly hysterical, and it took a bit to get her calm enough to leave the car. Just as she cleared the window, the car slipped a bit, and she panicked and jumped, knocking Chance off balance. He managed to spin around and push her toward us before he slipped and went over the side of the bridge. The rope kept him from falling to the creek. We figure his head hit the bumper of the car and he got knocked out. It took a bit to get to him and haul him up. Luckily, the rope held tight. The rest of the men arrived and managed to get the father out of the car and get him moving to the hospital."

Josie squeezed her eyes shut, her mind playing the scene out in vivid color. She felt as if she would be physically sick at any moment. *Damn Chance for having to be the hero…the guy who rescues others.* She felt anger at him and at the people who got themselves into such a mess and had to have others risk their lives to save them. She wasn't able to be very charitable in the moment.

"You said he was knocked out. How bad is it?"

"The paramedics couldn't say, but they looked really concerned. They wasted no time getting him in the ambulance and hitting the highway as fast as they safely could."

Josie had no idea what waited for her at the hospital. It seemed to take days to get there when it was a little more than an hour. As soon as the vehicle came to a stop under the covered arrival area, she was out and running toward the doors of the emergency room. It was a sick feeling of déjà vu all over again…first her dad, then her mom, and now…Chance. Tom tried to keep up. News had traveled fast, and there were more than a few concerned faces waiting for her arrival. She had no time for any of them. Her eyes sought out Dr. Winters. He seemed to sense her arrival and came through the double doors just as she approached.

"I don't need another patient on my hands right now. Take a deep breath, Josie." His hand covered hers, and his fingers felt her pulse. "You're whiter than a sheet right now."

"I'm fine," she said, only the word fine came out with a tremble in it. "Where's Chance?"

"Sit down over here," he said, leading her to a chair and waiting while she obeyed him.

Josie wanted to scream the question again, but she also knew that the sooner she followed his orders, the sooner he would answer her questions. She bit her bottom lip to keep control.

"We've got his body temp warming up nicely now. He has a nasty lump on his forehead; however, the scans are clear. We'll be monitoring him during the night and see where we are in the morning. The best thing for him right now is to be quiet and let his body rest."

"When can I see him?" Josie knew she wouldn't be able to begin to have any peace of mind until she could actually see him for herself and touch him.

"There really isn't anything for you to do here this evening…" he began but didn't get very far.

"With the weather like it is, it wouldn't make sense for me to leave not knowing if I could return in the morning or not. Besides," she pointed out, "I'm not going without making certain he's okay. I won't be sleeping much until I can be assured of that, so I'll stay here."

The doctor gave her an understanding smile. "You're a determined young lady, Josie. I'll have the nurse take you to his room, and we'll see about a cot for you."

"How's the family doing that was stranded?" she asked before he walked away.

"Some bumps and bruises and a scare they aren't likely to forget for a long time to come. The dad had an epileptic seizure and lost control of the car and it went into a skid on the bridge. One thing is for certain; they aren't likely to forget the man who saved their lives."

Josie didn't trust her voice not to break in reply, so she simply nodded her head and smiled her thanks. She did manage to clear the knot in her throat after a few moments, at least enough to speak with Tom.

"I can stay here, Josie. The boys can handle things at the ranch."

"No, you need to get home and get some rest, so that Mary can rest also. I'm sure she's worried about her husband, also. There isn't anything to be done here tonight. At first light, if the storm has died out, you and the boys will be busy checking fence lines and the pumps and troughs. There will need to be a crew out looking for stock in trouble. I'll be in touch when I know something definitive."

She accepted the well wishes and hugs of concern from the others who had waited for word on Chance. Josie was anxious to see Chance, so she didn't linger. The nurse led the way first down one corridor and then another. She pushed open a door in the middle of the third hallway and stepped aside for Josie to enter.

"I'll check on the cot for you and be back shortly," she spoke in lowered tones before leaving Josie alone.

Josie nodded her head, her eyes glued to the form lying

so quietly under a white blanket pulled up to just beneath his chin. Chance's face, which had a swath of bandage over the left side of his forehead, was pale as the pillowcase under his head. Josie stepped forward and stopped beside the bed, her eyes drinking in every feature of the man before her. There were monitors and wires familiar to her from her mother's stay not that long ago. She did her best to ignore them.

She sank onto the stool beside the bed, and her hand reached under the warming blanket, finding Chance's right hand. It felt cool to the touch but so very good. Something inside of her relaxed for a moment. The physical connection with him worked like a balm on her frayed nerves. Her eyes fell to his chest and watched the slow rise and fall of it.

All of a sudden, the tears began to fall. Josie tried to smother the sobs that threatened to break from her throat. It was as if the dam that had been threatening to crack all day finally burst. She laid her head on the side of the bed and tried to stifle the sniffles. She felt the tense muscles of her body begin to loosen after the hours of being stretched taut with worry. In the silence, holding on to Chance's hand, she had another conversation with God.

Josie only stirred from the position when the orderly came in with the "cot" which turned out to be a "sleeping chair" for her. He added two blankets and a pillow to it and pushed it into the corner. Josie thanked him as he left. She eyed the chair and knew she wouldn't be sleeping in it. She was content to stay where she was…in a stool as close as possible to Chance.

The only interruptions in the quiet of the room came

when a nurse would pop in to take vitals, adjust a wire or a tube, and record notes on the laptop on the small shelf next to the bed. When the door opened just before midnight, Josie recognized the woman who stepped into the room.

"Hi there, Josie. I'm so sorry that Chance got hurt today. Everyone in town is talking about it and so many have called the desk to check on him. You have to be very proud of your husband and what he did." Dee McNamara had been a grade ahead of her in school and was always friendly and had a warm smile for everyone. Josie wasn't a bit surprised when she heard she had become a nurse.

"Yes, that's Chance. Always going to someone's aid," Josie offered with a tired smile in return. "How's he doing? He hasn't moved since I arrived. Is that a good thing or a bad one?"

Dee placed the temperature in the record and then gave Josie an understanding smile. "His vitals are improving with each check. It's good that he's sleeping, although the doctor did give him a little something for pain, and that is probably helping him to relax. When he does wake up, he'll have a sore head." She came around the bed and laid a calming hand on Josie's shoulder. "I know that no matter what we say to you, you won't be completely eased until he opens his eyes and speaks to you. I seem to recall those gorgeous blue eyes of his, too. I had such a crush on him in the tenth grade." She chuckled at Josie's surprised expression. "But it was pretty plain from the get-go there was only one girl he ever had any interest in…and he married her. I didn't get a chance to tell you before now, but I hope you two will be very happy."

Josie decided this was her chance to ask the question that had come to her before. "You said it was pretty plain he only had interest in me. What makes you say that?"

If Dee thought her question strange, she just smiled and replied with a slight shake of her head. "It was clear to anyone who saw the look on his face whenever you would walk by or come into a room. And he was always so protective of you...and not in a big brother sort of way, either. Guys looked in your direction, but if Chance saw them, they got the message. I wondered how long it would take you to wise up and see it for yourself."

"I guess it did take me awhile to do that." She smiled softly as she looked at the man as he slept.

"You should get some sleep while you can. I'll be back later, but just press the button if you need me before then." The door whispered shut behind her. The room was in shadows except for the soft lights of the monitors and the night light over the bed.

Josie stood and changed out the stool for the chair. She looked upon the face of the man she had known for most of her life but realized she had never really seen him until a few months ago. Except, she had the oddest feeling that, while her mind had been on other things, her heart had known all along who Chance was and where it belonged...*with him*. If what so many others had said was indeed true, then Chance's heart might not be out of her reach. That possibility brought a smile to her face and hope to her heart. However, if he would just wake up and be okay, then her prayers would be answered, and she couldn't ask for more. Rising, she bent down and placed her lips softly against the side of his forehead that wasn't bandaged.

"Get better soon, Chance. I really need you to do that." She paused and then lowered her mouth beside his ear and whispered, "I love you, Chance Braxton."

Resuming her seat, she found his hand again, and laid her head beside it. Josie closed her eyes and, before long, she fell into an exhausted sleep.

Chapter Twenty-Two

THERE WAS AN elephant sitting on his head. That had to be it. Chance had use of one hand and with effort, he managed to raise it, and his fingers felt a soft lump of cotton material above his left brow. Slowly, he fought to open first one and then the other eyelid, taking in the strange surroundings. Sifting through his brain, the last thing he remembered was the biting cold wind and falling through space, a quick flash of Josie's face, and then it all disappeared as a blinding pain turned everything dark.

Josie. Where was Josie? There was a sudden need within him to find her. There were things he needed to say. He just needed to remember what they were. Chance's eyes focused more, and he realized the room he was in could only be in a hospital. How long he had been there, he had no idea. Something kept his right hand from moving. Had he injured it?

There had been a bridge and a fall. The details began to come back, along with an awareness of a growing dull ache in his head. His gaze slid downward, and he saw a familiar sight. Josie's head lay with her cheek on top of his hand, her lashes resting on pale cheeks, and she was asleep. More pieces of the puzzle came back to him. Among them was the conversation he had with her before Tom's arrival. There had been questions he needed answers to, but then he had to leave her before they could finish.

The most important thing he remembered was the fact that Josie had said she had chosen to not go away with Dev. *Not now, not ever.* And she had not helped Dev because she was in love with him. She had helped him in order to protect *him*…not Dev. Were his prayers being heard?

There had also been an incredible dream somewhere in the dark hours. He dreamed he heard Josie's voice telling him she loved him. Of course, it could have been the trick played on his head by a good hit. Her cheek stirred against his hand, and he watched Josie's head raise and her eyes flew to his face.

A broad smile of relief spread across her features, chasing sleep and worry away. Josie stood, a quick hand brushing loose tendrils of hair away from her face. She looked tired and most of her makeup was gone but she had never looked better to him.

"It's about time you woke up."

"How long have I been out?" His mouth felt stuffed with cotton as he tried to speak.

"Since yesterday afternoon, right after you decided to see which was tougher…your head or the bumper of a car."

"Not one of my better ideas."

"No, it certainly wasn't. You can never talk about my getting into trouble after this. And it has been verified…your head is definitely very hard." Josie's voice caught on some strange note of emotion. She reached for the call button for the nurse. He tried to move, but pain stopped him.

"Just take it easy. You should stay still until the doctor gets here."

"I've had falls before on the ranch. I'm fine. Or I will be once I get out of this place."

"Is that your educated, medical opinion?" Dr. Winters came through the door and caught Chance's words. The nurse followed close behind him.

"It's my years of experience having been stomped on by cows and other assorted ranch mishaps. This is nothing but a bump on the head. Do you concur?"

It had to be a good sign Chance was still trying to add a bit of humor in the situation, Josie thought. She would certainly take anything positive at the moment. She would have stepped back from the bed at the doctor's approach, but her hand was caught inside Chance's, and he was making no move to relinquish it. He probably didn't even realize he had claimed it when she stood earlier. Whatever the reason, she wasn't going to make a scene and take it back.

The doctor waited until after he had shined his penlight into Chance's eyes and did some movements of his neck and injured head and an eye exam in his examination before he stood back and returned the cowboy's regard. "You appear to be one very lucky man. Someone was looking out for you, and for that family."

"I can get out of here now. Just as soon as someone gets me my clothes." He moved a bit quicker than he should have, and he instantly halted, his mouth thinning when a painful reminder hit him.

"That's why you aren't going anywhere. Another night here won't do you any harm. If you went home, you wouldn't listen to my instructions and stay put for very long. Keeping you here, I can at least ensure you will listen for twenty-four hours."

Chance leaned back against his pillows, no sign of a smile at the moment. "I promise that I will follow your instructions. If I stay in this place, I won't get any rest. There will be someone poking, prodding, or generally keeping me on guard against being stuck by the next needle and that doesn't allow for resting."

Josie wanted Chance out of the hospital almost as much as he wanted to be out. She looked at the doctor, who wasn't moved by what Chance had just said. She spoke up. "I think you can give this place one more night. The food isn't all that bad, and you can have cute nurses at your beck and call. What else could you ask for?" She fixed a smile on her face and hoped he would agree.

Chance shifted his head ever so slightly on the pillow to look at her. "I could tell you what else, but it might make you blush in front of these nice folks." He was in rare form even in his injured state. He brought the blush to her cheeks as easy as ever…darn him!

"He'll stay, and he'll behave," Josie spoke up, drawing her eyes away from his. "Or you can just give him a huge shot and put him out of all our miseries for a few hours."

Doc Winters chuckled. "The boss concurs with me, it seems. You're staying put for another twenty-four hours…just settle in for a spell. I'll be back this afternoon to check on you." He turned toward the doorway but gave a pointed look at Josie before he departed. "Take a break, young lady…get out of this room and get some food…some sleep in something besides a chair. You'll need your strength to keep him in line once he does get out of here."

Josie returned his grin and nodded. Once the door closed behind him, the nurse took over.

"We'll be freshening your husband up a bit and getting some vitals checked. Then he needs to get some more rest. This would be good time for you to do the same and then return later in the afternoon."

Josie hesitated, not wanting to leave. Chance squeezed her hand.

"Go on, Josie. I'm not going to run off. I doubt I could get very far, even if I tried."

A few minutes later, Josie walked down the hall, retracing her steps of the evening before, until she was standing on the front steps of the hospital. Her eyes took a moment to adjust from the inside light of the hospital to the bright sunshine that glared off the blanket of snow that covered everything outside. Any other time, she would have taken time to enjoy the natural beauty.

Her mind was too numb to take in much except the fact she needed to get to the ranch, shower and change, and get things in place for Chance's return home…hopefully tomorrow…and get back to the hospital before nightfall. Tom arrived a few minutes later to pick her up. He gave her a report on the conditions at the ranch, which had come through the snowstorm with loss of only two cows, and a partial collapse of a roof of one of the hay sheds. It all could have been far worse.

Once at home, Josie shed her clothing and spent a long time under the hot spray of her shower. The water helped unknot her stiff muscles and allowed her to begin to return to normal.

As her body began to relax, the tiredness began to set in. Once out of the shower, she toweled off and dried her hair. She pulled on a freshly laundered nightgown and laid down on the bed, pulling a quilt over her, intending to just close her eyes for a half hour or so.

Something woke her up almost an hour later. She just didn't wake slowly…she sat bolt upright, a strange constriction in her chest causing her breathing to be shallow. Josie sat still, listening. Had there been a noise? A knock? No sound came. Tossing back the cover from her body, she swung her feet to the floor. At the window, she pushed back the curtain, and her eyes scanned the landscape outside. *Nothing out of the ordinary.*

The ringing of her cell phone brought her around quickly. As she grabbed it off the nightstand, her eyes caught the name of the hospital…an immediate stab of fear shot through her. *Just like Momma.* At that moment, she was reliving the call that came to tell her that she needed to hurry back to the hospital. But she had arrived too late. Josie tried to fight back the fear from her voice when she answered.

"Josie? Is that you?" Dee's voice filtered through her thoughts and brought her to reality.

"Yes…I'm here."

"Josie, I don't want you to panic or anything. You might want to come back to the hospital." It was clear Dee was trying to choose her words carefully. Josie's grip on the phone tightened like a vice. She didn't panic. She stilled into a strange clarity. "What's wrong? Is Chance…is he…"

"He's not dead, Josie. Don't think that. The doctor can explain it to you when…"

"I'm on my way." Like a shot, Josie tore open drawers, extracting clothing. The one thought in her head was that Chance was alive. That was the main thing. She needed to get to his side as quick as possible. Other dark thoughts tried to crowd into her mind as she dressed and flew down the stairs, grabbing coat and gloves along the way, but she shoved them away. She wasn't going to focus on anything else.

She saw Tom's truck parked next to the barn. Josie ran across the yard…slipping and sliding but remaining upright. She yelled across to him as he came to the doorway and gave him a briefing as she climbed into her truck, jabbing the key into the ignition. She waved away his offer to drive her. There was not a second to waste in her mind. The roads were still pretty rough going, even with the snow plows and sanding trucks running along them again. A couple of times, the sliding of her truck reminded her to take care if she wanted to arrive at all. She slowed a bit but did not let up. Bounding through the doors of the hospital, she didn't pause but navigated the hallways quickly.

Dee saw her first and stood from behind the desk. However, Josie didn't pause, passing her and pushing into the room. Only then did she come to a sudden standstill. The breath sucked out of her chest, which was the only thing that kept the scream locked inside her when she caught sight of the empty room…no bed, no Chance. *Oh, God, I'm too late.*

"Josie," Dee said, her arm going around her shoulders and a look of pure concern on her face. "He's okay. He's just been moved to ICU. You can see him shortly. First, we'll talk to Doc Winters. Chance is okay."

Josie looked at the woman, and she heard the words, but they were slow to filter through her mind. The reassurance in her voice and in her eyes helped the process along. The fact that Josie could get a breath of air into her lungs again also was a good thing. "What's wrong? What happened? Why did he get moved? ICU?"

"Let's go to the doctor's office. He said to bring you along when you got here."

Minutes later, she was seated in a chair, a cup of water in her not-too-steady hands, while she faced the doctor across his desk. Dee stood a couple of feet from her chair, watchful.

"Now Josie," the man began, "you can, and probably are, imagining all kinds of awful things. Don't. Did you hear what I just said?" He paused and looked at her over his bifocals.

Josie nodded. Before she could speak, he continued.

"I'll tell you what is going on. After you left, the staff was doing what they normally do with each patient. Chance was awake, but began to complain about a headache. I had ordered some medication for him. Not long after that, the nurse noted a change in his speech pattern and he indicated the pain had increased instead of decreasing. I was called. We immediately took him in for another scan, and I had the neurologist there also…searching for any possible bleeders we might have not seen before. Thankfully, there were none. After conferring with the other doctors, and more tests, it seems Chance had a reaction to the medication combination. Once we discovered that and took the steps to correct, the pain has eased, and he is resting again."

"Why is he in ICU, then? Are you…"

"He is in ICU because they can monitor him better there, and we needed his room on the third floor for another patient coming out of OR soon…simple as that. I was afraid that if I let Dee call you, you would think the worst. Yet, I knew if we didn't, and there was something…it would be worse also." His voice did soften at that point. "I know it's too soon after losing your mother in this hospital and all…and I know what the mind can do in these circumstances. But I want you to know that Chance should and *is* making a good recovery. This had nothing to do with his injuries. We just know now that he has an allergic reaction to those meds, and we won't ever use them again should the need arise….just like your allergy to penicillin."

Josie felt herself almost melt into the chair, as every muscle and nerve in her body suddenly began to release. If she had been standing, she might have fallen to the floor at that moment. She took another sip of her water, and then she smiled at the man and woman. "Thank you for calling me. I did think the worst. Can I see him now?"

Dee escorted her to the next floor and, in a small room with a glass front, she found a sleeping Chance. Dee gave her another hug and left her there. He looked perfectly fine…except for the bandaging and the monitors. He looked more than fine to her. Without warning, her eyes turned on the faucets, and tears of relief began to trail down her cheeks. She hastily wiped them away. She needed to get a grip.

For the next three hours, Josie had a pattern. Since he was in ICU…even though he wasn't listed as a critical ICU patient per se…she was only allowed two, fifteen-minute visits each hour. Chance slept through those visits. That was fine with Josie. He was there, and she could hold his hand. She would be grateful for that.

Doc Winters stepped into the room, along with another tall man in a white lab coat, just as the sun was setting outside the window. He introduced him as Dr. Doug. "I would attempt his last name, but I always butcher it up. He's head of our neurological unit, and I wanted you to hear it from his own mouth." He looked at the man.

"Mrs. Braxton, I know you are most concerned for your husband's injuries," he spoke, his Austrian accent sounding odd in a hospital full of Texans. "Please be assured that we have found no reason to believe that he has any serious residuals from his accident, other than what is visible. He will have a few headaches and general soreness where his body took a bit of beating in the accident. I see no reason why he won't be able to leave here in the next day or so."

"Now that is the best thing I've heard." The fourth voice in the room was wobbly and came from the man lying in the bed…his eyes trying to focus on each of them. They came to rest on Josie, and a hint of a smile took shape. "Quick…before they change their minds…get me to the truck."

"Not so fast, young man. You aren't going anywhere until tomorrow…if then." Doc Winters stepped in with that statement. Chance's eyes had no problem with focus at that point. He fixed them on the man. Josie knew that look well.

"Come on, Doc. You guys need this bed for someone who is really sick. You've already moved me once you said…that proves that point. I can rest even better at home in my own bed. Tell them, Josie."

Three pair of male eyes rested on her. Josie had to stifle a bit of smile. It seemed she just might have the upper hand at the moment where Chance was concerned. She looked at the man, who watched her with his sapphire eyes…a mixture of challenge and question in their depths. After a few long moments, she made up her mind.

"Chance would be able to relax better at home. And I will make sure he follows your orders, or I'll haul him right back here myself."

She felt a grateful squeeze of her hand, but she kept her eyes on the doctors.

"You think you can control this stubborn man?"

Josie flashed a quick look at Chance and then right back at the physician. "I believe I can."

Dr. Winters looked at his patient over the rim of his glasses, considering the situation. "I tend to think you just might be able to make him behave where no one else can. I'll send you home with some strong pain meds, and they'll tend to keep him sedated enough to rest."

"Thanks for getting me out of this place." Chance spoke after the doctor and nurse left the room. "Hospitals are okay as long as you're just visiting them. I've got things to do and can't lie around while daylight is wasting."

Josie gave him a long look, slowly extricating her hand from his. That got his attention.

"I meant what I said to the doctor. You will do exactly as he instructs, or I promise you will be delivered back here and deposited on the front doorstep so fast it will make your head spin even more than it already is. Do I make myself clear?"

Chance's mouth curved into an amused arc. "You really think you can tell me what to do?"

"I can ask you to do what you know is the right thing to do given your circumstances at the moment." She didn't want to give herself away, but the moisture was threatening her eyes. She gritted her teeth and tried to get the words out. "I can ask you to do that because I have lost everyone else in my life, and I really can't take any more right now. Where is the nurse with the paperwork?"

She used the first thing that came to mind to allow her to make a hasty retreat from the room. If she hadn't escaped when she did, Josie was afraid she would make a total fool of herself, and Chance would see far more than she needed him to see where her feelings were concerned. The last thing she needed or wanted was for him to feel pity for her. That was the last emotion she wanted from him.

IT WAS ANOTHER beautiful day with the blue sky and sunlight sparkling across the snow. The temperature was barely above freezing. The highway was cleared, so they made good time to the ranch.

Chance sat in the rear seat of the double cab, his head laid back against the seat, eyes closed. Josie kept glancing in the rearview mirror, checking on her patient. She was concerned, but not for the obvious reason. She was concerned because, since before they left the hospital even, Chance had been almost docile in his demeanor. Even when they brought in a wheelchair and told him he had to use it to leave the hospital, she had seen the flash of annoyance in his eyes, but he had not said a word. He just slowly took his seat in the chair. Even Doc Winters had sent her a surprised look as they followed the orderly and Chance out of the hospital.

Josie drew up at the end of the sidewalk that one of the hands had evidently shoveled free of snow earlier, just prior to their arrival. Tom stood waiting for them. True to Texas weather and its propensity for quick changes, already the melting snow and thawing icicles were dripping off the eaves of the roof. Josie gathered Chance's bag of personal items from the back seat and quickly moved around the truck, while Tom eased Chance from the seat, giving him his arm and shoulder for support, as Chance moved very slowly up the sidewalk. Josie darted ahead and held the front door open for them.

Moving in front of one of the wing back chairs situated

by the fire, Chance sank down into it. "Thanks, Tom. I can manage from here. You've got work to do, so I won't hold you back."

"No problem. The men have the last of the downed fences back up, and we should have the hay shed roof back in place by late today."

"Thanks again, Tom. Tell Mary thanks for stopping by and getting all that extra food I made earlier and taking it to the men for lunch today." Josie added her grateful smile with the words.

"Will do. I'm on the radio if you need anything."

Josie shut the door behind him and walked back into the living room to find Chance with a frown on his face. "Is your head hurting? You can have a pain pill now if you need one."

"No, it's not my head. It's probably best we came here and didn't confuse Tom with taking me back to my ranch and then you coming here. If you'll hand me my cell phone from the coat pocket, I can call and have one of my men come over and pick me up in the truck."

Josie did not move. She wasn't getting his cell phone. This was where she needed to stand her ground. "There won't be any of that nonsense. You've done enough moving around for one day. Besides, I promised Dr. Winters I would keep my eye on you and make you behave and that is exactly what I plan to do. So you can keep arguing, but you'll do it with yourself. I'm going to fix lunch, and then you're going to bed."

She didn't wait for a reply. Turning on her heel, she left him sitting in the chair, a very surprised look on his face. He could make of it whatever he liked. She did make a small detour to the coat closet, reaching in and taking possession of his cell phone. Good luck with him trying to find it. He was going to do as told...for once.

Josie set a tray out on the table, and then withdrew the pot containing the chicken soup from the refrigerator that Mary had made for their arrival. While she heated enough for their lunch, she also took out some lettuce, tomatoes, cucumbers, and grated cheese. A salad would be good to go along with the soup. Cutting a couple of thick slices of the bread loaf, she lightly buttered them and then toasted them under the broiler. Chance would probably prefer coffee, but he was going to be content with a glass of milk.

Once she had the tray arranged, she carried it carefully back into the living room, setting it down on the coffee table before she quickly opened the closet and took out a couple of wooden TV trays. She set one up in front of Chance. She ventured a quick glance in his direction while she reset the food on the trays. It was clear that he wasn't too pleased with the current events, yet he managed to say nothing. Something else which surprised her.

"We'll eat in here to keep you from moving more than is necessary. It's nice anyway, in front of the fire. Tonight, I'll make you some enchiladas. Provided you behave yourself and eat all your lunch now."

"Where is your lunch tray?"

"I'm going back for it. Is there anything else I can bring you?"

Chance looked over the food before him and then back

to her. "Nope. I have to admit this is much better than being stuck with a tray of hospital chow."

Josie responded to his smile with one of her own and felt something else respond inside of her. Something that remarkably felt like contentment beginning to build. She hurried back to the kitchen and soon returned with her own food tray. She sat in the other chair across from Chance. He hadn't touched his food but waited until she was seated and ready.

They ate in companionable silence for much of the meal. Her gaze kept drifting over to him, making certain there were no telltale signs of pain or any other distress. She intended to take her job of nurse and protector very seriously. *Whether he liked it or not.* So far, Chance seemed to be a docile patient. That worried her.

"Would you like more soup?"

Chance placed his fork down beside his plate and shook his head, but abruptly stopped, a rueful grimace crossing his face. "I'm good. Thanks."

Josie stood and reached for his tray. "You are *not* good. We're going to get you to bed, and you're going to take a pain pill and sleep."

"You're taking your watchdog role a bit far," he called after her retreating back.

Coming back into the room, she motioned for him to stand up. "Call me what you want, but what I say goes, or you go back to the hospital. Stand slowly and put your weight on me."

He stood. His arm slid around her shoulders, and she

stepped against him, sliding her own arm around his waist. She was his nurse. She didn't need to have thoughts other than medicinal ones about her patient, but that was easier said than done. Touching Chance was like touching a live wire that you couldn't let go of because of the current. Biting her bottom lip, she concentrated on taking one step at a time…in more ways than one.

Chance didn't say a word all the way up the stairs, which were very slow going. Josie had a feeling he was doing his level best to put up a brave front, one that would not have her rushing to call the doctor. He did hesitate when Josie opened the door and took a step into the bedroom.

"It might be better if I took the guest bedroom. I wouldn't want to keep you awake if I can't sleep or whatever."

Did he not want to share a room with her any longer? Or was he doing it out of deference to her? Was he still hung up on her wanting to be free to be with Dev? They hadn't finished that particular conversation, yet, but Josie wasn't backing down. She continued into their room.

"Sit down on the bed. I'll help you with your boots. You can work on the buttons of your shirt."

"I can undress myself. You're taking your Florence Nightingale duties a bit far."

She looked at him with hands on her hips. "We can waste time arguing, or you can just be quiet, and do as I say."

"Be glad I'm an invalid right now. Or you wouldn't be the one giving orders."

She ignored him and picked up one booted foot and

worked his foot free, and then did the same with the other one. Chance had handled his shirt and was slowly shrugging it off one shoulder and then the other. He tossed it onto the chair across from the bed.

"Unbuckle your belt and then your jeans. I'll help you slide them off." Josie knew she sounded a lot braver than she felt at the moment. What was the saying, "Never let them see you sweat?" Well, that was easier said than done. Particularly when faced with a shirtless Chance, leaning back on his hands, and a darkly hot look focused on her.

"I guess that walk up those stairs was a lot rougher than I thought it would be. Guess I need your help, Nurse Josie."

She had been adamant that he listen to her and do as she told him and not overdo things. Now he was admitting he might need help after all. She could ignore him, and he would know that he was affecting her in ways he could certainly take advantage of. Or she could follow through and not let him get to her. *Right.*

Josie stepped closer to stand between his legs where they draped over the edge of the bed. Another vision of the last time they were in their bedroom popped into her mind, and she quickly popped it right back out. She reached out, hoping her hands didn't appear as shaky as they felt. The metal of the buckle was cool to the touch. It was undone fairly quickly.

The zipper was next. Unfortunately, there was nothing cool about its feel…just the opposite. The heat from the bare skin of his flat stomach met fingers that weren't steady any longer. Her tongue slid over her bottom lip in a totally nerve-driven reaction. *Just keep things in perspective.* She looked up and caught the amusement lurking as he watched her hesitation.

Flicking the button through the hole, her fingers closed over the metal zipper. She could feel the temperature rising quickly along her neck and across her cheeks as it was very apparent Chance's lower body was quite *awake.* The zipper eased down and then her hands went to grasp the denim at his hips. With a determined jerk, she was none too gentle. She didn't appreciate being the source of his amusement.

With an easy movement, he helped the material slide down his legs. Josie stepped away and jerked the covers of the bed down. "I think you can manage to get in the bed."

She disappeared into the bathroom. Holding a paper cup under the faucet, she filled it. Then opening the pill bottle she had been given from the hospital pharmacy, she tapped out two tablets in her hand. Josie marched back to the bedroom, where Chance was reclining against the pillows, on top of the covers. She kept her mind centered on the matter at hand, and tried to not be distracted by the hard, tanned, male body that was almost naked, save for the black briefs.

Josie stopped at the side of the bed and held out her open palm with the two tablets. Chance eyed them.

"Those aren't necessary. I don't like being dependent on pills."

"For now, they are. You're going to do exactly what the doctor wants. Take them."

"And if I don't?"

"I'm not having this conversation again. I meant it when

I said I would call Tom and take you right back to the hospital. Then they can stick needles in you and do whatever else they want, if it means you'll behave and get better."

Chance's smile changed from being amused to one of gentle understanding. His hand reached for the pills, and he popped them into his mouth, took the paper cup, and emptied it of the water. Then, he swallowed. Josie went to turn away, but his hand caught her wrist, and she found herself hauled down until she was almost sitting on top of his lap. She managed to quickly turn and ended up against his side.

It didn't help that his voice lowered to gentle tones that were undoing her resolve. "Look, Josie," he began, obviously making an effort to choose his words. "I realize that, being in the hospital again, so soon after losing your mother there, brought back some things that hit you in a raw place. What you said about losing everyone…it hit home. This is just a bump on the head, and I'm going to be okay. You don't need to worry about me." The grin returned and caused her heart to flip flop against her chest. That and the slow circles being drawn on the flesh above her wrist by his thumb just above where his hand held hers. "You can't get rid of me so easily. I intend to stick around for a long time…if that's what you really want."

"I thought you wanted to be rid of me? You didn't want to be around any longer? Those papers downstairs on the table prove that."

"Those papers prove that I will do whatever you need me to do to make sure you have what you want and are happy."

"You did them for *me* and not for you?"

"Yes." He seemed to want to say more but for some reason, he seemed to be having a bit of issue focusing his thoughts and words.

Josie saw that the pills were beginning to weave their magic on him. Unfortunately, it meant their discussion was about to be postponed...again. Just when she was finding her courage to ask him just what it was he really wanted from their relationship. *Great.*

"Lie down and be quiet now. The meds are taking over." She stood, but he still had her wrist.

"Promise me that you'll sleep next to me tonight? I might need you, Nurse Josie. Promise?"

How could anyone deny him anything? His eyes were heavy, but he was fighting to stay awake long enough for her reply.

"I promise. I'll be right here all night." She was rewarded with a smile that faded slowly, as he allowed his body to relax. Taking her hand back, she pulled the covers up and over Chance to his shoulders. She stood watching him for a few more minutes, relishing the fact that she could look upon him and not have to hide her feelings. Josie left the room then, making certain the house was secured and lights out downstairs. Then she made her way back upstairs and undressed, replacing her day clothes with a soft, blue cotton, eyelet, gown.

Quietly, she slipped under the covers of the big bed and turned on her side, her eyes seeking Chance's sleeping face on the pillow beside her. Slowly, she reached out and laid her hand on his upper arm. The connection with him made her rest easier. Chance was home. She wasn't going to lose him, at least not like she had her family. For now, that was all she could ask for.

Chapter Twenty-Three

JOSIE WOKE WITH a start. Her eyes open, she lay still under the covers. Her ears were tuned for other sounds. Or rather the lack of them. She sensed she was alone and that brought her upright in the bed, her gaze flying to the empty pillow beside her. Chance was not there.

Tossing back the covers, she swung out of bed and padded on bare feet over to the bathroom door. Listening, she heard nothing. There was no response to her soft knock, nor when she spoke his name. Her eyes lit on the fact that his boots were not next to the chair where she had placed them the previous evening. That meant he had them on.

Immediately, she headed toward the door of the bedroom, grabbing the crocheted throw off the quilt rack as she passed. She didn't pause for shoes. That man was not where he was supposed to be, and if he had ventured out of the house, she was going to let him have more than a piece of her mind!

At the bottom of the stairs, she was just about to throw open the front door when she heard voices coming from the living room. She turned and hurried into the room, stopping just inside. Her eyes landed on the tall man with his back to the fire and a cup of coffee in his hand, while his other was stuffed inside a pocket of his jeans. Chance saw her the moment she entered, and a sheepish grin creased his face.

She advanced a few more steps into the room, and that was when she finally became aware that he was not alone. His ranch foreman, Clem Dawkins, and Tom were also standing in the room with him. Both men turned their attention in her direction, hats coming off their heads.

"Morning, Josie," Tom spoke up.

"Morning, Mrs. Braxton," Clem echoed.

"Good morning, gentlemen," she returned, but her eyes stayed on Chance.

"I think we're done here. Thanks for the updates, and thank the men for all the extra hours in the bad weather." Chance clapped a hand on his foreman's back as the pair turned to leave. They bid their goodbyes to Josie as they passed. She waited until she heard the click of the front door. She opened her mouth to speak, but Chance threw up a palm first and beat her to it.

"I'm okay. I feel fine. My head doesn't throb any longer…just sore to the touch. I slept quite well, thank you, and I managed to make my own coffee this morning. I met with the boys over here this morning because I knew you would have my head and theirs if I dared go outside this house today. Which I have no intention of doing. It's just you and me and no interruptions today. Now, you can speak." He lowered his palm, but then it quickly shot upward again.

"Just one more thing," he added. Stepping forward, he leaned down and placed a quick kiss on her slightly parted, very much surprised mouth. "Good morning, Mrs. Braxton."

It took a couple of blinks and some hasty brushing away of the morning fog of her brain to take in all he said right before the unexpected kiss. He definitely had caught her off guard.

"I might also suggest that, from now on, you might want to dress in something a little less alluring than your nightgown to come down for daily morning meetings. As much as I enjoy it, I would prefer that we just kept it for my eyes only."

Josie glanced down at that moment and, while she would hardly refer to herself as alluring, her cheeks went crimson to think she had stood so nonchalantly in her nightgown and bright pink and white throw, without shoes, and probably with a crazy case of bed hair. Her only thought had been to find Chance and keep him from further injury to his head, and here he stood before her, looking far too good in his tight jeans, boots, and long-sleeved chambray shirt. He had obviously showered and even shaved.

There was a delicious hint of his cologne still filling her senses from when he had dropped the swift morning kiss on her lips. Added to all that was the fact he seemed to be in a particularly good mood for someone recuperating from such a blow to the head. Maybe that was the reason he was acting strangely? What if he were having some sort of relapse? Worry furrowed her brow as she looked at him.

"Are you certain you're feeling better? Perhaps we should have the doctor just take a look at you to be on the safe side."

"Josie, for the last time, just stop your worrying. I promise I am fine. However, you'll be the one sick if you run around barefoot on these wooden floors." Chance set his mug on the mantel before seating himself on the raised hearth, his hand patting the spot next to him. "Sit here and get warm in front of the fire. This is as good a place as any for us to talk."

"I should probably go upstairs first and put some clothes on…in case anyone else stops by."

"No one is stopping by and, if they do, I have instructed the guys working out in the corral to tell them that we are not available. But if you feel you must run away upstairs to find your courage, I'll wait." He folded his arms across his chest and stretched his long legs out in front of him. He was prepared to wait her out.

"I have never run away from anything or anyone. My courage level is just fine, too." She gathered the throw around her shoulders as if it might be a royal robe and took her seat beside him.

"Good. Shall you go first, or shall I?"

"You're the invalid here; perhaps you should begin."

Chance slid a semi-warning look in her direction to not push it too far.

"First, I want to say thank you. You stepped in and took care of me, even when I might not have been the best patient." She raised her fine brows at that statement, and he took note of it, but chose to continue. "Frankly, I'm not used to that…having someone worry about me and want to take care of me. If I seemed ungrateful or unappreciative, I wasn't. It was just strange. But it was something that I could definitely get used to. I also know it was hard for you to be back at the hospital so soon again. I'm sorry I put you in that position."

"Thank you," she responded, losing some of the rigidity she felt when she first sat down beside him. Chance always had a way of getting around each defense mechanism she came up with over the years. "I admit I might have overreacted a little bit. You weren't really that bad a patient. Besides, that's what people do who…care…about each other. So… no thanks are really necessary." She almost tripped up and said "love" but quickly managed to come up with another word.

"We were in the middle of an important conversation when we were interrupted a few days ago. Phillip Banks called me earlier and wanted to know what he should do with that paperwork today. I said I would have to call him back after you and I finished our discussion today."

Josie felt her heart plummet to her feet. Chance was talking about the divorce papers. He said they would be filed today. She had tried to not think about them and recent events with Chance, and the accident had helped her do just that. It was evident that Chance was determined not to put it off any longer. There was too much pain in the center of her chest at the moment for her to think of something to say in response. She would let him do the talking since this was what he wanted.

Chance gave her a long look when she didn't respond. He noted she didn't meet his eyes but kept hers on the table in front of the couch. He cleared his throat and decided that it was now or never. "You surprised me when you told me about why you gave the money to Dev, so he could pay his debt. I had it figured that you were trying to help him because you still cared for him. If you still cared for him enough to do that, then I didn't want to stand in the way of what would make you happy. I thought you wanted to be with him when he left."

"I will always care for Dev. He was a big part of my life growing up. I admit I had a silly crush on him for a long time. However, when he came back here, and maybe even before that, when he never seemed to settle down and went through two quick engagements…well, maybe I realized the difference between a childish fantasy and reality. I can even feel sorry for him."

"Your fantasies seemed pretty real to me when I had to change my shirts each time you dried your tears on them after he did something stupid." Chance tried to make light of it, but Josie realized that she had indeed run to him more times than she could count.

"I'm sorry about that," she replied softly. "I guess whenever Dev didn't live up to my childish expectations, I felt like you would understand, and somehow I always felt better after unloading my heartbreak on your broad shoulders. You were always so patient, and you shouldn't have been. You should have told me to get lost."

"That wasn't an option. I guess I figured sooner or later you would grow up and you wouldn't need my shoulder any more. Whenever I thought about that, I didn't care for the feeling I would get. I can't remember when you weren't around. And I have no idea what to do if that day were to ever come. I confess that made accepting your mother's request a lot easier for me. I knew that I would at least have more time before I might have to watch you fall for someone else and not need me any longer. It sounds pathetic when I put it into words, but that's the way of it."

Josie looked up as his words stirred a faint flame of impossible hope inside her. Her eyes searched the dark ones watching her reaction with a solemn stillness. Her chest felt heavier, and it was harder to breathe. They were moving toward some unknown cliff, and she didn't know what was beyond it.

"Is that why you insisted we get married?"

"I didn't want anything being said that would hurt you...from any of the gossips in town. But I also hoped it would buy me even more time."

"Time for what, Chance?"

His voice softened along with his gaze. "You want me to lay it all out for you. It's times like this that I envy my brother his ability with the smooth lines and romantic stuff. That's what females like. It's what you deserve."

"I don't want a smooth line. You've always spoken straight with me, and that's what I want now."

His hand covered hers where they lay curled in her lap. The warmth moved through her in a comforting wave. Her gaze stayed steady on his.

"I realized a while back that I was jealous of my brother. I wanted to be the one who lit up your eyes when I came into view and be the one you fantasized about and dreamed of kissing. I wanted to be the one you gave your heart to. Because I also realized some time ago that, not only had you cut your teeth on my heart, but you stole it and carried it with you."

"So, I decided that I had to be patient and wait for you to grow up and maybe you might see that there was a Braxton who had loved you for years and would until the last breath left my body." Two long fingers reached up and rested under her chin, the touch almost as reverent as one touching the most delicate china. Warm, dark, sapphire blue light poured over her face from eyes that held his heart for her to see. "I love you, Josie. I want to stay your husband for the next sixty years at least. I promise to do my best to make you happy every day we have together. The question is, do you think you could find room in your heart for me one day?"

The knot was huge that formed in her throat. Tears weren't far off from her eyes that shimmered with moisture as she looked at the man who had always been there for her…just waiting. Josie slowly shook her head, hardly able to believe how much happiness could fill a person so fast that it seemed you could burst at the seams from it.

"I also realized some things over the last few months. I had blinders on for far too long where Dev was concerned. It was a girl's crush…perhaps it was more the *idea* of Dev…as a dashing prince charming, who would sweep into my life now and then. But that wasn't reality. Reality was totally different."

"I realized that, in every moment of my life...in the good times, but also in the worst of times, there was one constant. There was one person who was always there for just me. You gave me a shoulder for my tears, but you also knew when to give me a straight talking to and dust me off and tell me to get back to work. You were there to challenge me and to cheer me on. I took you for granted after a while, and that was wrong. As I grew up, I resented you. Because you were always right. You knew me better than I knew myself, and there were all sorts of feelings that I couldn't understand."

Josie took a breath. The man beside her deserved to know how she felt. He deserved so much more than she could put into words. "I wanted to prove to my parents and the other people in town that I could run this ranch. But I realized that it was really you that I wanted to prove to what I could do. Your opinion mattered. And, the more I fought you, it seemed the more I couldn't imagine my life without you. And then, one day, the truth was right there. I can't say that it happened in the blink of an eye. It happened over all the days of my life that you were in it. You gave me the strength to try and succeed, and you gave me understanding, and used so much patience, when anyone else would have walked away. You deserved so much more, and I didn't know how to make you understand that it was you all along, *you* were the Braxton in my heart...the only one there ever has been."

Josie entwined her fingers through his, as his hand still covered hers. There was no more pretense, no more barriers, and she allowed her heart to fill her gaze for him to see. "You asked if there was room in my heart for you. *You* are my heart. It's as simple as that. I love you, Chance Braxton. I always have, and I always will. And I'm staying your wife as long as I have a breath in me."

Two strong hands cupped her face and lips claimed hers in a kiss that rocked the earth beneath her and promised the world would forever be theirs. They were home, and tomorrow was theirs to walk together.

The End

If you enjoyed this book, please leave a review at your favorite online retailer! Even if it's just a sentence or two it makes all the difference.

Thanks for reading *True Blue Cowboy* by Debra Holt!

Discover your next romance at TulePublishing.com.

TULE
PUBLISHING

If you enjoyed *True Blue Cowboy,*
you'll love the next book in....

The Blood Brothers series

Book 1: *True Blue Cowboy*
View the series here!

Book 2: *Homeward Bound, Cowboy*
Coming March 2020!

Book 3: *Her Secret Cowboy*
Coming April 2020!

More books by Debra Holt

The Texas Lawmen series

This series features three of the sexiest lawmen ever to wear a badge. Two of them wear the silver star of the elite Texas Rangers. One is a United States Federal Marshal. Besides having the law in common, they are good friends with their friendships having been forged over the years. They keep their bonds of friendship and have each other's backs whenever needed. Dedicated to duty and their badges, their private lives are solitary ones until the day each of them meets their match in the opposite sex.

Book 1: *Beware the Ranger*

Book 2: *The Lawman's Apache Moon*

Book 3: *Along Came a Ranger*

Book 4: *The Sheriff's Christmas Angels*

About the Author

Born and raised in the Lone Star state of Texas, Debra grew up among horses, cowboys, wide open spaces, and real Texas Rangers. Pride in her state and ancestry knows no bounds and it is these heroes and heroines she loves to write about the most. She also draws upon a variety of life experiences including working with abused children, caring for baby animals at a major zoo, and planning high-end weddings (ah, romance!).

Debra's real pride and joys, however, are her son, an aspiring film actor, and a daughter with aspirations to join the Federal Bureau of Investigation (more story ideas!). When she isn't busy writing about tall Texans and feisty heroines, she can be found cheering on her Texas Tech Red Raiders, or heading off on another cruise adventure. She read her first romance, Janet Dailey's *Fiesta San Antonio*, over thirty years ago and became hooked on the genre. Writing contemporary western romance is both her passion and dream come true, and she hopes her books will bring smiles…and sighs…to all who believe in happily-ever-after's.

Thank you for reading

True Blue Cowboy

If you enjoyed this book, you can find more from all our great authors at TulePublishing.com, or from your favorite online retailer.

TULE
PUBLISHING

Printed in Poland
by Amazon Fulfillment
Poland Sp. z o.o., Wrocław

60764779R00204